DEATH COMES CALLING

R. G. Anthony

BALBOA.
PRESS

A DIVISION OF HAY HOUSE

Balboa Press books may be ordered through booksellers or by contacting:

Balboa Press
A Division of Hay House
1663 Liberty Drive
Bloomington, IN 47403
www.balboapress.com.au
1 (877) 407-4847

Because of the dynamic nature of the Internet, any web addresses or
links contained in this book may have changed since publication and
may no longer be valid. The views expressed in this work are solely those
of the author and do not necessarily reflect the views of the publisher,
and the publisher hereby disclaims any responsibility for them.

The author of this book does not dispense medical advice or prescribe
the use of any technique as a form of treatment for physical, emotional,
or medical problems without the advice of a physician, either directly
or indirectly. The intent of the author is only to offer information
of a general nature to help you in your quest for emotional and
spiritual well-being. In the event you use any of the information in
this book for yourself, which is your constitutional right, the author
and the publisher assume no responsibility for your actions.

Any people depicted in stock imagery provided by Thinkstock are
models, and such images are being used for illustrative purposes only.
Certain stock imagery © Thinkstock.

Print information available on the last page.

ISBN: 978-1-5043-1106-9 (sc)
ISBN: 978-1-5043-1107-6 (e)

Balboa Press rev. date: 11/08/2017

Contents

Overview

This story revolves around an Australian undercover federal police officer, Glen Johnson, who is on compassionate leave after the tragic death of his wife and daughter in an apparent car accident. He has turned to alcohol to drown his sorrows. He is suddenly drawn into something far more sinister by the death of his closest mate, and his investigation involving treason, drugs and betrayal. Glen and his mate's wife take it upon themselves to find out the truth and bring his killers to justice. Little do they know just how deep the corruption has penetrated and who is involved. Death becomes their constant companion, the deeper they probe into the murky world of drugs the more complex it becomes. Hostage taking, kidnapping attempts are in play before Glen, Mary, along with their new recruit Mike Lord forces the issue on an isolated property in the Warragamba dam area; and justice wins out, or does it.

R.G. Anthony

Acknowledgements

Darryl Knapp, Gina Chalker, Ngaire Soley and the staff of Grenfell record. For all their help and encouragement in the completion of this novel.

Any resemblance between any characters appearing in this novel

And any person living or dead is entirely coincidental and unintentional.

Chapter One

A cry for help.

It was about two o'clock in the morning when the telephone dragged Glen back to consciousness from his alcohol-induced sleep. Snatching it irritably, he snapped, "Johnson."

"Glen—Neil. Help—urgently—hurry."

"Where are you, mate?" asked Glen, sitting up and regretting the action as his head throbbed. He forced himself to listen as he scribbled down the address. "I'll be there, mate."

"Hurry, mate—run, and trust no one; these bastards are playing for keeps." The phone went dead.

Glen swung his lithe body out of bed. Raising his right hand to shield his bloodshot blue eyes from the harsh glare of the overhead light, he dressed quickly, pulling on his trench coat and beanie. He could hear the rain pounding on the roof.

Grabbing a Glock nineteen automatic and four full magazines from his gun safe, he scooped up his car keys and ran for the door of his apartment.

He ignored the teeming rain as he ran to his vehicle. Climbing in, gunned the motor, and turned onto the highway, peering through the windscreen wipers, headed for the old Sydney docks.

Their conversation gnawed at him, the tension in Neil's words. His cry for help would not shift; the urgency to get to him became supreme. He pushed the Mustang harder. *Trust no one? Why—what was the reason?*

Twenty minutes later, the car slid into a secluded parking spot alongside an old, battered brown Ute not far from the docks. He walked cautiously along a darkened street towards an old, abandoned warehouse. Thankfully, the rain had eased off. Staying close to the shadows of the building, with aching eyes, he probed the surrounding ground for any movement. The tension within Glen was rising; his hands shook uncontrollably. The truth dawned on him; physically and mentally he was in no fit state to cope.

As he approached a telephone box, his body began to tingle, a sixth sense warning him of impending danger. Slipping his hand into his coat pocket, he grasped the automatic, slid it from his pocket, and eased the safety catch off.

Sticking to the dark patches, he carefully slipped from one to another, his eyes straining for any sign of movement or danger.

Headlights lit the street when a car swung onto it. It raced up the road before screeching to a stop alongside a phone box. Two stocky men of average height jumped out, their features hidden by dark overcoats and hats. They walked to the phone booth, both armed with pistols and torches.

"He's around here," shouted one of them in a harsh European accent. "There's blood all over the place; the bulb is broken. If I catch him, I'll slit his throat," he said, drawing his finger across his throat. "I swear on my mother's grave—I will."

"Look around. That bastard couldn't have travelled far, not with that hole you put in Henderson" barked the driver. "If you find him, kill him and be bloody quick about it."

Glen shuddered at the callousness of the cultured voice; for some vague reason, he recognised it but was unable to place when or where he'd heard it.

He turned his attention back to the two men. Their torch beams swung back and forth, light bouncing off walls from side to side across the street. They crisscrossed the darkness. They were slowly working their way towards him when a clap of thunder sounded, and the heavens opened. Torrential rain pelted down, helping to clear his head and at the same time forcing the men to run for their car. He watched in stoney silence, shivering from the cold, listening to them argue among themselves. Moments later, the car started up and drove off. Swinging into a side street alongside the park, it travelled slowly; torch beams cut into the darkness, searching for their prey. Glen watched them vanish over the hill.

If nothing else, his army experience had taught him to be patient and watchful. Therefore, he waited as minutes slipped by. With ears straining, he caught the faint hum of an engine approaching and saw no lights. When the motor died, he moved farther back in the shadows. A concrete loading ramp hid his presence. Cocking the automatic with his left hand, he waited, shivering uncontrollably as drenching rain seeped through his coat.

The alcohol slowly receded, and Glen felt the tension within him ease. But although his mind was clearing, his anger rose. Mulling over the few scant details available, he couldn't shake the disturbing thoughts. *What in the hell is Neil investigating? What has he discovered that could cost him his life?* While he sifted through these ideas, his eyes did not leave the two men searching along the perimeter of the old warehouse. Bending down, one peered into an opening below floor level. "What about here?" the shorter of the two said, shining his torch into the narrow gap. The torch beam swung from side to side, lighting brick pillars supporting the floor and spreading the light, making it difficult to see.

"I go in," his mate said. "If I find him, I'll slit his throat like a baby goat."

"Your funeral, Nicky," came the curt reply.

"No—his." There was a sadistic chuckle as the speaker slithered into the gap and disappeared into the darkness.

Minutes dragged by. Glen, having heard every word, moved closer. If Neil needed help in a hurry, he had to get closer. Reaching the building's corner, he could keep both parties under surveillance while giving covering fire if needed.

Twenty minutes passed, but no one appeared. The man's mate knelt down, calling out, "Nicky—did you get him?" Silence. "Nicky, answer me, damn you. Did you get him?"

"Yes," came a muffled reply. A gunshot rang out, hitting the kneeling man's head, driving his lifeless body to its side.

For a brief moment, Glen's eyes strayed towards the gap. He saw a figure crawl from it, staggers to his feet, and shuffle in his direction, vainly trying to escape.

A car door opening caught his attention. A tall man scrambled out, raised a pistol, and fired at the stumbling figure. Glen squeezed off two rounds. The first whipped the hat from the killer's head. The second hit his right wrist. The shooter screamed in pain as a bullet smashed through bone and tissue. The impact forced him to drop his gun and scramble back into the car. The startled driver sped away at the sudden turn of events.

"Glen—Glen, is that you?" gasped Neil, his breathing shallow and rapid.

"Yeah, mate," said Glen, rushing to his side. "Talk to me." Glen cradled Neil's head as the other man grasped at his arms. He could feel Neil's fingers sinking into his biceps.

"Treason, drugs, and money laundering." His breathing was laboured. Blood poured from multiple wounds. "Some real deep trouble, mate. Big shipment coming in. Time is short…" Neil's grip relaxed, and he gave a deep sigh. His head rolled sideways. Glen's friend was dead. Anguish tore at his heart. "Ah!" Glen screamed. "You filthy bastards will pay for this—my God, you will."

He focused his attention on the crime scene. Pulling rubber gloves from his pocket and slipping them on so as not to leave trace evidence, Glen searched all the bodies. As he did so, an idea flashed into his mind.

Strolling across to where he had fired from, he knelt, searching for spent cartridge cases.

He picked them up and slipped them into his pocket. Moving back to Neil's body, he gently opened his hand, removed his weapon, and fired two quick shots across open water.

He then wiped Neil's gun carefully and returned it to his dead friend's hand, choking back raw emotions while carrying out the task.

Going to the road, he found the dropped weapon. He poked a pen up the barrel and carefully examined the gun. It had no serial number. That had been removed, most probably filed off. Ejecting the mag, he judged three rounds were missing. He replaced the mag, then the weapon.

Going to the phone box, he made several phone calls to people working in the Australian Federal Police and to his answering machine—messages asking for help. Then, as the heavens opened and rain pelted down, he made his way to his car and the battered old Ute.

Ten minutes later, he slid to a halt at another phone box. He placed an anonymous call to the police with a handkerchief muffling his voice, knowing the department's policy to record all calls "There's been a shooting at Walton's old, abandoned warehouse on Regan Street. There are three bodies."

Thirty minutes later, he arrived at his apartment. He poured a cup of coffee. His hands trembled as he raised the mug to his lips. As he moved into the lounge room, his eyes fixed on the portrait of his wife, Laura, and Alison, his eight-year-old daughter. Glen felt tears rolling down his cheeks. An ice addict travelling at high speed had hit their car as they were returning from a photographic assignment, instantly killing them both. Now, with Neil's death, his emotions threatened to overwhelm him, derailing him from the arduous task ahead.

Struggling to bring his emotions under control, Glen refocused on the events that had just occurred. He had no idea what was going on. Wiping tears away, he wondered what Neil had uncovered that cost him his life.

So many questions drifted through his mind, and he needed answers fast. How was he to find them? Neil said not to trust anyone. That comment was in earnest. *Treason was one word used. Drugs, money laundering? A police officer? Possible. How high up had it climbed?*

Stripping off his wet clothing, he stepped under a shower, letting hot water cascade over his body. The sudden heat, penetrating his icy body like red-hot needles, was relaxing, easing his tension.

Then, just as he retired to bed, his mind jolted him. "Bloody hell!" he exclaimed, sitting bolt upright. "Mary and the kids!" Engulfed in his own confusion, he'd forgotten about Neil's family. What was he going to tell them?

Neil had neither notebook nor identification on him. He wondered if he had left any clues at home. But Glen could not approach Mary until she knew about Neil's death. Only then could he see her and offer his sympathy at her loss. Asking relevant questions about his work was going to be difficult, if not impossible.

He had dozed off, it was daylight, and a ringing phone roused him once more, bringing him to full alertness. "Johnson."

"Glen –Mary Henderson. Have you heard from Neil?" She asked, in an emotional tone.

"No – Mary," lied Glen. "Why - what's wrong?"

"He is missing, and I have not heard from him in over twenty-four hours."

"How do you know?" asked Glen, a worried look clouding his weather-beaten face.

"I just had a visit from a strange man, looking for him."

"What's his name?"

"I can't remember. Delanco- no – Delacey I think. I'm not sure."

"Do you know what this bloke wanted?"

"He asked if I had heard from Neil in the past twenty-four hours."

"When I said no, he seemed upset. Wanted to know if Neil would ring someone else."

"What was your response, Mary?" asked Glen, rubbing coarse stubble on his face; worried she might have given out his name.

"There was something about him I didn't like so I said no."

"What did he look like, tall, short, fat or thin?" asked Glen, breathing regularly again.

"He was tall, with one arm, either missing or covered and wore a dark overcoat."

"Did he show any identification?" said Glen.

"No – I just took him at his word."

"Is he still there?"

"No - left about ten minutes ago. This bloke hasn't gone far, about half a kilometre away, parked as if waiting for someone."

Glen worried about Mary and her children's safety, just in case it had been the assassin from earlier that morning. "Mary – ring the local police - tell them about this bloke and that he knocked on your door and now parked up the street. Tell them that you are frightened by his presence."

"I'll do that right now."

"Mary – don't tell anyone that you have spoken to me. I'll poke around – to see what is going on."

"Okay, thanks." The phone went dead.

Minutes later Glen was headed for Mary Henderson address. Wanting to catch sight of this bloke before a police wagon arrived. He approached her house from a different direction and stopped around a corner. There was only one car to be seen. It was a light grey late model Falcon sedan with local plates.

"That's interesting," mused Glen. He strolled around the corner as a local police car arrived. The driver stepped out and spoke to them for a few brief minutes.

Glen could see him produce some identification that satisfies them. The driver slammed his door shut and left.

Running back to his vehicle, Glen drove off after the Falcon. Making a mental note of the registration and driver's description, he wrote them down at a stoplight. The Grey Falcon was four cars ahead; Glen radioed in for a record check to headquarters.

"It belongs to one Richard Delaney, 20 Chandler Street, Kogarah," was a swift reply.

"Does this individual own other cars?"

"Yes-a 1988 Brown Falcon Ute. Registration. Delta – Echo – Victor - 666."

"Thanks - Over."

Glen headed for the address when an image flashed into his mind. Remembering a battered Ute from earlier that morning, he altered direction and headed for the docks. Twenty minutes later slipped in alongside it. The plates matched.

He approached the Ute With caution. Finding the doors were unlocked. Glen did a quick search of the vehicle which revealed nothing helpful.

"*Is he the shooter?*" said Glen, running both hands through his light brown hair.

Glen had more questions than answers. *Why is time critical?* He had to go back and ask Delaney. He did not like it, but he had no choice, he needed something to go on. Time was growing short.

It eleven thirty in the morning when he pulled up outside Delaney's house. The man was working in the shed, his overcoat was slung on the back of a chair. Glen knew this was not a killer; he had only one arm, his left.

The man looked up when Glen approached. "Good day Mate," he said, "What can I do for you?"

"Keys," said Glen, with a relaxed smile. "I believe these belong to you." Dangling Ute keys in front of him.

"He hasn't crashed it?" Delaney asked, taking them.

"No - nothing like that. Neil gave them to me yesterday, told me to drop the keys off to you," lied Glen. "Do you want a lift to pick it up?"

"If you don't mind, mate. My wife sick, and I can't leave her for long."

"No sweat," answered Glen.

Chatting as they drove back to the docks, Delaney told Glen how Neil wanted to borrow his Ute for twenty-four hours, no questions asked. Neil had helped him through a rough patch when he lost his right arm in Afghanistan years before, and they had been friends on and off since. Glen watched Delaney drive away, happy to have his Ute back.

Without thinking, Glen swung into Reagan Street, heading for the old warehouse. He came to a sudden stop. A police car was blocking the road. He turned past the park and headed home. He noticed several days' mail protruding from the mailbox. Parking the car walked back and collected it. Reaching his front door, he found it ajar. Alarmed, confident he had locked it. Eased the automatic from his pocket. He nudged it open and slid inside. He moved carefully through the apartment, checking each room.

Finding no one in his apartment and at first, nothing missing, and it puzzled him until he noticed his answering machine tape was missing. "Damn it to hell," he muttered. Then it dawned on him, someone was checking him out. His suspicious nature believed someone may have access to police evidence or knew of Neil's death. Glen knew his life was in danger.

A slight click behind him caused him to spin around, just in time to see the front door closing. Glen reacted instinctively, racing for the door. Wrenching it open, he charged after a fleeing figure. Taking stairs two at a time, He tripped, crashing heavily to the floor. Regaining his feet quickly enough to see a dark-coloured car disappear into the traffic.

"Damn," he growled fiercely. "Whoever you are mate, we'll meet again. You can bloody well count on it."

He walked back to his apartment. Wondering they had been able to find him so quickly. Why would they want a tape from his machine? It puzzled him at first, then it dawned on him, messages he had left the night before. Neil had been right – trust nobody.

AS he gathered his scattered mail from the floor, an unstamped letter with Neil's handwriting caught his attention. Ripping it open, a small slip of paper fell out onto the benchtop. It consisted of groups of three numbers, flashing at him like a neon sign. Breaking the code was the next step.

After studying it for several seconds, the penny dropped. Glen knew that it was a book cypher. One they had used several times before. The Oxford dictionary was a standard book used, same year and publication. Most homes had them, and they did not look out of place. The first group of numbers marked the - page. Second - line - third - word. That narrowed the search. Grabbing his dictionary, tirelessly worked his way through groups. "You're a cunning old bastard." Thought Glen, his spirits soaring. He was positive he had the right destination. *I'll get them for you mate, or die in the attempt,*" he vowed, fervently.

He left his apartment again, this time with the deadlock firmly secured. He carefully checked the perimeter, looking for anything out of place. Then worked on his car, looking for hidden electronic tracking bugs. Finding nothing, headed into Sydney at a steady speed, regularly checking the rear-view mirror for any surveillance. Satisfied he was not followed; parked and headed into Sydney central station. It smelt of coffee, unkempt homeless people, a strong smell of urine and stench of grease pipes from takeaway cafes. His nostrils flared at overpowering odours. Thankful, there were few people around. It took him several minutes to find triple six lockers, because of the remoteness of the location.

He opened it, reached in and grabbed a bag and contents. Pleased to find Neil's I.D and notebook. Locating a quiet corner in a nearby café, Glen flipped through pages, surprised at details and names within. Reading on, uncovered a list of ships, shipping containers numbers, and related dates. Two had been a circle in red pen, with notes scribbled in the margins. Important - container floors are examined thoroughly for ice - large shipment - around a (billion dollars street value). Glen whistled quietly to him. No wonder these bastards were willing to kill. Significant amounts of money

Slipping the book into a pocket, sipped his coffee and examined the small crowd inside cafe while his brain processed new information, wondering what his next move would be. Knowing he was in a tight spot, the most significant problem who to trust.

While he sat there, a tall man entered, dressed in a dark-coloured overcoat with his right wrist heavily bandaged, resting in a sling. He placed an order and sat down facing the entrance. Glen watched, as dark-haired man toy with his coffee, growing impatient, as if he was waiting for someone to arrive or perhaps leave.

Minutes ticked by before another man joined him. He was of Islander appearance, with dark curly hair. In direct contrast to his companion, he was a few inches shorter and stockier in build and had a look of a dangerous man.

Whoever this bloke was, he was taking no chances – he slipped a package to his companion under-the-table and received a small box in return. The Islander then left. His friend waited a few minutes, then followed.

Intrigued by the two, Glen casually left and began trailing the injured man at a safe distance. He knew the odds of this man being involved in Neil's death were astronomical, but a feeling gnawed at him, telling him he had the right man.

Minutes later, he was face down on the platform, his vision swimming from a blow to the side of the head. He heard a shout, then running feet before passing out. He came to a few moments later, helped to his feet by two railway security guards who had witnessed the attack.

"Are you okay?" asked one of them, while Glen searched his pockets.

Relieved that nothing was missing. "Yes– I think so. What happened?"

"Three young thugs jumped you. Lucky we were close by. We yelled, causing them to bolt. They have been causing problems for the last week or so," stated the senior guard.

"Come to the office. We need a statement. We will have the nurse check you over. Just to make sure you are okay."

Nodding his approval, Glen followed the two guards, discussing the night's event. He made a statement and was medically cleared by an attractive young woman. Thanking them for their help, Glen left. He was angry being unaware of his surroundings and being caught off guard. Most of all losing his quarry. He made his way back to the car and headed for home, hoping to study Neil's notes and plan his next move. The throbbing in his head had eased from the punch. The painkiller was doing the job, enabling him to concentrate on the traffic. Annoyed that he could not follow his suspect. Luck may have led him to someone more important in the chain. Now he would never know. Regardless of the result, he would remember these two.

Safely back at home, he checked the apartment thoroughly to ensure nothing else had disappeared and that it was secure. The phone rang it was Mary Henderson. She was in tears.

"What's wrong Mary?" he asked, dreading the answer.

"It's Neil - he's dead. Murdered."

"You are kidding me?" He said, acting in surprised while hating the deception.

"Last night at the old docks. Shot several times. I have to identify him. Can you come with me please?" she pleaded, fighting her emotions.

"No problems."

"As soon as possible. Tomorrow morning?"

"I'll pick you up as soon as I can," said Glen, "The kids -What about them?"

"My neighbour will look after them," she said.

Glen felt sorry for her. An only child and both her parents deceased. He knew she had no one else. The one glimmer of hope arose, he could ask questions about Neil's case without arousing any suspicion of his involvement the previous night.

He laid in bed, thinking of three children and one grief-stricken woman before falling into an uneasy sleep.

The next morning he arrived at the Henderson's in time to see Mary closing the front door and walk towards the car. She was a small, slender woman in her thirties, of Irish extraction, with red hair and flashing green eyes. Except for today, they were red from crying and with dark rings.

Glen opened the door for her, closing it and climbed back into the driver's seat and headed straight for the morgue, and waited for her to speak.

"I must look a wreck?" she said, softly, her head bowed.

"You look beautiful," replied Glen diplomatically.

"You are a liar - Glen Johnson. I look like hell, and you know it. So don't try to con me."

"Would I do that to you?" He asked, grinning sheepishly. He'd forgotten how direct and challenging she could be.

"Yes - but God bless you anyway and thank you for your kind words." She said wiping her eyes.

"Mary, can I ask you a question if you feel up to it?"

"Yes. About Neil?"

"Yes – do you know what he was working on?"

"He refused to tell me any important stuff, said it was for my protection."

"Do you know why?" asked Glen, looking at her.

"He said it was to protect the kids and me. That's why I freaked out yesterday when that strange character turned up," she answered rubbing at her eyes, "Why was he killed?"

"I don't know Mary; I'm hoping you may be able to help me find out. What has he told you?"

"He said he had stumbled onto something big. That it involved someone reasonably high up in the Australian Federal Police."

"Did he say who?"

"No – said, he would know for sure this weekend," answered Mary, looking at him. "Do you think he found out?"

"Yes – that's obvious now. That's what cost Neil his life."

"You will try to bring them to justice?" She said, quietly. Her pain filled eyes staring deep into his.

"You can count on that," he vowed in a bitter tone. "Neil was my best friend, and I will try to bring his killers to justice one-way or another."

Mary looked shocked for a moment at the hardness of his voice then said. "Neil told me something else. If things got really tough, I could go to you for help. – No one else. He trusted you."

Glen responded frankly. "We've been friends a long time and face some scary stunts together, especially in Afghanistan. We depended on each another constantly for mutual protection. That's how Special Forces worked"

She asked. "How will you find the men responsible?"

"I don't know at the moment. I have nowhere to start, or who I can trust," answered Glen truthfully. "I'm hoping to get some answers today."

"At the morgue?" she asked, wide-eyed.

"The calibre of bullet that killed him. Information in general."

"I see," she said, her eyes hardening.

"Problem?" Glen asked, looking at her in a new light.

"Neil has some timetables at home which he thought was important."

"How important?"

"Important enough to lock in the floor safe," came her reply.

"Oh – I see," Glen said his interest aroused.

Reaching their destination in Glebe, Glen parked the car, and they entered a building and head for the coroner's office. Glen whispered urgently in Mary's ear. "Don't let on about Neil telling you anything or bringing work home."

"Reason?"

"We don't know who to trust. It's important, so be economical with the truth."

She nodded, as they entered the office.

Mary tearfully identified Neil's body, backed up by Glen. The lab technician had them sign some paperwork, Mary commented. "I hate to think he died alone."

"He didn't. He took two others with him. He went down with a fight," volunteered the technician.

Glen intervened. "What type of weapon killed him?" Briefly distracted by a toe tag, protruding from under the sheet.

"His back had three gunshot wounds and a stab wound in his upper arm," replied a technician. Going on the size of bullets removed. I would say a Colt forty-five or something similar."

"How Did the other two die?"

"A head wound with nine millimetres. The other, his head bashed with a brick."

They both thanked him, had turned to leave when the door flew open, a senior officer strutted in. Spotting Glen - barked. "What are you doing here Johnson? You are on compassionate leave." Before Glen could reply, Mary let fly with a tirade of her own.

"Who in the hell do think you are?" She raged, as anger and grief took over. "A member of Hitler's Gestapo. That is my husband laying on a slab, having done his duty to his country. This officer escorted me here to identify my husband body. To help a woman in distress." With that, she flounced out of the room, closely followed by Glen, a broad grin on his face. It was the first time he had observed McWilliams cut down so expertly by one so small. He enjoyed it.

As they drove away, Glen was still grinning. Seeing it, Mary asked. "What's so funny?"

"I just loved your way; you lowered the boom on that narcissistic bastard."

"He just ticks me off. The arrogant pig. Upsetting a grieving wife that way, I hope it won't get you into any trouble?" She said apologetically.

Glen roared with laughter, saying." Lady in distress – never. A grieving wife yes."

She gave a weak smile. "I laid it on a bit thick. I cannot stand that man. He makes my skin crawl every time I see him."

"Let's forget about him," said Glen, "What about that paperwork Neil has in the safe? It is urgent that I see them. The first forty-eight hours are significant in any investigation."

Mary nodded. "Neil used to say that as well. Soon as we reach the house."

Knowing she was hurting emotionally, Glen drove the rest of the way in silence. Thinking about the meeting with McWilliams, his presence at the coroner's office. The sudden outburst. *What triggered it, McWilliams knew that Neil, and he was friends. It was only natural that Mary sought his help. Why the angry outburst?*

Engrossed in his thoughts, Glen came to a halted outside Mary's house. Exiting the car, opened the door for her and followed her inside.

"Sit down while I get the file, then I'll make some coffee."

A few minutes later, she returned, handing Glen a manila folder saying, "This is everything on the case. I hope it will help?"

"As I said, every little bit helps," Glen replied, slowly going through the paperwork. He paid particular attention to the timetables, making notes on several items of interest. Then continued to examine the file, looking for any information about the rogue officer or officers.

He glanced up as Mary entered the room, carrying two cups. She handed one to Glen, asking. "Did you find anything that may help?"

"Several – unfortunately - nothing pointing to a rogue police officer," said Glen, sipping on the hot coffee. He let the warm amber fluid caress his throat as he looked into Mary's eyes, taking in the pain that radiated from them. It tore at his heart, attacking his resolve.

"What are we going to do? Nothing?"

"What's this we?" said Glen, looking up sharply.

"Neil my husband, the father of our children. Think again - Glen Johnson. If you think I am going to be excluded, you are in for a battle."

Her anger bubbled to the surface; she stared at him with a determined look. Her tiny hands closed into fists, daring him to challenge her.

"Look, Mary - be sensible. You have three beautiful children to consider. What if the worse happened to you?" said Glen. "They are orphans."

"Neil parents would take them in. They love the kids dearly," said Mary defiantly.

"They have already lost their father," said Glen, throwing his arms into the air and glaring back at her. "Do you think endangering your life will help them? Come on be fair," pleaded Glen, shaking his head in anguish sharing her pain. She missed Neil but had no idea of what he knew, it would be difficult to let her know what he had discovered.

"I need to do something, or I will go mad," she pleaded, bursting into tears. Her tiny fists hammering against Glen's chest. "I need to help in some way."

Taking her by the shoulders, he held her close to him. "I need you to hold together. Keep your eyes and ears opened. Let me know if anyone comes around looking for this," showing her the manila folder. "Listen to the questions and conversation carefully. They may let something slip. Can you do that?"

"Yes," she sniffled.

"Lock this back in the safe," handing her the file, "Then -- forget they both exist. Also, I may call around, to let you know how the investigation is going. Whatever you do, do not use house phone or your mobile to contact me. There is a good chance your calls will be recorded."

Glen watched her leave the room to lock away the file. On returning - Mary made another coffee, and they sat talking when they heard a car pull up. Mary went to the window,

"McWilliams and another man," She whispered. "What in the hell do they want?"

"There's one-way to find out," said Glen softly.

"How, pray tell?"

"Open the door and let them in."

Mary heard a knock, waited a few moments, and then opened the door. "Hello, gentlemen. Surprise, what can I do for you?" She said, through a half-opened door, deliberately masking Glen from sight.

"I have come to collect your husband file in this case, also his notebook," said Mcwilliams's; his voice was firm, icy, but polite.

"What file? – What notebook?" asked Mary, looking puzzled. "Would you like to explain what you are talking about?"

"I assumed your husband would have kept a file on the case," suggested McWilliams becoming a little agitated with her as she prevented his entry.

"The notebook you picked up this morning at the morgue?" said McWilliams companion sharply.

"We received nothing from the coroner's at all," said Mary, opening the door wide. That's right isn't it Glen?"

Both men took a step to the rear, shocked, as Glen stepped into view. "Yes, that's right," replied Glen, "He'd have kept the file in his desk, Mary?" he continued, his eyes not leaving the pair for a moment. Glen studied McWilliams's companion, taking notice of the man cultured voice and the sharpness of the question. Glen knew the voice, having heard it not that long ago.

"We can always look," replied Mary, with a surge of cooperation, grasping Glen's train of thought. "I'm only too willing to cooperate to help find the killers of my husband. This way gentleman."

They searched the desk and the filing cabinet thoroughly. Finding nothing, both men bid Mary and Glen an abrupt farewell, storming from the house without a thank you.

Chapter Two

Uninvited Visitor

Glen watched with hooded eyes as they drove away. He lifted a finger to his lips warning Mary to be silent. Then walked over to where the second man had been standing alongside a pot plant. Parting the leaves, he removed a small listening bug with his forefinger and thumb, hidden, when it seemed no-one was watching. However, McWilliams companion was unaware that Glen had detected a slight hand movement and become suspicious.

Glen grabbed a fist full of tissues from a nearby box, placed the bug inside them and walked to the kitchen. With conscious control of his actions, he opened drawers quietly until he found plastic lunch bags. With a finger to his lips, signalling with his fingers to Mary to remain quiet while he called her over. Opening his hand, he peeled away the tissues to reveal the bug. With his free hand, he made a movement to indicate speaking and then pointed to his ear. Mary stepped back, startled. Tears filled her eyes as she bit the edges of her lips to prevent crying out. Leaning close to her face, Glen whispered, "I need cotton wool."

He watched as Mary opened a cupboard to reveal a medicine chest. Glen flipped the switch on the radio to let the music disguise any noise her movements made, as she pulled out other objects before handing him a bag filled with cotton wool.

Smiling, he pushed the lot inside a glass and signalled with his head for Mary to follow him to the front door. There she watched with a puzzled look on her face as he deftly placed his palm over the open mouth of the glass, flipped it upside down and shoved the glass deep into the potting mixture of the pot.

Mary followed Glen into the kitchen and wiped at her eyes. Glen patted her shoulder, "That was to listen in on our conversations," he explained.

"Why do…?" she said before it dawned on her. "Because they are looking for the file?"

"We have two worried men who don't know what to think or do?"

"Do you think they are in on it?" asked Mary, a stunned look on her face.

"That's a strong possibility. It's beginning to look that way," said Glen. "Proving it? Now that's a different story."

"Do you mean they'll get away with their treasonable and murderous actions!" exclaimed Mary, horrified.

"No way," said Glen, "It's going to be difficult, but not impossible."

With a tight grimace, she snapped, "I'd kill both of them without hesitation," she said, eyes flashing with anger, distorting her beautiful features.

"I know how you feel, Mary. Believe me," said Glen. "Let's put them in jail, not ourselves. But first, let's make sure they are the people we want beyond any shadow of a doubt."

"Would proving it be difficult?" queried Mary, regaining her composure.

"The first thing we need is some outside help. Someone with muscle if needed."

"Such as?" asked Mary, intrigued by his ingenuity.

"I'm working on that. First, we need your kids out of danger and in a safe place. Do you have any suggestions?" asked Glen.

"What about Neil's parents. They live Queensland and would love to have them for a little while," suggested Mary, her face crestfallen.

Neil could see any prospect of her separated from her children, even for a short time, was a huge ask. "See what you can arrange," said Glen, rubbing at his eyes, as if filled with grit instead of tears.

"Meanwhile I am going to look up a colonel I know at the Australian Crime Intelligence Commission."

"Do you think that's wise?" said Mary.

"The wrong idea?" asked Glen.

"The Australian Federal Police Commissioner is the chairperson for ACIC."

"You must be kidding," said Glen, looking at her in astonishment. "How in the hell do you know that?"

"Neil and I met him several months back when we went to Canberra for a meeting with him," said Mary. "We met with him often, nothing new in that." Glen was shocked by this revelation, unaware they had ever met the Commissioner.

"It was a shortly after that, that Neil received this case," said Mary.

"You didn't sit in on any meetings, by any chance?" he asked, realising at once how dumb the question was.

"Don't be silly. After we'd had lunch with the commissioner, Neil told me all about him and ACIC, when we flew back to Sydney."

Glen's mind was racing as he digested the information. "You know what? You're a bloody wonder," he said, rubbing the back of his neck to ease the tension building up inside him. "He's the man we need to get in touch with. Neil was working undercover for him."

"I never thought of that possibility," said Mary, raising her right hand to her chin. She nervously chewed on a fingernail, realising just how valuable the information was. "I'm sorry Glen," said Mary, "I didn't think the trip, and your investigation had any connection whatsoever. I had no idea how important this was."

"That makes two of us Mary. I had no idea Neil had spoken to the boss, let alone met him. The trick now is to see him without his staff running interference for him or informing McWilliams."

"Ah, ha," said Mary, raising her finger. She picked up her purse from the table and rummaged through it. "Here's his card," she said, handing it to him.

"You're joking!" spluttered Glen.

Once again her mood changed, her mind drifting off to a happier time. "In Canberra, I expressed some reservations about his job and how dangerous it was. The Commissioner gave me his card and told me to call him day or night if an emergency arose. I would say this constitutes an emergency, wouldn't you?"

Glen reeled in surprise. He was struggling with all the valuable information Mary had contributed. She had given him so much more to work with to explore her husband's death. Far more than he'd expected.

"That's bloody outstanding," said Glen, regaining his composure. "Looks like I have a new helper."

"Thanks, Glen. To keep my sanity, I must help," replied Mary, wiping her eyes again.

"I'm sorry to upset you. It's your family I'm concerned about… I don't want any more of you hurt. This'll be dangerous," he said, looking deep into her green eyes. He was mesmerised by her strength of character, charm, and courage. "You're one hell of a woman Mrs Henderson. I'm proud to call you friend."

"Neil always reckoned you'd kissed the Blarney Stone. "He was right."

Mary, embarrassed by Glen's comments rose to her feet and continued. "I'll ring Neil's parents and arrange for the kids to stay for a couple of weeks. Then I'll ring the commissioner and try to arrange a clandestine meeting. That's all I can do."

"Mary," said Glen, "Impress on him how urgent it is. That it's important, we speak to him in person, away from prying eyes and ears. He'll get the drift."

"And if he doesn't?"

"Tell him it's an emergency. If that doesn't get his bloody attention, I don't know what will," said Glen. "Explain that it's already cost Neil's life, and he has rats in his organisation. At least one large suspect."

Mary looked up at Glen for a moment, shaking her head. She knew he was playing a dangerous game, with death as first prize.

Mary walked to the phone and dialled the number. Seconds later, she abruptly hung up.

"What's wrong?" asked Glen, a puzzled look on his unshaven face.

"I heard a click on the line as I started to dial. I think we may have rats. It's either that or I'm becoming paranoid," answered Mary, in a soft voice.

"Hell, they didn't waste any time acting, they must be desperate. Using an illegal phone tap," said Glen. "They haven't had time to get a bench warrant."

"What will they gain?" Mary asked, chewing on her hair, worry etched on her face. "What do they hope to achieve?"

"Information."

"But we don't have any information. Nothing of any importance," Mary said, clenching her fists tightly.

"For some obscure reason, they think we do."

"Nothing we've discovered so far points to them. It's McWilliams stupid actions that are making them suspects," stated Mary, walking to the kitchen and flicking on the jug. She rinsed out the mugs and made another cup of coffee. "Question is, what are we going to do?"

Glen smiled deviously, saying, "Nothing. Absolutely nothing. We are going to drive the bastards' nuts."

"May I ask how?"

"With monotonous routine," explained Glen. "There is nothing so tedious than listening to endless hours of numbing brain chatter. First hand or recorded".

"So what's next?" asked Mary, giving Glen a mug of steaming coffee.

"Ring Neil's parents right now," said Glen, pointing to a phone. Arrange for your kids to stay." Taking a drink of coffee, He continued. "Next, go online and book a one-way passage for the Gold Coast for all four of you." Raising his hand in expectation to Mary's interjection, he added, "You return on the first available flight. Email these details to your computer, and I'll pick you up from Mascot."

"May I ask why you are staying here?

"It may attract an unwelcome visitor if the place appears empty," said Glen, clasping his hands together. "If that happens, they'll receive a rude shock. Your dog Sam and I will be patiently waiting."

"Oh, I see," said Mary," disappointed at missing out. "A nasty little surprise party."

"Don't look so glum about it," argued Glen, "It may not even work."

"Well," said Mary, standing up, "let's set a trap to catch giant rats." She walked to the phone and rang Queensland. The necessary arrangements were quickly made. A few minutes later, she hung up and said, "Everything's arranged, and the rats are active."

"Good, let's see if we get a nibble," said Glen, rising to his feet. "I'll let you sort out things here. I have items to collect from my place. Don't forget to leave me a password to the computer and a front door key. Importantly, ring the commissioner from the airport. Let him know what's going on."

"You already know the password. It's your wife's name with a capital L, followed by the first four numbers of her birthday. Here's the key," answered Mary, handing it to him. "Now go, I have work to do."

Driving back to his apartment Glen checked his rear view mirror several times. A white Commodore sedan attracted his attention by its erratic behaviour, swerving in and out of traffic trying to stay close to him. Becoming suspicious, Glen pulled into a shopping mall to buy some groceries.

Several minutes later he came out carrying plastic bags of shopping. After loading them into the trunk of the car, he pulled out into the traffic. The Commodore was five cars back. Smiling, Glen murmured, "The rats are active."

As soon as he arrived home, he grabbed his shopping, locked the car in the garage, and walked inside to his apartment. He placed the bags on the floor, found one of Laura's digital cameras and fitted a telephoto lens. He walked to a window which looked down into the street and peered cautiously through the curtains. Sliding the window open, he raised the camera and snapped a handful of photos. He closed the window and walked to the computer.

After removing the memory card, he inserted it into the computer. Glen studied the photographs carefully, recognising the tall-injured man from the café. *"Well my murderous friend. You and I have a date with destiny,"* vowed Glen bitterly. *"A date I'm eager to fulfil."*

Running a registration check, he had the man's details within minutes. One John Mason. Discovering Mason had several outstanding warrants for unpaid speeding fines and a lengthy rap sheet. Glen stretched back in his chair, wondering how to use the information to his advantage. He needed to buy time and the freedom to move around.

Walking downstairs to a building pay phone, Glen rang the local police station and lodged a false complaint using a fake name. He supplied, make, colour and registration of the Commodore. Then he returned to his apartment and waited to see what would occur. Twenty minutes had passed before any police arrived. An argument accompanied by physical confrontation followed. The driver was arrested and driven away. Witnessing the noisy quarrel, Glen smiled. His ruse had worked. He'd also photographed the entire incident as documentary proof.

"That's one problem temporarily solved," thought Glen, rubbing his hands together. He needed time to organise for the night. He was confident that someone would turn up. The frontal assault had not worked; a covert operation would be the next logical step.

Glen walked into the spare bedroom where all Laura's photographic equipment was. He rummaged around in the boxes trying to find Laura infrared animal cameras with motion sensors. He was planning to set them up both outside and inside the house in the hope of gaining photographic evidence.

During his search he stumbled across a cam recorder, fitted with infrared lens and motion detector. "You bloody beauty," he cried. "This is perfect." He checked them carefully to ensure they were in perfect working order before stashing them in a bag.

Walking to the window and parting curtains, he looked down into the street to check on the Commodore. It was still parked.

Although he wanted to search the car, he decided against it. Caution seemed the wiser decision.

It was late afternoon when Glen reached the Henderson house. Letting himself in, he quickly set up the cameras in strategic locations in the backyard, focusing his attention on one window in particular. At the same time, Glen made it easier for an intruder to gain access into the house.

Looking up, Glen caught sight of Sam, Henderson's big Siberian husky cross, sitting quietly behind him. Sam had been watching his every move with keen interest. He was a well-trained dog who gave a little throaty growl when danger was threatening. Should an intruder try to enter the house? Sam's low snarl would provide a warning. However, and most importantly, he would attack when commanded. Glen had worked with him before and had great faith in the animal's training and ability

Finished outside, Glen walked back into the house, silently followed by Sam. Sensing something was amiss, Sam followed him from room to room giving him funny looks.

Glen entered the laundry and opened the window a couple of centimetres, just enough to gain entry without making it look obvious. Glen wanted them to come this way. So he could control the action to his advantage.

Going into the lounge, he found a site for the cam recorder with a full sweep of the room. He was hoping to catch the intruder in the act. He rechecked house security, ensuring the deadlocks, and the windows were locked.

Satisfied with his efforts, he moved into the kitchen and made himself a cup of coffee. Feeling peckish, he went to the fridge. To his surprise, he found a container of sandwiches and a handwritten note. "Just in case you get hungry – Take care. Mary."

"That mistress of yours is wonderful woman Sam. Come on, mate; we'll share the sandwiches."

Sam wagged his tail in agreement and followed Glen into the lounge room. They shared the couch and devoured the food. Then Glen curled up with a couple of pillows and blankets that Mary had thoughtfully left out.

A small growl from Sam alerted Glen that they had a visitor. His watch showed three thirty in the morning. Placing his hand on the dog, he whispered softly, "Quiet." He flicked on the cam recorder and silently cocked his pistol.

A figure appeared from the laundry, using a thin beam of light to guide him. The intruder stealthily worked his way towards the main bedroom. Remaining hidden, Glen could hear the intruder opening and closing drawers, giving the room a thorough search. "Reynolds said it was here," muttered the intruder.

Glen's ears pricked up at the mention of the name. Sergeant Dave Reynolds, The man who accompanied McWilliams when they called on Mary yesterday. The bug planter.

Unable to find the file, the man came out into the lounge, muttering angrily. "I'll burn the damn place down. That'll teach the silly bitch a lesson." He began stacking magazines against the lounge

'Not bloody likely," shouted Glen, flicking the light on. "Police – you're under arrest for breaking and entering and attempted arson."

The startled man hurled the magazines at Glen, then dashed for the back door.

"Attack, Sam!" commanded Glen. He watched in satisfaction, as Sam dragged down the fleeing man. He screamed in terror, trying to fight off the snarling dog. Sam sank his fangs into his right forearm. "Call him off! Call him off!" bellowed the man. "I give up."

"Heel, Sam," commanded Glen. The dog obeyed and moved to his side. Eyeing the cowering man, ready to attack again.

"Roll over onto your stomach and put your hands behind you!" ordered Glen, pulling a pair of handcuffs from his hip pocket.

As he went to cuff him, the man lashed out with his foot. The kick caught Glen off guard, hitting him in the groin and causing him to grunt in pain. He tripped over Sam and fell backwards. The intruder jumped to his feet and bolted for the laundry, slamming the door shut behind him.

Painfully getting to his feet, Glen was too slow to stop the man from scrambling through the open window. He heard him clamber over the boundary fence and take off down the street. Moments later, he heard a squeal of brakes and then a dull thud.

"Damn him to hell," snarled Glen, angry for being caught unawares for the second time in two days.

Walking into the lounge, Glen turned on the computer, picked up a camera. He continued on to the main bedroom, photographed the mess, then tidied up the room, switched off the light and closed the door and returned to the computer.

There were two emails, one giving Mary's flight details saying that she would arrive at twelve thirty that afternoon. The other email was curious. "Your sister is in Perth and won't be back until late tomorrow." Mary knew he did not have a sister, so Glen immediately grasped the meaning of the text.

As soon as it was daylight, he began removing the memory cards from the cameras and inserting them into the computer. He downloaded their contents and copied three good images of the intruder to the hard drive and also to a flash drive.

Turning his attention to the cam recorder, he was pleased to find some real footage. The excessive white light had ruined some of it, which had occurred when he switched on the overhead light. The recording of the intruder's voice caught his attention. It was sufficiently audible to hear Reynolds' name mentioned.

"It's not much," thought Glen, nodding his head slowly. "But now, we have a reasonable idea who's behind Reynolds."

He made a dual recording, plus written reports, with copies of all the photographs in his possession. He hoped to supply the Commissioner with enough evidence to continue working on the case.

With time growing short, Glen headed out to Mascot Domestic Airport to pick up Mary, wondering how she had made out. Working his way through the traffic, Glen regularly checked his rearview mirror, looking for a tail. Not noticing any he continued to his destination.

He walked into the terminal in time to see Mary's aircraft land. Five minutes later, Glen saw her coming through security. He gave her a brief nod and waited for her to collect her bag before heading out to the car. Seconds after getting in, she asked, "Well, what happened? Did we get visitors as you expected?"

"Yes. One intruder."

"Did you catch him?" asked Mary, flushed and excited.

"Yes and no," answered Glen, somewhat sheepishly.

"He escaped on you?" said Mary, looking at him in disbelief. "What happened?"

"It wasn't easy, believe me. As I went to cuff the bastard, The bastard lashed out with a foot, catching me in the groin and causing me a great deal of pain. As I staggered back, I tripped over Sam. In that brief instant, he jumped to his feet, bolted for the laundry and slammed the door behind him."

"Did it hurt?' she asked, smiling wickedly, unable to stop laughing.

"Of course it bloody hurt woman! What are you, a damn masochist?" retorted Glen, feeling embarrassed and insulted at the same time.

Laughing, she grabbed him by the arm, "Come on. I'll make you coffee when I get home. By the way, the Commissioner contacted me."

"Good news I hope!" said Glen, still feeling aggrieved at her treatment of his misfortune.

"Well, I think so. I managed to speak to the Commissioner briefly this morning."

"You managed that," asked Glen, in a subdued tone, "When he was in Western Australia?"

"When I rang yesterday, I spoke to his wife. I explained the important details to her. She said she'd get him to contact me. Asked me where I was and wanted Neil's parents' phone number. Just before I left for the airport this morning, I received a call from him. He was upset to hear of Neil's death and was flying back. I arranged to meet him at a Chinese restaurant called the Golden Dragon at seven thirty tonight. It's about a block from his home and fitted with private booths."

"Wait a minute," interrupted Glen. "He lives in Canberra?"

"That's right. We have seats booked on the five o'clock flight," answered Mary. "Aren't you lucky you have such an efficient sidekick?"

"Oh, my God! Save me from this woman," pleaded Glen. "She's gone nuts!"

Ignoring the slur, Mary continued. "Now that that's settled, I want to go home, have a hot shower and change into clean clothes."

The trip was uneventful and mainly in silence. Asking Mary how the kids were taking their visit was his opening move.

"Hard, as you can imagine," she answered. "Especially young Emily. She loved her father dearly."

"And her mother? How is she coping?"

"Just," she answered, tears welling in her eyes.

Leaving it at that, Glen drove in silence. He wanted to tell Mary what he had achieved but decided to wait for a more appropriate time.

Thinking carefully about it, Glen decided to run his idea past Mary. She had a sharp eye for details. If she approved, they would take a copy of what information they had and put it before the commissioner, seeking his reaction. His need to work on this case was overwhelming, the thirst for justice strong. Nevertheless, the Commissioner's permission and backing were essential if he was going to examine McWilliams and Reynolds. For that, he would need substantial proof. Finding evidence was the question.

Walking out of the bedroom, Mary stopped, puzzled at the magazines piled against the lounge. "Can I ask a question?" she said, looking at Glen.

"Sure, what do you want to know?"

"Why are the magazines piled up at the end of the couch?"

"I'm sorry about that," said Glen, looking up from the computer, silently cursing himself for forgetting them. "When our visitor couldn't find the file, he decided to burn the house down."

"Burn the house down!" she exclaimed, fuming at the thought. "You must be joking!"

"Unfortunately, I'm not," said Glen. "Remember, I said it could get rough."

"You weren't kidding, were you?" said Mary, horrified at the possibility of losing the house. "And you let him get away?"

"No," replied Glen calmly. "Look at these photographs. Tell me if you recognise this individual."

Walking to the computer, Mary studied the photos for a minute or two and then said, "Evil looking character."

"He's the person that broke in about three thirty this morning looking for the file."

"H-h- how did you take the photo?" Mary stuttered in amazement.

"I used some of Laura's animal traps, using infrared lens and motion detectors. I set them up outside and inside the house." Playing the recording, Glen said, "Now look and listen to this."

"Oh, my God! Who is Reynolds?"

"You've already met him," said Glen bluntly.

"Not with that name."

"Yesterday, right here."

"Do you mean the man with McWilliams?"

"Exactly. The man's name is Sergeant Dave Reynolds, a crony of McWilliams."

"How come you didn't recognise him yesterday when they were here?" asked Mary, enquiringly.

"I knew the face," answered Glen, "But I couldn't put a name to it until I heard it mentioned this morning. It was then, every detail fell into place for me."

"So there's no doubt they're crooked?"

"Beginning to look like it. Mind you, the intruder could mean someone else with the same name. Yesterday, after I left here, I picked up a tail; a tall, thin man, with one arm, strapped up. He was driving a white Holden Commodore."

"The one-armed man that called here?" interrupted Mary.

"No, look at this photograph," answered Glen, bringing it up on the computer.

"That looks a bit like him, but it's not the same man. I'm sure of that," said Mary, studying the photograph carefully.

"If you ever see him hanging about Mary, let me know at once. He's dangerous," stressed Glen. "He's a killer."

"Did he kill Neil?" asked Mary quietly.

"That's a strong possibility," answered Glen cautiously, hating to deceive her.

"The man who called?" queried Mary.

"He was a friend of Neil's from Afghanistan. His name was Delaney, and he lives nearby. Neil borrowed his work truck, no questions asked," said Glen.

"So he came here looking for his truck," guessed Mary. "What do we do?"

"I want you to arrange all the information and photographs in chronological order and download them onto a couple of flash drives. Include Neil's file in the safe. Also, make a separate file for the Commissioner, with a laser disk of the recording," directed Glen. "Do you think you can do all that in the time we have left?"

"I don't think that will be a problem. I'll just make one file and download it," answered Mary, happy to be doing something productive.

With Mary on the computer, Glen went to shower. He changed into the spare set of clothes. Walking into the kitchen, Glen flicked on the jug and made them both coffee. He carried the mugs to the computer, placing one next to Mary.

"Thanks."

"How's it going?" asked Glen, sipping on the coffee, feeling the hot liquid lifting his spirits.

"Good," answered Mary, gathering paper from the printer and putting it in a manila folder before handing it to Glen. "The paper for the Commissioner. One disk, one flash drive. What's next?"

"Using an old film case, mark the disk with the movie title, put them together and place them in a carry-on bag. Hang the flash drive around your neck. When you go through security, just throw the flash drive into the tray as if it doesn't matter," advised Glen. "Enclose the paper copy in a brown paper container and seal it shut. Finally, pack it at the top of your suitcase."

"That's all?" said Mary, slightly puzzled at the precautions he was taking.

"No, I want you to make up another file, just using the first part of Neil's report. Exclude the shipping timetables. That's important. Instead, add these two coded names to it," finished Glen, writing down groups of numbers and handing them to Mary.

"What's this file for?" asked Mary, looking up at him.

"That's cheese to catch a giant rat," said Glen, grinning. "This file we'll hand over to McWilliams before flying to Canberra. I hope this will take the heat off us."

"I'm interested in how?" asked Mary.

"After I set the cam recorder up for regular use, you're going to ring Mr McWilliams. Tell him you found a sealed file hidden in Neil's dirty laundry basket. You're sure it's the file he was asking for."

"Do you think he'll go for it?" said Mary, feeling a little nervous about the whole idea.

"Yes, I do. To have it handed voluntarily? McWilliams will jump at the chance. To stir the pot," said Glen grinning, "ask him if he wants you to open it to check the contents. Let's see the reaction we get," answered Glen, setting up the cam recorder. "One more thing. Tell him you want a receipt, to protect yourself legally. Otherwise, you won't release it."

"You think McWilliams is on the take?" said Mary, smiling.

"Yes, I do. And I believe that there are millions of dollars involved. However, we need hard evidence, material that will stand up in a court of law," said Glen, angrily punching his right fist into his left-hand. "If these bastards are dirty, they are a threat to every clean police officer and dishonour everything they stand for."

"If you're wrong?" reasoned Mary.

"If I am, I'll stand corrected. It means the end of my career in the Australian Federal Police. But I know in my heart," said Glen, pointing to his chest, "that I'm not. This man's an arrogant character and is never wrong in his own eyes. He believes his intellect is far superior to anyone else's."

"Thanks, Glen. Now I know we're doing the right thing," said Mary, tears welling up in her eyes. "I don't want Neil's death to be meaningless."

"Neither do I, Mary." said Glen, Neither do I," Putting his arm around her shoulder. "Let's set this operation in motion."

"Yes, let's get cracking," answered Mary, walking to the phone. She dialled McWilliams' number and spoke to McWilliams in person. A few minutes later she hung up as Glen walked back inside with Sam by his side.

"No problems?" he asked, a laundry basket in his hands.

"He'll be right over. No, do not open it. Extensive evidence could be in it, which could be substantial. His words, not mine," said Mary, her hands trembling slightly.

"Good, the bait's working. Let's see what happens. Meantime, find an old folder or file that doesn't look new and hide it under all the clothes," directed Glen. "Then place the basket on the table in full view of the camera. Most important, get him to sign the receipt here."

'Anything I should remember?" asked Mary.

"Yes, be yourself and act natural, but keep Sam inside with you, just for added protection. I'll be in the kids' bedroom listening."

Mary rushed around following Glen's instructions, ensuring everything was perfect. Satisfied with the arrangements, she walked to the kitchen, washed up the mugs and put them away. As Mary walked back into the lounge, she spotted the plant pot and removed it from sight, uncertain if McWilliams would be alone.

Glen opened the bedroom door and whispered, "He's just pulled up, and he is on his own."

Mary gave him the thumbs up sign and waited for the knock at the door. When it came, she called out, "Coming." Opening the door, Mary smiled briefly, "Come in commander."

"Thank you, Mrs Henderson," he said, strutting into the room as if he owned it. "Where's this file you've found?" he asked stiffly.

"Over here on the table," answered Mary, leading the way. She removed the clothing from the basket. "I think this is what you were looking for," said Mary, picking up the wrinkled paperwork.

"Ah, yes. That seems like the one your husband showed me," lied McWilliams, eager to get his hands on it.

"I'm so glad that's cleared up. I need you to sign a receipt, releasing me from all legal responsibility, and the file is yours."

McWilliams took a pace towards Mary as if to snatch it when Sam stood up, his fur rising, emitting a low, throaty growl. Rethinking his position, McWilliams muttered something vague and signed the receipt.

Walking towards the front door, Mary expertly escorted him out of the house, handing him the file. Then stood at the door and watched him walk to the car and drive off.

Glen opened the bedroom door and walked out beaming. "Brilliantly executed, Mary. That was a magnificent performance. It deserved an Oscar."

"I don't know about that. I'm shaking like a leaf. At one stage, I thought the bastard was going to snatch the file. However, Sam put him in his place. Good boy," said Mary, kneeling and giving the dog a big hug. Sam responded with a whimper and tail wagging.

"Mary, scan that receipt into the computer and print off a copy. Place it on the Commissioner's file. Then we must go if we're going to catch our flight," said Glen. "I'll check the recorder and grab the memory card."

Glen walked to the camera. "Damn it to hell!" he exclaimed. "The bloody recorder isn't working. The battery's dead."

"Did you get anything at all," asked Mary

"I don't know. We have no time to check it now. We'll do that later."

"That's disappointing," said Mary, knowing how important the video would be as evidence. "While I'm thinking of it, how come our narcissistic friend didn't spot your car?"

"That's simple, I parked it in your garage while you were flirting with him on the phone," answered Glen, a massive grin on his face.

"Flirting with that man! I'll give you flirt, Glen Johnson," exploded Mary, threatening him with her tiny fist.

Laughing at her empty threat, Glen picked up the cases and headed for the car. Time was growing short. He reversed the car out of the garage and waited patiently for her, knowing from past experience that that comment was going to cost him.

Chapter Three

The Commissioner

Glen sent Mary ahead of him, through airport security, following her, about four passengers back to ensure there were no problems. They walked to the gate and waited patiently for their flight.

Soon they were airborne. Fifty odd minutes later, they were over Canberra. They landed without incident, collected their baggage and caught a cab to their motel. Walking to their rooms, Glen whispered in Mary's ear, "Check to make sure the Commissioner's file is intact." Mary gave a quick nod and disappeared into her room.

They reached the Golden Dragon with several minutes to spare and were shown to a booth. The Commissioner and his wife had already arrived. Going through the usual formalities, Mary opened the proceedings.

"Commissioner, as you are aware, my husband was brutally murdered two nights ago, while working undercover for you. Would you say that is a fair assessment?"

"Yes."

"Since then, my house has had a listening device installed, my telephone messages and conversations have been recorded, and my home has been broken into and nearly set on fire," stated Mary, in a matter of fact tone.

"Believe me, Mrs Henderson, I have no knowledge of, nor have I authorised any such action against you," said the Commissioner emphatically, his British accent recognisable.

"We are well aware of that sir," said Glen cutting in. "We have some preliminary evidence, suggesting that a couple of our members are involved in some type of illegal activities."

"That is what your husband was investigating on my behalf before his death," said Commissioner Worthington, nodding. "I've had my suspicions for several months."

"Why is that, Jack?" asked Mary, using his Christian name.

"Over the past few months, several important operations have failed. At first, we thought our intelligence had been wrong. Then I began to suspect an internal leak. Neil's death proved that I was right. Unfortunately, I'm no better off now than I was before."

"Can I ask a question?" said Glen interrupting. "Were all of these operations located in Sydney?"

"Yes, all but one, which was in Newcastle. Why do you ask?" queried Jack, glancing at Glen.

"Sir, we have a file, partly compiled by Neil, Mrs Henderson, and myself, with photographs, recordings and written reports that indicate the behaviour of two individual officers in the Sydney office that might be involved. Sir, I do stress the word might."

"Don't worry Johnson, your job is safe. Neil recommended you as a backup, in the case of a mishap."

Mary handed the envelope to the Commissioner, and she and Glen sat back, as the man read through the file without interruption. They heard him mutter at one stage, "Those two. That wouldn't surprise me for one moment."

A few minutes later, the commissioner looked up, asking, "Do you have any more?"

"Some, sir," said Glen. "Mary has a CD with a recording we feel you should hear. We want your opinion on it."

"Go ahead, let's hear it."

Playing the recording several times, Mary looked apprehensively at Glen before the commissioner indicated he had heard enough.

"You have done well to gather this much," he said. "Do you have any more?"

"Maybe sir, but I'm not sure if the camera was working. The battery went dead," answered Glen. He pulled the memory card from his wallet and passed it to Mary. She pushed it into the slot of the laptop and hit enter.

The Commissioner watched in silence as McWilliams entered the frame, received the envelope, had the minor confrontation with Mary and Sam and signed the receipt. It was at that point that the camera had gone dead.

"What exactly was in the envelope?" asked the Commissioner.

"A preliminary report sir, with all the vital information removed and particular groups of numbers added which suggested names of participants."

"Supposing, McWilliams cracks the code, what then?" asked the Commissioner, leaning back and placing his hands on his head.

"If he does he'll be the first man in history to decode gibberish, sir," replied Glen, "I needed to buy time and freedom of movement. It was imperative that we met in secret."

"This is important to know," said the Commissioner. "Neither McWilliams nor his crony had any authority to collect the file or to have any part of the investigation, mainly because all the failed operations came under his jurisdiction. Admittedly, I thought the leak was lower down the chain of command. This evidence has proven me wrong," said the Commissioner, shaking his head. "It's unbelievable, that a man with eighteen years in the Australian Federal Police, nominated at one stage to be a director, has betrayed his country and colleagues."

"Sir," said Glen, breaking in on the Commissioner's train of thought.

"Yes, Johnson? What is it?"

"Sir, I would like to volunteer to carry on this investigation, with your permission and backing of course."

"That goes without saying, my boy. Neil Henderson spoke highly of you. He wanted to use you as back up. I said no because you had just lost your wife and daughter in that horrific traffic accident."

"I wished you had agreed to his request, sir. You may have done us both a favour," answered Glen, his mind returning to that day six weeks ago. "I've been through hell since then."

"Of that I'm sure. Hindsight is a beautiful thing, Glen. Whatever resources you require will be placed at your disposal. Anything else?"

"Yes, sir. First, I need to get out of McWilliams' control, giving me freedom of movement. Secondly, I want Mrs Henderson made a special deputy, so I have someone I trust that I can bounce ideas off," said Glen, "and can come to you in an emergency."

"How does that suit you, Mrs Henderson?" said the Commissioner, turning his head. Only to find both women had left the booth unnoticed. "Well – I never, where did those two disappear too."

"I'm sorry sir, I didn't notice them slip away."

Moments later the curtains parted, both women walked in chatting away. "What?" said Mary, a cheeky grin on her face? "Don't tell me you missed us." Sitting down both women smiled sweetly and giggled.

"As I was about to say, Mrs Henderson," continued the Commissioner, "Glen asked me to make you a special deputy. How do you feel about it?"

'I would appreciate it immensely. Mr Johnson needs someone to watch his back and make his coffee for him and keep him out of trouble," replied Mary, with a wide grin, pleased that Glen had kept his word by bringing the subject up,

"Glen, there is one thing I'm not too sure about. The man in Mrs Henderson home, what did you do with him?" asked the Commissioner, setting his wine glass aside. "Did you hand him over to the local police?"

Mary spluttered in her glass, trying to suppress her laughter. She knew this was a sore point with him, especially after the crack she made."

"In a roundabout way," he said, giving Mary a disapproving look. "He broke free and managed to get away from the house. He went over the boundary fence and was hit by an oncoming truck."

"Dead?"

"No sir, he's in a coma in St Vincent's Hospital, Kings Cross. He's not expected to live, sir," said Glen, looking straight at the Commissioner, holding his stare.

"Were you chasing him at the time?"

"No, sir. I heard the squealing of brakes, then a dull thud and shortly afterwards, the sounds of screaming sirens and flashing lights close to the house," answered Glen.

Sitting up straight, he continued. "Making inquiries the next morning, I discovered his name and address. Not being in pursuit, I didn't feel it was my responsibility to follow it further. Remember sir, I was trying to keep a low profile. It's all written down in this letter," said Glen, passing him an envelope.

Receiving it, the commissioner read, "For your eyes only," glanced up at Glen, his facial expression deadpan and slid it into the inside pocket of his suit coat. "I'll read it later when I have more time."

For the next two hours, they chatted, enjoyed a good meal, and then parted company. On their way back to the motel, Mary commented, "That seemed to go well."

"Yeah, better than what I thought it would," said Glen, feeling empowered to act more robustly. He wanted to lean on McWilliams, just to stir the bastard up but knew he would have to wait. His chance would come.

"Glen," said Mary, breaking into his thoughts, "Thank you for asking Jack about me becoming a special deputy."

"No sweat," answered Glen, "You've proven how valuable your assistance can be. And you are pretty steady under pressure. More importantly, you can think on your feet in the time of crisis. The primary factor, however, is this; I know I can trust you. At the moment, that's essential."

"What's next?" asked Mary, as they arrived back at their motel.

"At the moment I don't know," said Glen. "Things have been moving so fast, I haven't had time to think things through."

Deciding to call it a night, they headed for their individual rooms. Opening the door to his room, he caught sight of a man leaving by his room window. "Hey you, stop, or I'll shoot," yelled

Glen, whipping his pistol out and lining it on the intruder's back. The tall, dark-haired man halted, stepped back into the room, his hands in the air. His brown eyes mesmerised by the steadiness of the pistol aimed at him.

"Turn around," Glen ordered, stepping over to the window and closing it behind him. The man turned around, eyeing Glen off. "Do you know it's illegal to point pistols at a police officer?"

"Really?" said Glen, "Show me your badge. Well come on, let's see it."

The intruder pulled out his badge and showed it to Glen. "Satisfied?"

"No. Why is one police officer illegally searching the room of another police officer?" demanded Glen, pulling out his badge.

The man looked stunned as he peered at Glen's badge intently. "I don't know what to say, mate. We received notification three days ago that, if you turned up in Canberra, we were to follow you. Record where you went and who you spoke with. Then…"

"Report back to the Sydney office to either Commander McWilliams or a Sergeant Dave Reynolds," cut in Glen savagely. "I hope for your sake that you have not reported my presence to those two individuals."

"No, sir. The information we received that you were a drug dealer. Not a police officer," answered the young constable, in a state of confusion.

Picking up the phone, Glen rang Mary's room. "Mary, sorry to disturb you, but can you come to my place? It's an emergency. Right, thanks."

A few moments later, Glen opened the door to Mary's knock. "Come in and meet my guest, Constable Mike Lord of the Australian Federal Police."

"What's he doing here?" asked Mary, looking confused.

"Illegally searching my room. For what, I don't know. For whom, I do," said Glen.

"Don't tell me – McWilliams and Reynolds," said Mary, a look of disgust clouding her features.

"You see, Mike, a few nights back, Mary's husband was murdered by a drug cartel. He was one of us, working undercover. At the time, unknown to us, there was a fly in the ointment. McWilliams and Reynolds," said Glen, finishing with a flourish.

"Since then," cut in Mary, "They have tried just about everything to discover what we know. The unfortunate fact is we don't know anything. It's their stupidity and actions that have alerted us. We came here today to arrange my husband's funeral," continued Mary, bending the truth a little.

"If you doubt our word, Mary can ring the Commissioner right now, and you can verify everything yourself," added Glen, taking over from Mary, in an attempt to place the young constable under more pressure.

"How do I know you're not fabricating this story?" asked Lord, resenting the fact.

"I can help you there," said Mary, chiming in. She pulled the Commissioner's card from her pocket and handed it to him. "You can ring him yourself."

Mike Lord looked at the card and decided he was not going down that path. "What do you want me to do?"

"One, forget you ever saw us. Two, if any more of these requests come through. Contact me by email. Let me know what information they're after. In return, we'll forget that you entered my room illegally," said Glen, writing down his email address. "Mike, remember, we are the ones that saved your arse from being caned."

"One thing I will promise you, Mike," said Mary, interrupting. "For cooperating with us, we'll file a report with the Commissioner, saying that you supplied information vital to this case."

"But that wouldn't be true," said Mike, defensively.

"Why wouldn't it?" asked Glen. "The information you just gave us is essential. If you hadn't volunteered to help us, we'd have been caught completely unawares. Knowing our movements were being illegally monitored for purposes of gain and evasion, for that we are incredibly grateful."

With that, Glen ended the conversation, dismissing the young constable and watched him depart the premises. Looking at Mary, he asked, "What is your gut feeling about this young bloke?"

"I believe he's telling us the truth. He's obviously a new man on the block. He was doing his job as he saw it," answered Mary. "It's clear he's inexperienced. It's his belief he was showing initiative, trying to prove his worth."

"The question is, do we take him at his word? Or let the commissioner know and he deals with it?" said Glen, a thoughtful look crossing his face.

"Maybe we can split it in half," suggested Mary. "Let the Commissioner know, and he can deal with it first thing in the morning plus cover Mike's butt at the same time. Tell him that Mike gave us valuable information, how McWilliams is using our organisation against us to keep track of our movements."

"Yeah, that could work," said Glen. "It will give the young bloke a chance to prove his loyalty and keep our word to him at the same time."

"Good, we'll go with that," said Mary rising to her feet and walking to the door. "I don't know about you, but I'm tired, and it's past my bedtime. See you in the morning."

Calling on her the next morning, Glen was surprised that Mary had gone out and had been away for about an hour. He was sitting down to breakfast when she walked into the dining room and threw a set of car keys on the table.

"What's this?" asked Glen, looking up at her.

"Our transport home. I rang the Commissioner first thing this morning and told him the story we decided on last night. He asked me to call on him at once. He arranged for a vehicle to be placed at our disposal for an unlimited period. Also, he gave me this letter for you, stating that the bearer has full rights to act on his initiative," said Mary, sitting down at the table. "He gave me a curious message. Quote, "Tell Glen I fully understand.""

"I see," answered Glen, shoving a fork full of bacon into his mouth. The first decent breakfast he'd had in several weeks.

"Well, I don't," complained Mary, annoyed at being left out of the loop.

"It's about the letter I gave him last night regarding the bloke who broke into your house, the accident and his details," said Glen, leaning back in his chair.

"You've not only kissed the Blarney Stone, Glen Johnson, but you also married it. I know bullshit when I hear it," whispered Mary fiercely, her eyes flashing like emeralds in sunlight.

"Oh, come on Mary. You were there when I told him about it," answered Glen, amused by her false rage.

"Well then, tell me this. Why didn't you mention it to me?" said Mary in a calmer tone.

"Because we were flat out like a lizard drinking and it slipped my mind," answered Glen, unable and unwilling to tell her the whole truth.

An hour later, they were heading for Sydney. Originally Glen had intended taking the most direct route, but after the incident the night before with Mike Lord, a voice deep within told him that was not the smart thing to do. He decided to go via Lithgow, a far more indirect way. Though time was critical, it gave them more options should they pick up a tail.

Mary drove at a steady pace. With kilometres slipping by, she pulled into a service station, refuelled the car and grabbed a drink for each of them. Walking back to the car, she noticed a red sedan had stopped a little way ahead of them.

Climbing in, she said, "Glen, see that red car. It's been following us for some distance. I'm not sure if it's tailing us or not."

Looking at the car ahead, Glen said, "Change places. We'll soon find out."

Slipping the car into gear, Glen eased out onto the highway and picked up speed. The red sedan waited a few moments then followed. It stayed several cars back, making no attempted to catch up.

"I'm not sure," said Glen, putting his foot down a fraction more. The car picked up speed and started to draw away. Once out of sight, Glen turned off into a side street and waited for the red sedan to pass.

"There's something familiar about that car,"

"Do you reckon it's hostile?" asked Mary, concerned she may have made a mistake.

"I don't think so. But I know it from somewhere," said Glen, racking his brain, trying to remember.

"Could it be someone from your past?" asked Mary, trying to be helpful.

"I don't know. That's what's bugging me. I make an outstanding cop. The past could bite me on the arse, and I wouldn't see it coming", answered Glen, frustrated with himself.

"Don't be so hard on yourself, Glen," said Mary, "You've been through hell the last few weeks. Hitting the booze the way you did wouldn't have helped."

"How in the hell do you know that?" said Glen, stunned by her admission.

"You don't remember. Neil and I called around several times, trying to help you get through your grief. We were the only ones that knew how hard you took Laura's and Alice's deaths. Your world was destroyed in one brief moment," said Mary in a consoling tone. "Now you're there for the kids and me, helping us to come to terms with our grief. It's just as real and devastating for us. But I had to be strong, for the kids."

"I'm sorry Mary, I never knew," said Glen, realising for the first time, how far into the abyss he had sunk.

"It was Neil who organised your compassionate leave. Made sure you ate, showered and dressed," explained Mary, in a soft yet ruthless tone. "It was him who dragged you back from the depths of despair."

With tears rolling down his face, the truth gushed out. "I tried to save him, but I was too late. He died in my arms."

"You, you were there?" stammered Mary, "When he died? Why didn't you tell me?"

"I didn't know how to. I was too much of a coward. I couldn't face you and the kids. Worse still, I couldn't face myself. Not after failing him and ruining your lives," said Glen, miserably.

"Don't talk like that. You could have died that night. You haven't failed us; it's your strength and ability I'm relying on," said Mary, sharing his misery.

Feeling the guilt lifting from his shoulders, Glen said, "I promise you this; I'll do my utmost to bring Neil's killers to justice, even if I die in the attempt."

"I never doubted that for a moment," answered Mary, looking at him. "Neil told me how you and your section were ambushed. The other two men killed." Brushing her hair to one side, she continued. "Neil was severely wounded, you refused to leave him. He told me how you stayed with him for several hours, fighting off six Taliban rebels until a passing Apache helicopter pilot came to your aid. On being picked up, you had only four rounds left."

"But Mary, that was different," growled Glen, stubbornly trying to defend himself.

"Those were not the actions of a coward. I don't care what you say. Your actions gave me my husband, three beautiful children and twelve years of marriage," said Mary, tears rolling down her face.

Turning his head, Glen focused on the road ahead while his mind tried to erase the turmoil within and come to grips with the task ahead. The red sedan worried him. Who in the hell owned it? Where had he seen it before? He glanced over as Mary checked the G.P.S. "Problems?" he asked.

"No, I've been thinking. If that red sedan is following us, somewhere, it will pull over and stop, waiting to see if we've turned off."

As they approached Lithgow, Glen caught sight of the sedan as it pulled into a service station. Making a split second decision, he pulled in behind it. Mary looked at him sharply, sensing his intentions.

"Do you think this is a wise decision?" she asked bluntly.

"I don't know. I'm sick of constantly looking over my shoulder. If this red car is following us, I want to know why," growled Glen, getting out of the car. "I think it's time to take some decisive action. So why not now?"

"If that's the way you feel, let's get to it. Direct action can get quick results. Maybe this is one of those times," said Mary, vacating the car.

As they walked towards the service station entrance, they kept a watchful eye on the pair, wondering what the reaction would be when confronted. As soon as they entered, Mary relaxed and smiled. "Hello, Mira. How are you?"

The small blonde woman spun around, surprised at hearing her name. "Mary! Where did you come from?" she asked, before spying Glen in the background. "Glen. It was you. I wasn't too sure."

"Hello Mira," said Glen, looking at his ex-sister in law and, in particular, her male companion. He was an active individual, thirtyish. Not Mira's usual taste in men. In fact, the complete opposite.

"Glen, Mary, this is Ken Reynolds. We met a couple of weeks ago at a dance," explained Mira.

Noticing Glen's body involuntary stiffen at the mention of his name, Mary quickly intervened. "Hi Ken, what are you doing out here in the wilderness?"

"I'm an artist. We've come out to get some photographs of the surrounding landscape."

"Whatever for?" asked Mary, in a questioning tone.

As Ken Reynolds explained the reasons behind the photographs, Mira pulled Glen to one side, whispering. "How come you are with Mary? Where's Neil?"

"Neil is dead. Murdered two nights ago," answered Glen bluntly. "I'm helping Mary with his funeral arrangements and other business affairs."

"Oh, my God!" gasped Mira, raising her hands to her face in horror. "I didn't know."

Changing the subject quickly, Glen said, "Who's this new bloke you've hooked up with Mira? Do you know much about him?"

"Not a great deal. Why do you ask?" Mira said, a frown clouding her suntanned face.

"We have a suspect under surveillance for Neil's death, with a similar surname. I'm wondering if he's any relation. That's all."

"He's never mentioned any family. I've never asked," said Mira, thinking back over the past two weeks.

"Whose idea was it to come here? His or yours."

"Why; his.

"Has he ever asked you about your family or Laura?" asked Glen, watching, as Mary moved further away from them with Mira's companion in tow.

"Once, when we first met. Ken asked if I had any siblings. When I said no, not anymore, he dropped the subject."

"Does he know who I am?" asked Glen, looking across the room.

"No, I told him you were an old friend whom I hadn't seen in months. That appeared to satisfy his curiosity," answered Mira.

"Good, leave it at that. I'd like to know more about this bloke. Find out what you can, then let Mary know. Whatever you do, don't ring. Her phone's bugged. Just call around to the house and see her," said Glen, his voice laced with urgency. "I don't want you hurt. So please be careful."

He watched as Mary made her way back to them with drinks in her hands. Her companion broke away from her and headed for the toilets. "Bloody good idea," muttered Glen, leaving the women and following.

He halted at the door, listening. Hearing Ken Reynolds voice as if he was talking on the phone, Glen pressed his ear hard against the door. He could hear fragments of the conversation.

"I tell you, Dave, I'm not sure.," said the voice, before it faded. "I'll do my best."

Having heard enough to make him cautious and highly suspicious, Glen returned quickly to the women. Grabbing them by the arms, he hurriedly ushered them outside and briefed them on the conversation he had overheard, particularly impressing on Mira the importance of not engaging in any discussion regarding them. "If he asks, tell him anything but the truth," said Glen, reinforcing his suspicions.

"We'd better get going, or I'll have to pay the babysitter extra," lied Mary, moving off towards their vehicle.

"Okay, I'm coming. Remember what I told you, Mira. If he's mixed up with this crowd, he could be extremely dangerous. I'll catch you later," finished Glen, walking to the car as Mary pulled up.

Leaving the service station, Mary headed for Sydney, when Glen instructed her to turn off and wait. Minutes passed, before the red sedan sped by, oblivious to them.

"Go back into Lithgow and take the Bells Line Road," said Glen, looking back over his left shoulder.

"What on earth for?" queried Mary, looking at him in bewilderment.

"To avoid any nasty shocks, from a particular group of people who would love to know our whereabouts," informed Glen.

"So, you think he's tied up with them?" asked Mary, glancing at him.

"To be honest, Mary, I don't know what to think. But until I know for sure, I'm taking no chances. Both our necks are on the line."

Satisfied with the answer, Mary nodded in agreement, then said, "This way will take us longer."

"Not that much more. At this time of day, the Blue Mountains will be bumper to bumper traffic all the way through to Parramatta. Besides, I have to pick up my car from the airport."

"Oh yeah, I forgot about that," said Mary, slowing down as they approached the road to Windsor.

It was nearly four, by the time Glen arrived back at his unit. He scanned the surrounding area for prying eyes. After locking his car, Glen made his way to his apartment. He checked it over thoroughly. Finding nothing amiss, Glen began to relax and plan his next move. He must have sat there for an hour or so, going over all the information in his mind, wondering what was the best way to proceed, when a knock came at the door. Getting up, he walked over towards it, calling out. "Yeah, wait a bloody minute."

Several shots rang out, the bullets punching through the door, narrowly missing him. Reacting instinctively, he hurled himself to one side while drawing his weapon. He held his fire. He waited a few moments before climbing to his feet. The sound of running footsteps attracted his attention.

Throwing caution to the wind, he ripped the door open, catching a glimpse of the tall man from the café fleeing down the stairs. With total disregard for his safety, he charged after him, knowing this was an excellent opportunity to take out Neil's killer. Another bullet chipped the brickwork above his head, some flying masonry nicking his face, forcing him to duck. He fired once, his round hitting the man in the head, flinging his lifeless body back into the wall. Looking down at the crumpled body of Neil's killer, Glen felt no remorse. Thinking. *"That's for you, mate, Mary, and the kids."*

At that moment, one of the residences poked his head out of the door. Glen growled. "Ring the police. Tell them there's been a fatal shooting. There's a federal officer on the scene."

The state police arrived within minutes, immediately taping off the site. Identifying himself as a federal police officer, Glen led them back to his flat, showed them his bullet-ridden door, and the spent cartridge casings lying in the hall. Moving back the way they'd come, Glen pointed to the impact of the bullet on the masonry, and from where he had fired the fatal shot, Still dabbing at the wound on his face, Glen looked at the men as they wrote it all down. He knew from experience they were analysing the veracity of his story. In his mind, it was a clear-cut case of self-defence. How they might view, it was something entirely different.

One of the officers asked, "What case are you working on at the moment?"

"None whatsoever. My wife and young daughter were killed in a traffic accident six weeks ago. I'm on compassionate leave. As I told you before, I've never met or spoken to the gunman." He failed to mention that he'd put a bullet into the man's shoulder a couple of nights earlier.

"There must be a bounty out on the Feds," interjected a burly, plain-clothes detective.

"Why is that?" asked Glen coldly, looking for some snippet of information.

"One of your blokes was killed a couple of nights ago down at the wharf."

"Do you know who it was?" asked Glen, hoping to gain information that could be helpful.

"No, but Commander McWilliams did. Do you know him?'

"Yeah, he's my boss."

"And don't you forget it, Johnson," boomed a voice behind him. "What in the hell has been going on here?"

Glen knew the voice without turning. "McWilliams," he growled to himself. Rolled his eyes in frustration, Glen turned slowly to confront his superior, ready, but unwilling to play his trump card at this particular moment. The first thing Glen noticed was that McWilliams seemed visibly shaken by the event.

"Well, Johnson," demanded McWilliams arrogantly. "I'm waiting for your explanation."

Before Glen could reply, the senior detective angrily challenged the way McWilliams was trying to hijack the investigation. He retaliated with equal vigour. "And who, sir, gave you the right to take over this investigation, without prior approval from our Commissioner. I'm sure he will have several words with your Commissioner on this subject."

Not wanting to involve his chief officer any more than necessary, McWilliams backed off. "If this man is guilty, I want to see him punished to the full extent of the law," spluttered McWilliams, overplaying his hand.

"If he is guilty of anything, it's lucky to survive an assassination attempt. He fired one shot in self-defence, the Assassin eight. I say that makes it a clear-cut case of self-defence. From information I've been told, he is on several weeks of compassionate leave," stated the burly detective emphatically. "Is that correct?"

"Yes," admitted McWilliams reluctantly, apparently annoyed at the demise of the gunman. With that, he turned and strolled away. Anger powering each step as he disappeared down the stairs.

"I'm glad he's on your side. With superiors like that, you don't need any enemies."

"You can say that again, mate. He's a narcissistic bastard," added Glen, grateful to the detective for his unexpected intervention.

"One more thing. If you need help at any time, day or night, ring this number and ask for Pat Murphy. That's from your Commissioner to mine, to me, with instructions to assist you in any way we can."

"Thanks, Pat. I don't know what to say."

"Don't thank me. It's your Commissioner you should be thanking. Besides, I've waited a long time to step on that cockroach McWilliams. It just made my day."

"I take it you've met him before?" asked Glen with a smile.

"Once or twice. By the way, do you have a place to spend the night?"

"Yeah, I have," answered Glen, thinking of Mary on her own.

"Good. We are going to be tied up here for a while. You can go."

"I need to get back inside for some clothes and car keys. And - do I keep my weapon?" asked Glen hopefully.

"I don't see why not," said Pat, handing it to him. "I know where to find it if I need it."

Gathering up everything he required, his keys and a spare automatic, Glen went downstairs to his car and headed for the Henderson place. Winding the window down, he let the breeze fan his injured face and thought about the unprovoked attack on him. *Why was it carried out in such* a clumsy manner? Most of all, why was it attempted at all?

At the moment he was no threat to them. The thing puzzling him the most; McWilliams turning up at that precise moment. Was he checking to see if his hired assassin had completed his contract and to give him aid to escape? There was no way it was coincidental. He no longer believed in coincidences. Most of all, he didn't trust McWilliams.

The commander was there for a particular reason. Money, loads of it. One billion dollars to be exact. The more he examined the facts, the stronger the nagging doubts grew. They had missed an important clue. But what?

Several minutes later, he was knocking on Mary's door. On opening it, she took one look at his face and exclaimed, "Glen, your face! What happened?"

"I'll explain inside," he said, as she opened the door to let him in.

"You can do that while I clean up your face," she said, ushering him inside and sitting him down. "Stay there; I'll be back in a moment."

Glen sat ashen-faced through her nursing, saying nothing until she had finished. "Well, what happened?' she demanded, admiring her handy work.

"Our friend, with the bad arm, paid me a visit shortly after I arrived home today. He knocked on the door. Lucky for me, I was about a meter away when I called out. Next moment a fusillade of bullets ripped through the door. I managed to throw myself to one side, narrowly escaping injury."

"He tried to kill you?" Mary exclaimed, in shocked disbelief.

"I think that was the intention," answered Glen, a wry smile on his face.

"This is no joking matter. Did you ring the police?"

"Not straight away. I chased after the assailant. That's when I received this," he said, indicating the wound on his face. "He fired at me again from the stairwell. His bullet hit the corner of the building, and some masonry chipped off the wall, hitting me, forcing me to duck as I fired. My round hit him in the head, killing him instantly."

"Is he the one that killed Neil?" she asked, a nervous tremor causing her hand to shake.

"Yes. There's no mistake."

"Neil can rest easy in his grave now. He didn't deserve to die. He was a good man. I'm glad that bastard is dead," she cried, holding her head in her hands, her body shaking uncontrollably.

Glen rose, walked to her and placed his arms around her. "Let it out, Mary. Let it out," he said softly, amazed she had held together for so long. Wrapping a blanket around her, he convinced her to lie on the couch. "You calm down," he said as he stood up. "I'll make some coffee."

As he moved around the kitchen, he could hear her sobbing. He understood how she felt. Picking up the mugs, he walked back into the lounge and placed them on the table. Mary sat up, took a sip, wiped her eyes, had another sip letting the amber fluid work its magic on her tormented spirit.

"If you feel up to it, I have a bit more to tell you," said Glen, returning his mug to the table.

Mary brought her emotions back under control, "Go on," she said. "Let's hear the rest."

"Not long after the police arrived, McWilliams showed up, visibly shaken at finding me alive."

"What was he doing there?"

"I don't know, but I intend to find out," said Glen, his voice cold and harsh.

Chapter Four

The Hostages.

Early next morning a soft knock on the front door roused Glen from the couch. Springing to his feet, he armed himself and walked silently to the door. With the previous day's incident still raw in his mind, he stepped to one side and leaned against the wall. As he did, Mary walked from the bedroom, her eyes widening and then understanding. Moving behind a solid wall, she looked up at Glen, waiting.

Reluctantly, he gave a slight nod.

"Is that someone knocking," called Mary, in a clear, firm voice.

"It's Mira, Mary," came the reply.

"It's early. Are you alone?" asked Mary.

"Yes," came a stifled answer.

"Hang on a moment, I'm coming."

Mary unlocked the door and turned the handle. The door opened violently, knocking her over, with Mira sprawling on top of her. Ken Reynold entered the room, a thirty-eight calibre pistol clasped firmly in his right fist. "Okay, give me the letter," he demanded.

"What letter?" challenged Mary defiantly, engaging direct eye contact and holding it?

"The letter your bloody husband stole from the warehouse. The letter is incriminating certain people of influence. I want it, and I want it now."

"I don't know what you're talking about," argued Mary, trying to regain her feet, at the same time dragging Reynolds deeper inside.

"Stay still or else!" snarled Reynolds viciously, walking towards her. "Otherwise, I'll have to mess up that face of yours."

"I doubt that," growled Glen as he kicked the door shut and slammed the barrel of his gun across the man's wrist. Reynolds screamed in pain as both bones in his thin wrist snapped, causing him to release the weapon.

Like a vulture, Mary scooped the gun from the floor, kneed Reynolds in the groin, forced the revolver into his mouth, and cocked it, all in one fluid movement. "Threaten defenceless women," screamed Mary, anger burning deep in her emerald green eyes. It was at this point that Reynolds soiled his trousers, fainting during Mary's tirade.

Withdrawing the gun and lowering the hammer, Mary handed it to Glen saying, "That man scared sh... witless of me." With that jibe, she walked over to Mira and helped her regain her feet. "Coffee time, I think," she added, ambling into the kitchen with Mira in tow. Glen shook his head in disbelief at Mary's swift actions and equally strange behaviour. He wondered how close she was to squeezing the trigger. Or was it a bluff?

Either way, she had Reynolds bluffed. He decided that knowledge could work to their advantage. He would let Mary lean on the man when he regained consciousness. Cuffing the prisoner's left arm to the lounge, Glen watched as the women walked back into the room carrying three mugs of coffee.

"Well, Mira, how come you're involved in today's proceedings?" asked Glen, looking at Mira's trembling hands.

"He called. Said his mother wanted to meet me. I agreed, hoping to gain information that may have help you. Then, he asked me about Mary and where she lived. Like an idiot, I said nearby. The next moment I had a gun jammed into my ribs, and my mother is held hostage by a couple of his friends. He threatened to bash my face in if I didn't bring him here. When we pulled up, I recognised Glen's car. I felt so relieved when I knew he was here. You know the rest."

"Lucky for us. Otherwise, we could be dead or severely injured," said Mary bluntly.

"Give him the letter that's so important to him."

"We can't give him the letter," said Glen.

Baffled at his reluctance, Mira asked, "Why on earth not?"

"For two simple reasons: one, we don't have it. Two, its federal evidence in an investigation," answered Glen, giving Mira a withering look of distrust. "We had no idea it existed until Reynolds mentioned it," said Glen, thankful for the breakthrough.

"That explains a great deal," added Mary. "That's the reason we're under all types of pressure. And it also explains the attempt on your life yesterday. Now, this incident today. They're becoming extremely desperate."

"Oh, my God! What have I done," cried Mira, lowering her head in shame? "I was desperate, they're where holding my mother hostage, and if we didn't return by a particular time, they threaten to kill her."

"Not if I can bloody well help it. I couldn't save Laura or Alice, but I am not going to stand idly by when I can help her mother," said Glen, jumping to his feet. "Mary, walk next door and ring this number. Ask for Pat Murphy. Tell him we have a package for him to pick up and keep isolated for at least forty-eight hours. Also, we have an urgent need for a particular detail, and we have to act quickly."

"What package?"

Glen nodded his head at the prone figure. "Him."

Ten minutes later, Mary returned, her face beaming. "The troops have left. They're calling here first to collect our prisoner. Then onto Mira's place. Pat said needs as much information as possible if we are going to free Mira's mother."

"Right, Mira. How many men are there at your mother's place?"

"Two. Strange looking individuals, acting as if they're on drugs. Solidly built, dark-skinned. Non-European," said Mira, panicking over her mother's safety.

"They sound like friends of our late-night visitor," said Glen, looking at Mary. "Do they have weapons, Mira?"

"They both have pistols like that," said Mira, pointing to one they had taken from Reynolds.

"That's all?" asked Glen.

"As far as I know."

"Did your friend here give you any hint as to the time you had to be back by?"

"No, none. Reynold's remained silent in regards to the time we had to return."

"We haven't any time to spare. When Pat and his men arrive, and this germ is in protective care," said Glen pointing to Reynolds, "we will move against the two holding Mira's mother."

Several minutes later, several state police arrived led by Pat Murphy. Ken Reynolds had regained consciousness and looking fearful by the number of police gathered in the house. With his wrists handcuffed and in great pain. Reynolds was walked out to a police wagon and transported.

Gathering around the table, Glen explained the layout of the house and the blind spots from which to approach it. "Pat," he said, "There are a couple of details you should know. Mira's mother is feeble and cannot move fast. Also -- she happens to be my mother-in-law. I'm very fond of old Jess, so I don't want her harmed."

All nodded in approval. "This has to be quick and clean," added Glen, moving among them. "From the information we've been given, they're armed with thirty-eight calibre pistols and possibly of Islander descent. So be careful, these boys like to play rough."

"We can handle ourselves if we have to," said Pat Murphy, a sparkle in his brown eyes. "Glen, can I suggest another idea add to yours?"

"Go for it," said Glen, keen to listen to any suggestions that might make the plan feasible in its execution

"What we need is a decoy to distract them so we can take advantage of it," added Pat.

"Any suggestions?" asked Glen, looking around the room.

"I have one," said Mary, stepping forward. "Mira told me earlier, that the men at her place asked Reynolds to send a couple of pizzas to them. I'm the smallest here and know the local pizza parlour owner well. I could fit into the uniforms reasonably well and borrow one of his delivery vans."

"Are you sure?" asked Pat. "Do you think you can handle it?"

"No doubt whatever," replied Mary, confident in her competence.

"What do you think Glen?" Pat asked, uncertain about Mary's claim.

"If you think I'm going to stop her, think again, Pat. I know what she can do," replied Glen, remembering that she'd won the National Karate Championship three years in a row. With all agreement, Glen gave Mary permission.

Mary quickly arranged for the uniform and the delivery van while the rest planned the other part of the operation down to the last detail. At the last moment, Mira remembered the pizza had to be the Meatlovers Special. It was a minor detail, but essential to the plan. With all aspects in place, they put it into action.

For extra protection, and unknown to the others, Mary slipped a thirty-eight calibre pistol into her clothing. Satisfied no-one could see it, she began her part in the deception.

With everyone in position, she stopped outside the house, grabbed the pizza, walked to the front door and rang the bell. Moments had passed before a short, stocky man opened the door. "What you want?" he asked gruffly in broken English

Ignoring his rudeness, Mary said, "Two Meatlovers Special pizzas for this address. Already paid for by Mr Reynolds."

"Moneybags finally paid for something."

Placing the pizza boxes in his hands to divert his attention to the food. A yell followed by a struggle inside turned his head a fraction, giving Mary enough time to knee him in the groin. Then with devastating effect, deliver a sidekick to his right knee, bringing the man crashing to the ground. As he rolled in pain and grasping himself, Mary drew the pistol, rammed it into his left ear forcing him to stop moving. "Try to run or resist, and I'll squeeze the trigger. Do you understand?" said Mary sternly. Her prisoner cowered and in pain, nodded his head.

Pat, the first to reach her, stopped dead in his tracks. He stared in disbelief at the sight that confronted him.

"Do you want to handcuff him or should I, Murphy?" asked Mary in a sweet, innocent voice. "Old man, you need all the help you can get."

Reacting to her jibe, Pat handcuffed the man and forced him back into the house.

"Young woman, don't you give me any of that old man garbage or I will put you over my lap and tan your rump," growled Pat, pushing his prisoner in front of him.

"Kinky! You might not be as old as you look," taunted Mary, bringing up the rear.

"I see you grabbed him, Pat," said Glen. "Good job. I was afraid Mary would be outclassed," said Glen, a big smile on his face.

"In a pig's eye! She had him on the ground with a pistol wedged in his ear before I arrived," replied Pat, guessing it was a ploy. "Glen, I hope you know payback is a bastard," said Pat, laughing.

"Thank you and your group for the help, Pat. I'm in your debt. If I can return your kindness, let me know. One more item; make sure those three do not talk to anyone for the next forty-eight hours at least. I can't stress how important it is that they're held incommunicado for that period, longer if possible."

"I'm sure we can work it out. These men are all facing several serious charges over today's events," said Pat, urging his group and the prisoners out of the house and into the cars. "We'll take good care of them. Of that I'm sure!" he shouted over his right shoulder, closing the door behind him.

Mira walked out of the lounge room. "I am glad they've gone," she said. "They interviewed both mum and me, each of us giving a statement. Glen, mum wants to see both you and Mary - to thank you personally, for what you did today."

"Come on, Mary, we'll go and see my mother-in-law. I haven't seen her since the funeral of Laura and Alice," said Glen solemnly, his eyes misting up.

They walked into the lounge to find Jess shuffling around in the kitchen, making a pot of tea and some sandwiches. "Hello, you two. It's been a fair while since I've seen you." Her voice shook from old age, shock, and hopelessness. She placed the pot and the tray of sandwiches on the table. Walking over to Glen, she put her thin arms around him and hugged him tightly. Softly she whispered, "I am sorry for our young women. We have to move on, son. We have no choice" Glen turned his head slightly, his emotions threatening to overwhelm him. He hugged the old woman back.

Shuffling over to Mary, Jess hugged her, saying how unfair it was about Neil. How society had turned violent and unpredictable. Mary hugged her back, tears rolling down her face, happy for a woman's touch and kind words.

"Come now, you two," called Jess. "Let's have a cup of tea and catch up on all the gossip. Mary, you can tell me about your three beautiful children." Her hands shook as she poured tea into the four cups and handed them around.

"Sandwiches, anyone?" asked Mira, passing them around.

Glen felt sorry for Jess. She had lost her husband in a car accident and her only son in Afghanistan when a landmine exploded. Now she'd lost Laura and her granddaughter. Glen shook his head in sadness; life had been cruel to old Jess. She deserved better.

After about thirty minutes, old Jess retired to her room to rest, the dramatic hostage event taxing her strength to the point of exhaustion.

Mira and Mary returned to the table. Glen asked Mira about Ken Reynolds.

"Mira, this morning when you arrived, Reynolds was raving about a letter Neil was supposed to have taken from a warehouse. Do you know anything about this claim?" asked Glen, standing up and stretching.

"They have the impression that you have it in your possession," answered Mira, reminding them of Reynold's wild claim.

"Well, we do not. We had no idea the letter even existed until Reynolds stormed in demanding its return," added Mary, thinking about the events of the day.

"Here's a question only you can answer, Mira? When you met this unsavoury character was it by chance or by design? We know you said you met him at a dance a couple of weeks ago," said

Glen, thinking hard about the sudden change in the plans of their opposition.

"Yes, that's right," replied Mira thinking back to that night. "At the time I figured it was purely accidental. Now, I'm not so sure."

"The reason I'm asking, I didn't become involved in this case until four days ago, the night Neil lost his life," said Glen, mystified at their belief that Mary and he knew all about this letter.

"I'm not a member of the Federal Police. I have no knowledge of this!" exclaimed Mira, bewilderment wrote across her face.

"That's what I don't understand," said Glen. "Your meeting was ten days earlier, well before I became involved."

At this point, Mary chimed in with a chilling thought. "Glen, do you remember when we were returning from Canberra that I told you that Neil and I had been around to your place multiple times over the past six weeks, helping you get back on your feet?"

"That must be the connection. Mira is my sister-in-law," Glen said grimly, understanding for the first time how twisted and profound this case was. They knew who Neil was at least ten days earlier. "They're assuming Neil had given me the letter. That explains the burglaries at Mary's and my place. It also explains the reason why McWilliams was so desperate to get his hands the file. Hoping and praying the letter was in it. When we handed McWilliams that dummy file and there was no letter, he must have thought we'd removed it," finished Glen, standing up and walking over to the sink and splashing water on his face.

"Whatever is in that letter must be dynamite for certain high-profile people who want no publicity or for others in high positions. Who is pushing hardest?" added Mary.

"McWilliams!" they all shouted together.

"We know the man is guilty, but without that letter, we have no substantial evidence to convict him. A drug shipment worth a billion dollars is arriving in Sydney. The drugs will be concealed in a sea container with a false bottom that's coming tomorrow or the next day. On which ship and at what time I'm not a hundred percent sure that's where those timetables come into play, I hope," added Glen, knowing the price Neil had paid to get the information.

"What's glaringly obvious?" cut in Mary, fiddling with her long red hair. "We need to find this ship and the docking date. Moreover, the container number."

"I agree with you, Mary. Time is running out quicker than I like," said Glen, standing up. "We have a great deal to uncover and little time in which to do it."

"Mira, if you and your mother are okay, we'll go and see what we can dig up," said Mary, following Glen's example and standing up.

Turning to Mira, Glen said, "Tell Jess I'll be back around to see her soon."

Mira kissed him goodbye on the cheek saying, "I will. Mum would love to see both of you again."

"Mira, to be on the safe side, I will arrange for police protection for both you and old Jess," said Glen, a serious look invading his face. "If I have my way, no more harm is coming your way." Going to the phone, he asked for immediate protection for the family.

Leaving the house, Glen followed Mary back to the pizza parlour to return the van and uniform, then back to her home where she parked the car in the garage.

Once inside, they examined the timetables thoroughly over the next two hours. The notes in Neil's Notebook made little sense. He had several matters marked, but neither of them made any sense of them. The initials ETB stumped both of them.

Finally, Mary called out loudly, "Coffee break!" Standing up, she went to the kitchen, flicked on the jug and readied the mugs. "What I don't understand, Glen is that Neil's so precise with matters of this nature. We must be missing some relevant information."

"I'm confident you're right, Mary, but what are we missing that's important?" reflected Glen, thoughtfully.

"I know what it is! It's that damn letter! If we find that - I'm sure we'll locate the information we're searching for!" exclaimed Mary excitedly.

"Can you tell me where Neil would stash something so damn important to the case?" asked Glen looking at her excited face. "You know your husband as well, if not better than, I do. Where would he hide a piece of evidence essential to his case?"

"I'd say in plain sight. Could be anywhere. Close enough to grab at a minute's notice, but obscured to people searching in a hurry," answered Mary, plainly baffled.

As they discussed their plans, Sam, at Glen's feet, sat up with ears pricked and emitted a low growl, the hairs on his back upright.

"We have company," said Glen, moving swiftly to the windows and parting the curtains a fraction. "McWilliams," he whispered. "I wonder what that bastard's after now?"

With Sam by his side, Glen opened the door to McWilliams.

"Ah, there you are, Johnson. I've been looking everywhere for you. Starting from tomorrow, you will be on special assignment in Newcastle," gloated McWilliams on delivering the news.

"I'm afraid not. I am no longer under your command, sir," replied Glen, in a polite but firm voice.

"What do you mean 'no longer under my orders'? Since when?" blustered McWilliams recoiling as if stung by the news.

"I've been asked to lead a special task force for the Commissioner. Here is the letter of confirmation," said Glen, showing it to his former boss. "I received it yesterday."

"We'll see about that!" stormed McWilliams, turning and leaving, mumbling obscenities at the world as a whole.

"Looks like they're going all the way to get rid of me, Mary," said Glen, watching his former boss drive off and closing the door.

"What do you think they'll do now? Harass us more or take more drastic action?" asked Mary, a shudder running down her spine.

"I don't know. Whatever has been planned will not be comfortable for us. You'd better keep the Commissioner advised of our latest dramas and of McWilliams trying to transfer me to Newcastle," said Glen, scared of the future and what might occur.

Continuing, he added, "Let him know about the hostage drama and the police protection arrangements for Mira and her mother."

"I'll be next door if you require me in a hurry," answered Mary, slipping out of the house.

A quarter of an hour later, Mary returned with a reassuring message. "Another man is coming to join us, adding to our strength.

The Commissioner is ordering extra protection for Mira and Jess, and giving you complete authority to take whatever action you deem fit."

"Any idea who the new man is?" asked Glen, thankful for another pair of eyes.

"None. Just that the man's reliable and willing to set the record straight."

"Hell, it's the young bloke from the other night!" exclaimed Glen, looking at her in apprehension. "He's still wet behind the ears!"

"Maybe, an extra pair of hands and eyes would come in handy," said Mary, pleased her children were in Queensland.

"I suppose you are right, but hell, I don't want to babysit him as well," growled Glen, with a slip of the tongue.

"Damn you to hell!" exploded Mary, hands on her hips. "Who else are you babysitting, Glen Johnson? Not me, that's for damn sure! I can uphold my end, and you damn well know it!"

"Come on, Mary. You know I didn't mean it like that although I do have to keep an eye on you to some degree. I feel responsible for the kids, for keeping their crazy mother alive and out of harm's way." Glen flinched in sudden realisation.

"Now I'm crazy, am I?" spat Mary, her temper bubbling to the surface.

Knowing she was about to erupt like a volcano, Glen gave voice to the first thought that came to mind. "Do you know you are beautiful when you're mad?" Then he dived to the floor as a magazine flew past his head.

Next moment she was attacking him, her tiny fists pounding his chest, venting the frustration and fear she was feeling. Tears rolled down her face as her battered emotions took control. The floodgates opened as she sobbed uncontrollably, the tears soaking his shirt. Holding her close, Mary released all her grief and anger out on him. They stayed there on the floor for about five minutes before Glen spoke.

"Mary, are you okay?" asked Glen in a soft, gentle voice.

"I'm not sure. Can I stay here for a while? I feel safe and warm," came her reply, as if she was floating on a cloud. "Glen I'm sorry

I lost my temper and acted stupidly," she said rolling off him and getting to her feet. "Everything was pulling me down. I was finding the pressure overwhelming me."

"There's nothing to be sorry for," said Glen, "I know what it is. A great deal has happened to you over the past few days, ripping and twisting the guts out of you."

"Yes, that's exactly what it's like. As if your whole life, no, your world's gone, leaving a dark space inside you."

The discussion would have gone longer except a knock at the door interrupted them. Taking no chances, Mary waited for Glen to take up his place at the door before answering. "Is there someone knocking?"

"My name is Mike Lord. I was sent to report to this address and to help in any way I can."

"Hang on, I'll be there in a moment," called Mary approaching slowly, giving Glen a strange look and signalling a problem. "It doesn't sound like him," she whispered. With a nod of Glen's head, she opened the door and stepped to one side.

The young man stepped through the door and halted abruptly as a gun barrel was pressed against his spine. "May I ask who the hell you are?" demanded Glen.

"I told you. My name is Mike Lord. I'm to report to you."

"Who gave the orders?" asked Mary. "You are not the Mike Lord we met in Canberra. You do not look or sound like him."

"I will ask you one more time," growled Glen, cutting in. "Who sent you?"

"I told you, the Commissioner. He asked for me. He was under the impression I'd helped you before."

"Let me see your badge?' demanded Glen, waiting until he received it. "Number checks out. Identical with the one shown in Canberra. But there's a problem: same badge number, but a different face."

"Where did you see this badge before? More importantly, when?" asked Mike Lord, puzzled by the reaction.

"A couple of nights ago in Canberra. I caught a man searching my room," said Glen. "When I challenged him, he claimed to be you. He even showed me his badge, this one."

"Dark hair, brown eyes, and a fraction taller than me," described Mike Lord.

"That represents him accurately enough. Who is he?" asked Glen, intrigued by the story.

"My former roommate. He stole my badge, broke into your room and pretended to be me," reasoned Mike Lord.

"This roommate of yours - does he have a name or do I have to guess?" asked Glen sarcastically.

"Henry James," stated Mike Lord. Then he rattled off his former address.

"That's possibly the reason we picked up a tail returning from Canberra," interjected Mary, turning her thoughts to that day.

"I take the point, Mary. We have a bigger problem on our hands. Two Mike Lords and one badge. The immediate task is separating the official one from the impostor. As our lives are on the line, we need to straighten out this charade quickly."

"I'm sorry, Mike, but we've been fooled once, and we won't repeat the same mistake," said Mary, cutting in on Glen.

"If you are genuine, you have nothing to fear. If not, you'll face jail."

"I have a clear conscience. The Commissioner himself made sure I was aboard the flight. He gave me these instructions to give to you on arriving here," said Mike Lord, handing Mary the documents.

She examined the paperwork, commenting, "They are genuine. Of that, I have no doubt. I recognise the signature. Also, Jack has enclosed extracts of his record plus a full description of our boy genius."

"Double check with the boss. That way we might stay alive a little longer." Lowering his weapon, Glen signalled to Mike to make himself comfortable. "Checking will take some time," Glen said. "Like a coffee while we wait, Mike?"

"A condemned man's last meal, why not."

Both men were at the table sipping coffee when Mary returned.

"Well, is he clean?" asked Glen, looking up at Mary.

"Yes, he's genuine. The commissioner had Henry James picked up. He matched our description and, when confronted, admitted impersonating Mike."

"I'm sorry, Mike, but we had to be certain," said Glen, shaking his hand.

"All these security checks, are they necessary?" asked Mike, relieved.

"Yes, mate, I'm afraid they are," answered Mary. "In the past forty-eight hours there's been a murder attempt on Glen's life, his in-laws have held hostage and threatened with violence or worse. There's been a forced entry into my home, I've been knocked to the floor and threatened with a firearm. Therefore, if we appear over-cautious, we have damn good reason. We both want to go on living," finished Mary in an angry tone.

"To make matters even worse," interrupted Glen, "They're chasing a letter we never knew existed until today." Then, deciding to give the man some slack he added, "It's an important piece of evidence that might implicate a couple of senior police officers."

"McWilliams and Reynolds," stated Mike. "And a billion dollars, worth of ice. The reason I know that is that the Commissioner explained the problem and danger just before leaving. He made it clear that orders came from you and no one else."

"I'm happy to know you've had a thorough briefing, Mike," said Mary, looking at Glen strangely as she continued. "How are you fixed for accommodation and transport?"

"I'm fine thanks. The boss arranged a car and for me to stay at a motel."

Noticing Mary's strange look, Glen asked, "Have you booked into your motel?"

"No, not yet. I came straight from the airport."

"Okay Mike, check into the motel and have a feed if you need one. Return here at six pm. Clear?" ordered Glen, checking the time.

"You're the boss. I'll be back here by six," replied Mike Lord, walking to the front door. "Catch you later."

Glen waited until Mike had left, before speaking. "Okay, what's up?"

"I don't know. A feeling I have. No, more like intuition. I think we should be careful, that's all," answered Mary. "Do you think I'm wrong?"

"I don't know what to think. Your instincts are sharper than mine at the moment," answered Glen. "Just to be on the safe side, we'll play it your way."

"Thanks, Glen, I am trying to be careful, believe me," said Mary, thinking about her children and wondering how they were coping.

"Come on, Mary," said Glen snatching up his keys. "I want to check out Mike and see exactly what he's doing or if he receives any visitors."

"I'm with you on that," replied Mary, grabbing her purse and pistol.

"I've meant to ask, where did that cannon come from?" asked Glen.

"Neil. I have a license, and I know how to use it. Also, I'm a crack shot," replied Mary.

"If Neil taught you, I could believe it," smiled Glen, scratching his head. "It might even give us an edge in a tight spot."

Using Glen's car, they headed for the motel Mike Lord was staying at. Glen searched for a sheltered parking spot with a good view of the lodge. Finding one, he parked and switched the motor off.

"What's next on the agenda?" asked Mary, sliding her seat back and stretching out, trying to relax the tension building within her body.

"We wait and see what develops," said Glen, picking up a set of binoculars off the backseat and scanning the motel room for any signs of movement. He watched as a car pulled into the parking space outside Mike Lord room. "He has visitors Mary!" exclaimed Glen in a loud voice.

"Who, do you know?" Mary asked sitting bolt upright in the seat.

"Not yet. The driver is still sitting in the car. No, wait. He's getting out now. It's bloody McWilliams!" exclaimed Glen. "That bastard Mike Lord is working for them."

As they watched, the two men met at the door. The conversation started friendly enough, then gradually descended into chaos.

Slipping out of the car, Glen crept closer until he could overhear the argument.

"Why didn't you report to me the moment you arrived in Sydney?" demanded McWilliams, arrogantly glaring at the young constable.

"The simple fact is, sir, I am on the job for the Commissioner, and I have to act under his orders and his rules alone," answered Mike calmly.

"So, can you please tell me what this job entails?" asked McWilliams, fighting his anger.

"No, sir – classified," said Mike, keeping his temper under control, playing on McWilliams sense of superiority.

"You will keep Lord! And so will that four-eyed little creep, the Commissioner!" snarled McWilliams storming back to his car and driving off.

Mike Lord watched McWilliams drive away, giving him a middle finger salute and returning inside.

Glen smiled at the gesture and agreeing with the sentiment, worked his way back to Mary and the car.

As Glen climbed back into the car, Mary asked, "Did you learn anything of interest?"

"A great deal about our young friend and what he thinks of McWilliams in general," answered Glen, a grin a mile wide on his face.

"Do you mean the middle finger salute?" said Mary.

"Just the way he stood up to McWilliams and didn't crack," added Glen, proud of Mike's coolness under pressure. "But that is not what's bothering me now. How did McWilliams know Mike was in town? And know his location?"

R. G. Anthony

"A leak in the Commissioner's office?" suggested Mary. "Someone else in McWilliams clutches?"

"The immediate question, if so, who?" asked Glen, rubbing his chin in deep thought.

Chapter Five

Evidence Search

It was precisely six pm when Mike Lord returned, an anguished look on his face. After entering, he sat down saying, "I don't know how or when my identity and location were known. I received a visitor, Commander McWilliams, demanding to know why I had not reported to him."

"What did you say?" asked Glen, pleased Mike had come right out and told them.

"The truth. I told McWilliams I was under the Commissioner's direct orders and his orders alone. He exploded, threatened to get even with me and called the big boss an interfering little creep."

"What happened next?" asked Mary, a grave look on her face.

"He drove away in a rage."

"You missed a minor, but important, detail," said Glen. "One we heartily agree with. In fact, Mary and I would like to add our contribution as well," both of them raising their middle finger.

"How do you know about that?" asked Mike in disbelief.

"We were coming to see you when McWilliams stopped there. We saw and heard every word that passed between you," answered Glen. "The fact that you told us was important. Otherwise, you were returning to Canberra."

"I'm glad I told you because I don't want to go back to Canberra. It's too bloody expensive," stated Mike. "Sydney's my hometown. This will give me a chance to see my parents."

"That will have to wait a while. We'll be busy for the next few days," said Glen, "We have work to do and not an enormous amount of time."

"What are you planning to do Glen?" asked Mary looking at him intently.

"We're going to the place where Neil died to search the warehouse. To find the letter."

"It's a possibility, isn't it, Glen, that we won't find it?" asked Mike logically.

"We'll cross that bridge when we come to it," replied Glen. "It's essential we discover the letter."

At that precise moment, a clap of thunder shook the house causing all them to jump with fright.

"Bloody hell that was close!" exclaimed Mike, putting into words what Mary and Glen were thinking.

At that point, torrential rain pelted down. The dark clouds rolled in blocking what little daylight there was.

"That's a blow," said Mike to no one in particular.

"No, mate, this will work in our favour. It'll keep people indoors, allowing us a free hand," said Glen. He continued, "It will, therefore, cover our movements, giving us some leeway to move about unhindered."

"We want it to keep raining, masking our movements. What's my role?" Mary asked looking at Glen, half expecting the worst.

"You will have two important jobs. You will be in the car acting as our security detail and driver. If someone comes along and starts poking around, fire up the car and rev the motor. We should hear it."

"What happens if we don't?" asked Mike.

"We have to think on our feet, cope the best way we can," said Glen bluntly.

"Maybe we can trace Neil's movements back to the place where he found the letter?" suggested Mary.

"Possibly the warehouse of the company the container belongs to."

"It's a chance. It could give us a lead of some description," added Mike, buying into the conversation.

"We need to move; time is running out. We need to take some risks if we're going to prevent McWilliams and his cronies landing those drugs," growled Glen. "Better still, to expose the bastards with their hands in the cookie jar."

"Wouldn't that be a coup?" smiled Mary at the mere prospect of nailing McWilliams' butt to the wall.

"First we have to find that damn letter and get the shipment date and container number," stated Mike.

"When do we start this hunt?"

"In an hour's time, we'll check the site out before going in. That should ensure that we remove any risks of detection," answered Glen, walking into the kitchen and flicking the electric jug switch. As he made the coffee, his mind was working at a furious pace, trying to build a list of their needs.

"Mary," he called, "do you have any thick material that will block out lights under the building. I want to prevent drawing attention to ourselves."

"How big a piece do you need?" she asked.

"A square meter should be enough," replied Glen, carrying the coffee back to the lounge room.

"I'll see what I can find." She returned a couple of minutes later with dark curtaining material with rubber backing. "I think this will do the trick."

Taking the material from her, Glen handed her a flashlight, telling her to go over to the light switch. Giving one end to Mike, Glen held the material up. "Turn the lights out, Mary."

The house was plunged into darkness. Mary turned on the flashlight aiming it at the centre of the material.

"Come closer," directed Glen, looking intensely at the back of the material.

She continued to walk forward until the light was pressed against it.

"This will do," said Glen. "It's blocking out the light at point-blank range. An excellent choice of material, Mary. What do you think, Mike?"

"Perfect for the job."

Time passed slowly as they drank their coffee and chatted about their needs that night. It was nine o'clock when they left the house and headed for the docks. They circled several times finding nothing. Mary let the men out and drove off to her parking spot.

Both men had slipped under the building when headlights appeared, halting alongside the flats.

"That should be Mary," whispered Glen, hanging the material in place and taping it so no light could escape.

"What exactly are we looking for?" asked Mike.

"I wish I could tell mate," said Glen. "Anything – a piece of paper wedged in an unlikely spot or plain sight. Where I cannot tell you."

"Thanks, but that doesn't help a great deal."

"I know, but that's all we have. You take this half, I'll take the other."

The men parted and gradually worked their way along the building. A couple of hours had passed when Glen stumbled on three letters written in blood, WCC, on a floor joist.

"Mike, I think this what we're looking for," called Glen, scrutinising the letters.

Mike crawled up to him and looked. "Bloody hell, is that what I think it is - blood?" he asked.

"Without a doubt, it's Neil's. He died that night," replied Glen sadly, the thunder, lightning and heavy rain outside reminding him of that night and his feeble efforts to save his friend.

Mike, noticing Glen's mood, asked, "What do you think these symbols mean?"

"They must apply to a business or a person," answered Glen, snapping out of the depression which threatened him. Taking out a small camera with a flash he took a couple of photos just in case the letters disappeared.

The sound of the motor starting up, then revving caused them to switch off the flashlights and crawl to the entrance.

Glen lifted the corner of the curtain and peered at two men who were walking along the footpath. They veered off across the street before disappearing into a block of flats. As Glen was about to strip the curtain down when both men re-emerged and headed back towards them. They waited several minutes; then after pulling the curtain from the opening went to the rear of the warehouse.

Mike stopped dead in his tracks, as lightning lit up a large company sign - "Wyoming Container Company."

"Look Glen!" exclaimed Mike, pointing to the sign. "That's what we want."

"Possibly. Check similar companies to see if the lettering's the same," said Glen. "Mike, keep an eye out for security; there'll be someone about."

They were busily searching when Glen found a small office with Warren Collins Pty Ltd - Importers/Exporters stencilled on the door.

"Mike," called Glen softly, "take a look at this."

Rushing up to him, Mike said, "Forget that for the moment. We have visitors approaching fast!"

The only hiding place available was a dumpster between two buildings. They climbed in and lowered the lid. Using a small block of wood to wedge the top open a few centimetres, they waited with weapons drawn. They watched in silence as a car halted outside the office. Three men climbed out and entered the building.

"See the plates, Mike?" whispered Glen.

"No, this angle's too sharp. On leaving they'll have to reverse towards us," replied Mike, analysing the layout.

"It's necessary that we identify the owner. Don't make any mistakes," advised Glen glancing at his watch, worried about Mary and her safety. "I hope Mary stays put."

Before Mike could answer, the men returned to the car, reversed and drove away.

"I wonder what that meeting was about?" asked Mike, writing down the registration and watching as the car disappeared.

"At the moment, I don't care. I'm worried that Mary mightn't be okay," said Glen, walking briskly out of the yard to the phone box. He flashed three short, three long and waited for an answer.

The car's high beam replied three times. It moved towards them quietly and slid to a halt for both men to climb in.

"Let's go," ordered Glen, strapping on his seat belt. "We have some information we need to check as quickly as possible."

"Well, are you going to tell me or am I supposed to guess?" asked Mary, irritated by the long wait and the lack of sleep.

"We found some newly carved initials on one of the beams," said Mike, trying to spare Mary feelings.

"We think a couple of companies found there are the ones we're after," cut in Glen, grateful for Mike's delicate handling of the truth.

"What're their names?" asked Mary. "Neil might have mentioned them in his investigation."

"One was the Wyoming Container Company," said Mike, his preferred pick.

"No, that's not it. I do remember Neil mentioning a shabby little office of some importer mob. I don't think he ever named them," said Mary. "Just that the office was located between two larger companies."

"Have you ever heard the name Warren Collins Pty Ltd - Importers/Exporters?" asked Glen, hoping the name might ring a bell.

"No, a name like that I would remember," answered Mary, slowly shaking her head.

"It's possible the two businesses are working together in some way," suggested Mike.

"That's a strong possibility, Mike. Nothing can be rejected at this stage," agreed Glen, deep in thought. "We might have to return tonight and try to find evidence which will lead us to the ship and container in question."

"Gentlemen, it may have escaped your notice, but it's nearly one in the morning," stated Mary, giving Glen a severe look as she drove into her drive.

Once inside, Glen headed for the computer, punched in his ID number and scanned for any report Neil had filed about the companies of interest. Finding none, he began looking for company directors. He looked up as Mike placed a coffee cup in front of him.

"Making headway with the companies?" asked Mike, receiving a negative nod. He pulled out his notebook. "Try this – Alpha Bravo Zulu Seven-Seven-Four."

Moments later, they had the information on the owner and type of car. "This bloke - what's his involvement?" asked Mike, looking intently at the screen.

"No bloody idea whatever," answered Glen. "Let's see if he has any form. Well, look at this! This bloke's mixed up with the drug trade for years. He is one nasty bastard and suspected of involvement in several murders."

"What's his name, Glen?" asked Mike, his curiosity getting the better of him.

Glen answered, his mind drifting back to the morgue and a toe tag on one of the men. "Stefan Dalca was born in a small Romanian village. He immigrated to Australia when he was eight years old. He's in his mid-forties. His criminal career began in his early twenties. He's come under suspicion for various crimes. No convictions. Mike, later this morning go to the morgue and check on the people that died with Neil. Keep it low-key. Find out what you can. The one I am mainly interested in had his head bashed with a brick," said Glen.

"Mary, I need you…," began Glen turning to find her asleep on the couch.

"She fell asleep over an hour ago. Not long after we arrived," said Mike, smiling.

"You take one of the kid's rooms. I'll take the other," directed Glen, covering Mary with a blanket.

It was nearly seven o'clock when Glen walked into the lounge. He found Mary sitting watching television. She looked up as he entered the room. "Glen, you may want to watch this. The wharfies have called a three-day strike over safety issues. No ship can unload in that time."

"That's great! We have a little more time before that container's unloaded. Mary, I need the file from the safe. I have to cross-reference some information," answered Glen with a sigh of relief.

"What do you look so bloody happy about?" asked Mike, walking into the room.

"A wharfies' strike. That will give us extra time to find what we're looking for," Glen answered looking up at Mike.

"We need to move then. I'll make us some breakfast while you work out the steps."

"You stay out of my kitchen Mike, or I'll cut your legs off at the neck," threatened Mary walking back into the room and handing Glen the file.

"Aw, Mary, I'm a growing boy who needs his nourishment," returned Mike, with a smile.

Ignoring their banter, Glen opened the file and extracted the timetables and a cargo manifesto. Looking closely at them, he moved his finger slowly down the list until he found a container for Warren Collins Pty Ltd. It was being carried by a Japanese freighter due to dock at three pm the following day.

"That's it, otherwise why would Neil take this manifesto?" said Glen loudly, noting down the container number and the ship's name.

"Are you positive?" asked Mary as Mike walked back into the lounge with plates of food.

"A cargo container for Collins," said Glen pointing to the manifesto. "Arriving tomorrow on a Japanese freighter."

"Well, eat this while it's hot," said Mary slipping a plate of bacon and eggs in front of him. "Then we'll discuss our alternatives."

After breakfast, they gathered around the table, discussing different choices. "Mike, that little job I mentioned last night, I want it completed as soon as the morgue opens. If what I suspect is correct, Mary will be in great danger."

"Whose toes have I trodden on?" she asked in bewilderment.

"Remember the man that died under the building while searching for Neil. I suspect he is either the brother or a close relative of Stephan Dalca."

"Dalca?" replied Mary. "What did I ever do to him?'

"Nothing personally. If these two are family, some of these people have a strong sense of duty. Eye for an eye, tooth for a tooth. Revenge is high on their list," answered Glen, looking at Mary. He watched as the information registered.

"That means I'm an open target for anyone," said Mary. "So are my kids."

"It's a possibility, Mary. As he is the only relative, he needs to be the one to come after you," added Glen.

Glancing at his watch, he said to Mike, "Take off and get the information we need. Make sure the photograph is outstanding. We might need it for facial recognition. Finally, keep a low profile and continually watch your butt."

"What've I done Glen? I've placed my kids in danger," said Mary shakily.

"This happened when Neil killed him in self-defence we'll have to guard against everything," answered Glen, trying to comfort her. "You have two strong he-men to take care of you."

Mary burst out laughing. "What garbage! You pair couldn't lead thirsty horses to water let alone protect me!"

Glen smiled gallantly, realising she was hiding her fear behind bravado. Getting up, he walked around to her and placed his arm around her shoulders. "We'll protect you to the best of our ability, unappreciated by certain people who shall remain nameless."

"I'm sorry, Glen. I'm not frightened for myself. It is the kids' safety that's worrying me. They've done nothing to have this mess taken out on them."

The sound of a car pulling up, a door slamming and footsteps made Mary jump. Glen walked to the window. Parting the curtains slightly, he caught sight of Mike strolling up the path.

The roaring of a motor and screeching tires followed by several gunshots, caused all three of them to duck for cover. Glen recovered quickly enough to catch sight of a black car as it disappeared down the street.

Opening the door, Glen raced outside and gave Mike a hand to regain his feet and helped him inside, closing the door behind them.

"Are you okay, Mike?" asked Mary, rushing to his side, shaken by the whole incident.

"Yeah, a slight graze, nothing serious," replied Mike as blood soaked through his sleeve and rolled down his arm.

"Mary, get the first aid kit. Then, go out the back door and ring Pat Murphy. Tell him what's happened, and I'll explain the rest when he arrives. Mary, please be careful and hurry in case our trigger-happy friends return."

Giving Glen the first aid kit, Mary disappeared through the back door.

Stripping away Mike's sleeve, Glen had a quick look. "You're lucky, mate. It's only a superficial wound." He wrapped the wound, placed Mike's arm in a sling then continued. "Pick up any information?"

"Yeah, a fair bit. That bloke's name is Nicu Dalca. He's Stephan Dalca's younger brother. What made you suspect they were siblings?" asked Mike.

"His toe tag was protruding when we went to identify Neil's body. The name was clear. It meant nothing until last night when the name Dalca came up. I started to put it together," answered Glen walking into the bedroom, grabbing a tee shirt and throwing it to Mike. "Wear that until we wash your shirt."

Seconds later, the back door opened and Mary walked in saying, "Pat's on his way bringing a doctor with him to check on Mike's scratch and a couple of men for added protection."

"Did you happen to mention Dalca to him?" asked Glen, waiting for a response.

"Yes, his exact words – Tell Glen to watch your arse. Dalca believes in the old ways, a back shooting, and no warning."

"A nasty sort of a bastard," added Mike, looking at Mary's pallid features. "One sure way of curing this son of a bitch's murderous ambition is a bullet placed in the right spot."

"What I don't understand," said Mary, "Is the fact that it took him so long to react. Is there possibly a simpler reason for this sudden attack? To divert our attention?"

Glen looked at Mary thoughtfully for a moment, mulling over her words. "You have a damn good point. They're trying to distract us from our primary task. It sounds like one of McWilliams' narcissistic schemes. It's the kind of sadistic ploy he'd use to buy time to protect his precious shipment of drugs."

"Why go to that length now? His ship is due to dock tomorrow," said Mike.

"Wrong Mike, time is on our side now. The wharfies' three-day strike has stuffed up their plans for three days or longer before the container can be unloaded and cleared by customs."

The sound of cars stopping outside caught their attention. Cautiously peering through the window, Glen said, "No worries, Pat and his men just arrived."

Glen opened the door and greeted them. "Good to see you again, Pat."

"This is Dr Benson. I dragged him along to check on the wounded," said Pat looking around. Spotting Mike with his arm in a sling he directed the doctor to him.

"Oh, Pat, Mike Lord, my other helper."

With introductions completed, Glen explained the problem to Pat and the others. "So you see we need pressure applied to this character, to give us room to move freely."

"Did you manage to get the registration, by any chance?" asked Pat with a hopeful look.

"I did, Pat. I wrote it down." He gave the number from the previous night, knowingly bending the truth to fit the situation "It was an imported job, - Black," called Mike, looking across at Glen.

"I can vouch for the colour. I was too busy ducking bullets at the time to worry about trifles like registration," answered Glen, backing up Mike story.

"Do you have any helpful information that might help, Mary?" Pat asked.

"When the shooting started I was busy introducing myself to the floor," answered Mary truthfully.

Turning to his men, Pat said, "Both of you check outside for bullet holes. If you find any, photograph their location, dig them out and bag them. I want to nail this bastard's arse to the wall," finished Pat.

"I hope all this hasn't interrupted your morning nap, old man," taunted Mary, taking great pleasure at his discomfort.

Having learned from his first meeting with Mary, Pat remained focused on his job.

"Mike, how were you wounded? Did a bullet come inside?" asked Pat, looking around for any damage.

"No, I was outside, walking up the path, when I heard the roaring of a motor and screeching tires. Turning around, I saw the car with a gun protruding from the window. This was followed by several gunshots. I dived to the ground. Going down, I felt a burning sensation in my left arm."

"When did you get the rego?" Pat asked, a dubious look on his face.

"As I turned around I caught a glimpse. I'm positive that's the number," said Mike.

"What concerns us most, is their custom of blood feuds. It places Mary and her children in an awkward position. Would he likely to carry out the threat?" questioned Glen.

"Mary said you think it's a ploy to distract you from your primary task, correct?" asked Pat.

"Possibly. The wharfies' strike has created a problem for them. They need to buy time," said Glen. "If we're busy watching our rear, we can't concentrate on them."

"How much time do you need?" asked Pat, looking at Glen.

"I need them distracted, Pat. The longer, the better."

"Wounding of a federal police officer while going about his official duties. Illegal firing of a firearm in a public place endangering the public," said Pat. "I think that will do to start with."

"Pat, if he's dangerous, take a lot of back up. I don't want to see you or any of your people hurt," said Glen.

An officer walked inside saying, "We found several bullets holes in the house wall, Pat. We're collecting and bagging them as we speak."

After Pat had left, Glen switched his attention to Mike. "How's the arm, mate?'

"Not bad. The doctor gave me a shot just to be on the safe side."

"What was the idea of giving Pat that registration from last night?" asked Glen looking at Mike, his mind working overtime.

"Okay, I didn't get the rego. However, I know my cars. I'm positive. Besides, Pat can't act without the registration. Anyway, I only arrived yesterday. I'd have no way of knowing his license plates," argued Mike using logic as a defence.

"That's not ethical," interjected Mary, looking at Mike with wide eyes.

"Maybe not," interrupted Glen, "but I feel a lot happier creating problems for Pat than the other way around. Also, Mike's quick thinking allows us to apply a blowtorch to McWilliams butt. He'll be too busy trying to protect their billion dollar shipment."

"So you tolerate Mike's methods?" asked Mary, looking unhappy.

"Yes. Just remember, this is the man that wants to harm you and your children. Mike did this to protect all of us from an unexpected attack. Remember, these bastards are ruining thousands of young lives every day of the week with this lethal crap. Sometimes you have to use unsavoury methods to get the job done," said Glen looking at her, slightly disappointed at her response.

"I don't mean to doubt what we're doing; I just don't want us to sink to their level," explained Mary.

"We do what we have to do to keep ourselves safe. Remember, Mary, I didn't pick up this injured arm by tripping over one of your garden dwarves. Some bastard was shooting at me, and I resent that. I'm allergic to blood, especially mine," said Mike, a smile on his face, trying to eject some humour into the conversation.

"I'm sorry, Mike. For a moment I'd forgotten how your injury occurred. A little to the right and you'd be in hospital or dead. I know both of you need to stay ahead of these mongrels." Accepting their argument, Mary said, "Coffee, then we can work on solving this case."

They sat in the lounge drinking coffee and devising plans to increase their advantage, somehow forcing them to make mistakes if possible. "Can we track their cars without them knowing?" asked Mary, looking for a simple solution.

"Yes, but the question is, whose car?" said Mike. "It needs to be someone worthwhile. A person who might lead us to someone more involved."

"There's only one person that comes to mind; McWilliams. He'd be the perfect candidate," suggested Glen. "There's only one drawback; he doesn't use the same car all the time."

"That makes the job harder, not impossible," added Mike. "How about tagging someone's car, who's I have no idea."

"Who has the lowest profile—attracts the least attention?" asked Mary. "McWilliams' ego rules him out. Wherever he goes, he draws attention, like a moth to a flame. He announces his arrival with a loud mouth and an arrogant attitude."

"You're right Mary. McWilliams is the wrong man," agreed Glen. "Who sails under the radar ninety-eight percent of the time? Sergeant Dave Reynolds! The man who planted the bug at the house. The cultured voice that gave the order to kill Neil. He's our man."

"Where's his car parked? Is it easy to hide a tracking bug without interference?" asked Mike casually.

"At work, no chance at all. His home's the best place," answered Glen.

"Where does the bug come from?" said Mike.

"The Commissioner supplied Neil with bugs and scanners several weeks back just for this task," said Mary.

"Get them," ordered Glen. "I need to judge their type and range." "Also, both you and Mary need to learn their uses."

Mary disappeared into the bedroom. Mike asked a critical question. "How are we going work this?"

"One of three ways. Have Mary dress in a tracksuit, jog past his car and, when she takes a tumble, she places the bug inside the chassis out of sight. She regains her footing and continues."

"Why Mary?" asked Mike. "Either you or I could do the same job."

"A couple of reasons. Mary is small, fit and quick on her feet. Her reflexes are fast," answered Glen. "With some training, Mary will be able to place the bug in the right position within seconds."

"Have I volunteered?" queried Mary entering the room.

"You're the right person for this job," answered Glen.

"In what way?" asked Mary, placing a box on the couch?

"You're the right size, quick and fit," said Glen. "Anyway, Mike can't do it. His wound would slow him down. And you have faster reflexes than me, Mary."

"Explain to me what job I'm doing."

Walking to the box, Glen removed a couple of bugs. "Come outside," he said, "And bring the car keys."

They waited as Glen reached under the car and found the spot to place the bug. "Mary, watch my hand. That's the position. Nowhere else."

Feeling for the place, Mike realised how confined space was. So, the reason for Mary's selection over him was apparent. The size of her hands, not his inexperience. Happier with himself, Mike stepped back, listening carefully to Glen's instructions.

"Okay, Mary - begin. The primary purpose of the exercise is delivering the bug without tripping the alarm," said Glen.

Nodding in acknowledgement, Mary jogged slowly towards the car, rolled, planted the bug and got back on her feet in twenty seconds. She repeated it several times, improving each performance.

"Well done, Mary," called Glen, as she walked towards them. "That was brilliant."

"What time of day?" asked Mary, "At night it could be slightly longer?"

"At night or early morning. Whenever he decides to come home. His movements are beyond our control," replied Glen.

"His car - what make is it?

"Same as the one you're training on," said Glen.

"That'll make it easier, knowing the car. I'll do a few more trials to ensure I have it right," answered Mary jogging away.

"Does this bloke keep regular hours, boss or do we have to guess?" asked Mike.

"I honestly don't know Mike. I was never curious to find out. We'll need to know now."

"How do we find out?"

"One way, Mike, one way. A good old fashioned police stakeout."

"I've never participated in one before."

"You're in for a treat mate. Bring plenty of hot coffee and doughnuts," smiled Glen, tongue in cheek. "That's what crime magazines say. It could turn into one long boring night."

They both looked across at Mary as she strolled towards them. "What are you pair chatting about so earnestly?" she asked. "I'm ready. When do we start this venture?"

"When we know he's settled down for the night, and no one will disturb us," said Glen bluntly. "We need this to flow as smoothly as possible."

"Sometime this year I take it?' came Mary's sarcastic response.

"Tonight or early morning. We have to watch Reynolds' place to know for sure."

"Okay, let's go inside and wait until dark. Meantime, I'll make coffee and sandwiches for later. If we plan to carry out this, I need to go as well. I'll be sleeping in the back seat with pillows and blankets, relaxing while the pair of you watch for our quarry."

After dark, they headed for Reynolds' home, hoping he'd arrive soon so that they could set their plan into action. After three solid hours waiting Reynolds returned. More time had passed before Glen decided to go ahead with the scheme. Waking Mary, he watched in silence as she walked briskly down the street to within fifty meters of the car. Then she started jogging, ready to put the sting into motion. Seconds later Mary had completed her task and continued down the road.

Several minutes later she was back in the car, her job finished with no mistakes. "Now what?" she asked.

"A long night and lack of sleep while we wait for Reynolds to make a move.

Chapter Six

Sgt Reynolds.

It was a little after three in the morning when Reynolds appeared, climbed into his car and drove off. "Here we go folks, our pigeon's moving. Where to? I have no idea." said Glen, firing the motor and switching on the electronic scanner. He then handed it to Mike.

Mike nursed the scanner. "He's turned right, travelling at fifty kilometres," said Mike, his keen grey eyes never leaving the screen for an instant. "He's taken the next turn to the left and increased speed."

"If he keeps going in that direction, he's heading for the docks," suggested Glen. "Maybe a secret meeting with his bosses or to pass on instructions to others."

"Yeah, looks like you're right. Reynold's turned into Regan Street and stopped."

Glen parked the car up near the flats and woke Mary. "Wake up. Mike and I are going to check out what's going on. Use the same signals as before. Can you please pass me the bag and the flashlights?"

After making sure Mary was fully alert, Glen turned to Mike saying, "Take out the interior light globe and leave it in the glove box."

Leaving the car both men made their way towards the warehouse, their eyes peeled for security guards or others. Working their way silently towards the little office, they spotted Reynolds' car and another parked. "Get the rego number. We'll check it out later," whispered Glen.

Crawling stealthy to the rear of the building, they found the approach easier as they slowly wormed their way under the structure. Hearing people moving above them, Glen quietly removed a sound activated bug, and a small tape recorder and transmitter and attached them to a floor joist. "With luck, we may gain some intel," Glen whispered.

Both men froze when they heard approaching footsteps followed by a knock at the door. It opened. A voice was heard. "Sorry to trouble you, Mr Harvey. I saw the lights. Just checking to ensure the office was secure."

"That's okay, Smithy. Keep up the excellent work." The door closed and the footsteps receded.

As they lay there, Reynolds bellowed to Harvey.

"What happened to the men you promised us? No one's turned up."

"I don't understand. I organised a hit on the house as you asked," replied Harvey heatedly. "They only had to make it look like a revenge killing to keep Johnson on the defensive for the next few days until the Eiko Maru docked and the container's cleared and removed."

"Shut your mouth! Never mention that name again. No one knows what's in that container and I want to keep it that way. Besides, there were no reports of shootings in that vicinity," snarled Reynolds worried about the lack of progress.

"What I don't understand is why Johnson hasn't acted on the letter before now. Is it possible he isn't aware of its existence?"

"That's bullshit. Johnson must know. The Henderson's were always at his flat for weeks." Reynolds snarled. "McWilliams is convinced he has it."

"I hope he's right. We're all in for the high jump. He'll lose a great deal more than the rest of us, considering he planned and organised the whole set up." replied Harvey, reflecting on what he might lose.

"Shut your bloody mouth. Any more negative talk and I'll blow a hole in you that a truck could pass through," snarled Reynolds, his eyes hard and hateful.

"A happy bunch of campers," whispered Mike listening to the conversation, "I think you've upset their little applecart."

"They're in for a rude shock. Wait until I've finished with McWilliams and his cronies!" whispered Glen fiercely. "They can commiserate together in jail."

Crawling to the front of the building, they peered out at the parked cars. Realising this was a perfect chance to get photographs, Glen opened the bag, removed an infra-red camera and took several shots of registration plates and the cars' makes and models.

Then he began to set up several animal cameras equipped with remote sensors until he was satisfied with their placement. He wanted to document any office traffic. He whispered to Mike, "These cameras will gather additional intel for us. We'll return to the car and listen to the bug; we may pick up additional information."

Both men slipped silently from beneath the demountable and walked out the gate, working their way to the car. They found Mary tuned into the bug, listening.

"Interesting conversation?" asked Glen, climbing in.

"Do you know what is McWilliams is doing with his share; running for bloody parliament at the next election?" said Mary casually.

"When did McWilliams turn up?" asked Glen, a look of disbelief on his face.

"You were walking back to the car as he drove in. Lucky for you that the parked semi and the dip in the road shielded both of you from him."

"I don't bloody believe it!" exclaimed Mike. "How did we miss him?"

"I know McWilliams has been ranting and raving about the reliability of people, their inability to do a simple job. They've not contacted him or Dave for help," said Mary, pleased they were upsetting the crooks well-oiled machine.

"Pat's doing a damn good job of keeping our trigger-happy friends from communicating with McWilliams and his cronies," remarked Glen, with a wry grin.

Ten minutes later, the meeting broke up. McWilliams, angry about the failure of his people, left first; the other two a minute or two behind them

"How do we continue now?" asked Mary. "Go after Reynolds or return to the house?"

"Return to the base. We've collected information we need to sift through. We need to try to build a profile on Mr Harvey and his connection with the drugs and his role within the group," said Glen. "Mike and I need to get what sleep we can. I have a sense the pace of this operation is going to intensify. We need to be fully alert and react swiftly. If any of us wants to stay alive."

Mary turned the car and headed for home. As she drove into the drive, she stopped suddenly. "Sam's not barking. He always does when I come home."

"Let's go, Mike," ordered Glen, drawing his weapon. He didn't question Mary's reaction. He had learned her instinct was infallible.

Both men approached the backyard gate gingerly. Opening it, they split, moving stealthily into the yard. Moments later, Glen found Sam on the ground, whimpering, blood seeping from a gash on his head. As he went to move Sam, a faint movement caught his attention. He threw himself to one side as a knife sliced through the fleshy part of his arm, causing him to flinch in pain. Glen heard a grunt as Mike pistol-whipped the assailant from behind, sending him crashing to the ground.

Following the assailant down, Mike rolled the man over, cuff him and sat him upright against the tree. Going through his pocket, he relieved him of his wallet and a couple more hidden knives.

"You right, mate?' asked Mike, turning h[s attention to Glen as he struggled to his feet, clutching his wounded left arm.

"Yes, I'll be okay. That bastard sliced my arm open with a knife. I'm more concerned about Sam and his injury. It looks like his head has connected with a lump of wood. He has a deep gash."

The yard flooded with light as Mary switched them on. Seeing Sam in Mike's arms, she rushed to him. "Sammy, my darling, are you okay?" cried Mary stroking his shoulder. The dog's tail moved in response, and he licked her hand.

'What happened to you? Did you fall over the dog again?" said Mary sarcastically, not seeing the blood dripping from his arm.

"No, I did not trip over the bloody dog!" snapped Glen defensively. "I was going to his aid when that bastard handcuffed to the tree tried to carve me up like a Christmas chicken. What do you think this is - bloody claret?"

Seeing his injured shoulder for the first time, Mary rushed to his side. "I need brighter light so I can see how bad that wound is. That injury's going to need a few stitches."

"No bloody kidding – a man could bleed to death. The dog receives more attention than I do!" complained Glen, feeling neglected.

"But he's a poor dumb animal! He can't tell us what's wrong with him," retaliated Mary defending Sam.

"I know exactly how Sam feels. Two dumb animals together."

At the mention of his name, Sam struggled to his feet, wandered over to Glen and sat down beside him.

"I'm glad someone around here understands, Sam," said Glen kneeling to check his head. Next moment the floor rushed up to meet him, then blackness.

Glen awoke later that morning, lying in bed, his arm tightly bandaged. He was struggling to sit upright when a strange soft voice said, "Don't try to move, Mr Johnson. The stitches may rip out making the wound worse," said a young nurse sitting by his bed.

"Where am I?" asked Glen.

"A private hospital near your friend's house. They rushed you here after the accident. Unluckily for you, the wound was deeper than they thought. You collapsed from the loss of blood, shock and pain

"Thanks for taking care of me but I have to leave," said Glen.

"No, you don't, Glen Johnson. You will stay put until the doctor signs the release. Jack said so," said Mary, walking into the room.

"Brilliant! Work to do, and I'm stuck in this bloody hospital," growled Glen, slumping back on the pillows.

"Glen, you have over fifteen stitches in your arm! Thank God your accident hadn't cut deeper," said Mary, her emerald green eyes boring deep into his.

"I get your drift. It's my arm that's injured not my brain," replied Glen. "What happened to that diseased animal we captured?"

"Mike turned him over to Pat at the animal shelter. He's well supervised."

"Here comes your doctor now. I'll see if I can take you home."

Walking to him, Mary spoke briefly. After a few moments, they both walked to Glen. The doctor checked Glen's chart. "All your signs are steady since arriving. Any after effects, come back. No strenuous exercise for at least a fortnight.

Glen looked at him, dumbfounded. *Who was he trying to kid?*

Mary and Glen left and drove to her place. "Where's Mike?" he asked as the painkillers slowly wore off.

"Picking Sam up from the vet, I hope. He was lucky as well. There are no cracks, but he's going to have a sore head for a few days. Do you know, Sam might have saved your life? He gave our visitor a hard time."

"Good for him. Sam's a damn good dog. I hope he enjoyed his clash," said Glen, bitterly, unable to interrogate their prisoner himself.

"Glen, I'm sorry. I had no idea how bad your injury was until you collapsed. You scared the hell out of us."

"I can assure you, it did nothing to help my state of bloody mind." Said Glen, "And why did you bring me to a private hospital? That's the damn part I can't understand."

"I was following orders, the Commissioner had arrangements in place for any injured agents to be taken there. My instructions? Limit the knowledge to the least number. After treatment and if it's not life-threatening. Get you out quickly, and answering the least number of questions possible. Besides I was trying to explain about the story, I spun to cover up your injury after you passed out,"

"You managed that part with extreme efficiency. As for the other, I understood the meaning, Mary. I said so at the time."

"Looks like Mike and Sammy are back," said Mary, pulling into her drive. Helping Glen from the car, she escorted him into the house. Mike and Sam, who wagged his tail at Glen, met them at the door and helped him to the lounge.

"You stay seated," ordered Mary. "I'll make breakfast and coffee. Mike, you can bring him up-to-date with our progress."

"She's bloody bossy for someone her size," said Mike, loud enough for Mary to hear.

"If you want to eat for the rest of this week, Mike Lord, I suggest you avoid any further statements of that nature."

Glen tried to stop himself from laughing, but pain shot through his arm, causing him to grab it. "What progress is she talking about, Mike?" queried Glen.

"Our new friend, Mr Joshua Harvey, a half owner and managing director of the Wyoming Container Company. He and his silent partner purchased it from Warren Collins about six months ago The Japanese government owns the freighter Eiko Maru. No previous connection with Harvey's company until now."

"Good job. What about our knife-wielding friend? Were you able to gather any information from him?" asked Glen, rubbing his arm gently, trying to relieve the pain.

Spotting his discomfort, Mary filled a glass, removed tablets from a bottle and gave both to Glen. "Take these. Strong painkillers – they'll ease the pain."

Glen swallowed them and then turned his attention back to Mike.

"Seemingly, he was in the same cell block as Dalca. He contracted him for the princely sum of ten thousand dollars to break in and kill Mary. After completing the task, he was to call on Mr Harvey, tell him where Dalca was and collect his money. The important part is that no one knew about Sam. When our friend, Wesley Weasel… Yes, that is his real name… "(Mike grinned wildly at Glen's sudden look of disbelief)"… jumped the fence, Sam introduced himself, scaring Weasel half to death. Sam tore several strips of skin from him before being belted unconscious with a lump of wood. He was about to be slash Sam's throat when we turned up. Mistaking you for Mary, he tried to kill you."

"Oh, my God! I'm not that ugly am I, Mike?" cried Glen, flinching as a wet dishcloth hit him on the side of his head for his random outburst.

"You watch your manners, Glen Johnson, or I'll have to beat you around the ears. For those cracks, I have a good mind to throw out breakfast!" threatened Mary.

"No don't do that," pleaded Mike, thinking of his stomach. "It must be the tablets you gave him that is causing him to act crazy."

"Don't hand me that garbage! Mike an all you're thinking about is your stomach," fired back Mary. "But -then again - Mike might be right. Those tablets could be undermining your judgment. Maybe we should take you back to the hospital and leave you there for a couple of days."

"Like hell, you will! We have work to do and a short period in which to complete it," exploded Glen, taking charge. "We need to concentrate on finding that damn letter, and the meaning of the initials E, T, B. You implied earlier, that Neil would hide it in plain sight. Could he have disguised it, leaving it in full view somewhere in the house? If so, which room would he pick?"

"Let's go about this logically," supplied Mike. "What's in the house that starts with E?"

"The only idea I can think of is Emily's room," said Mary, after some thought.

"That's a good place to start," said Glen, walking into Emily's room.

All three began to check every possible place that Neil may have used, but they came up with a blank. "If it's in here I have no idea where it's hidden," said Mary laying Emily's teddy bear back on the pillow. "It's not here. We'll search the boys' room."

For the next hour and a half, they searched the house, looking in every conceivable place. Nothing turned up.

"I'm bushed," muttered Glen, sitting down, feeling light in the head and unsteady on his feet.

"You're looking pale, Glen," said Mary in a concerned tone. Feeling his forehead, she exclaimed, "You're burning up!"

Forcing him to lay on the lounge, she placed a pillow under his head, covered him with a blanket, opened a container of antibiotics and pushed him to take a couple.

"Mike's making coffee, so stay there and rest. You are a sick man. That wound has affected you more than you realised. Not much we can do during daylight hours. After you've had a rest, we can plan our next move."

As they chatted and sipped the coffee, Glen spoke. "Mike - that bag in the car. Bring it in. I have several items I need to teach you. It's important you learn how they work."

Moments later, Mike returned with the bag and handed it to Glen. Taking out an animal camera, he gave it to Mike. Then systematically, went through each phase, showing him how to remove the digital card and replace it with a new one. Insert the replacement battery then reset it. Mike continued to practice. Satisfied with his progress, Glen coached him until he'd mastered the various uses of the tape recorder and power source.

As Glen watched, perspiration beaded on his brow. His body waging war against a raging infection, forcing him to lay back and rest.

Feeling his forehead, Mary made him take a break. Unhappy with his condition, she stopped the training session and gave him a couple more tablets. A little later, he was asleep. Sam lying by his side.

"I'm glad he's resting, Mike. Rest is what he needs at the moment," said Mary quietly. "We're going to need his expertise later tonight."

"What's his reason for teaching me to understand how to use all of this equipment? He understands it far better than me," replied Mike, baffled by Glen's insistence.

"Don't you get it, Mike? Glen's in no shape to go crawling under buildings. He should still be in the hospital a couple more days. Our job tonight is to replace all used items and return with the others," said Mary. "Meanwhile, files need work and evidence need

95

compiling. The more paperwork we have up-to-date, the less we have to worry about later."

Glen awoke mid-afternoon, his throat dry, his shoulder throbbing. "Water!" he croaked, trying to sit upright.

Hearing him, Mary walked to the fridge, grabbed a jug of cold water, a glass and another couple of tablets. Giving him the glass, she poured the cold water and watched him drink his fill. Mary gave him the pills, making sure he swallowed them. "How are you feeling?" she asked.

"My throat feels like sandpaper. My arm is throbbing. That aside, good. How long have I been asleep?"

"About four hours. Before you start arguing, your body was rebelling against being invaded by a knife, lack of sleep, infection and a high temperature."

"But Mary - we have important work to carry out," protested Glen, knowing deep down that he shouldn't be arguing with her.

"Glen," she said gently, "We understand time is critical. Cards and batteries in the cameras need replacing, and you are in no condition to do it. Mike and I are going tonight. You are going to be our security."

"I take it you've given this lots of thought?" asked Glen, eyeing Mary with approval.

"Yes, we have. It's time we take a share of the danger instead of leaving it to you."

"Is Mike with you?" asked Glen.

"Yes, I am, boss. I noticed you take more risks than the rest of us. That's undemocratic. I'm entitled to my share. So is Mary."

"If the two of you insist, who am I to stand in the way?" said Glen graciously, thankful that he didn't have to ask.

"Reynolds - will it be necessary to tail him tonight?" asked Mike.

"No, I think we'll gain more Intel from the office at the docks. Of course, that's provided we keep our cameras and bug powered, and we're not discovered during the changeovers," commented Glen, still concerned about their safety.

"Look, boss, I know how concerned you are about us. However, for this job you are unfit. Passing out is not a choice, it's suicide. Especially in the wrong place, it's bloody dangerous!" added Mike convincingly.

"Mike, I know what you say is right. You're like my babies, and I worry."

"All kids grow up and have to make their way in the world. Now our turn's come," said Mary softly.

"Wait a moment! I know how to even the odds. Mike, pass me the bag. Pull out two bugs and set them to another frequency. If you need help, I'll know. These are sensitive; I'll be able to check your progress. If problems arise and you split up, stay within two kilometres of the car. Give me your position. I will hear you. Interference occurs if you're trying to contact me at the same time. Any questions?" asked Glen.

"This equipment is old. Why aren't we using more modern gear?" said Mike.

"As you know, all our current gear's been encrypted. If we use it, sure people might overhear our conversation and realise we're on to them. Do not underestimate McWilliams. He's narcissistic and a stand over merchant, but he's not bloody silly. He's intelligent. If cornered, Mike, don't take him lightly."

With security arrangements in place and knowing that Glen could react instantaneously to any emergency, Mike and Mary relaxed for the next few hours. It was after eight pm when they left.

Once in position, Mike and Mary slipped from the car and swiftly manoeuvred their way to the entrance. Finding the office deserted, they slid under the building and started replacing the old parts. Thirty minutes passed, with one item still to be replaced. Several cars arrived, and a group of men entered the office and slumped into chairs.

"Okay Reynolds, we have a serious problem. Any idea why Dalca and his men are missing? What's happened to your brother and the two men with him?" asked an unknown speaker.

"Trying to avoid the police. Dalca could be hiding until the heat is off. Hell, there's been no reports of any shooting. My brother's a worthless piece of garbage at the best of times. He's with that scraggly old crow, humping her, while he's looking for that letter."

"Mira is not a scraggy old crow," growled Mary softly. "The first chance I get, I'm going to bust Reynolds in the mouth."

"I'd like to see that!" muttered Mike.

Glen, overhearing the conversation, smiled quietly. *"Careful, Mike. You are walking into dangerous territory."* knowing how fiery Mary could be.

"The strike's likely to carry on for several more days. I don't know how true it is."

"Great, that's all we need. The longer it goes on, the more chance of a search taking place," complained a voice.

"Not necessarily. Work will build up, applying pressure on customs to act quickly," stated Reynolds. "I would be happier if Johnson was busy elsewhere."

"Is he snooping around and making a pest of himself?"

"No information, Joshua. The lack of interest by him is puzzling. To put it bluntly, uncharacteristic. His lack of interest is troubling me a great deal. In fact, he has the potential to destroy us," replied Reynolds.

"As I said yesterday, he may not have the letter. It' is possible Henderson never let on about it. In that case, all you're doing is alerting him and drawing attention ourselves. The constant attacks by our forces have failed."

"Are you suggesting Henderson's wife is unaware of its existence as well?" snapped Reynolds angrily.

"Do you tell your wife every detail of your work?" queried Harvey. "I know my ex-didn't."

"Then _ what in the hell were they doing in Canberra?" demanded Reynolds.

"There is always the possibility they were arranging for her husband's funeral as reported."

"One report says they were in Canberra. Another says that they had no scheduled meeting with the Commissioner," raved McWilliams, bursting into the room. "Having no security during these meetings is stupid. Not one of you heard me arrive. I was standing at the door listening to every word spoken for several minutes. This deal will make us all wealthy. Now break this up before we attract attention. Joshua, can you wait a moment?"

Once the others left, McWilliams turned on Harvey savagely. "Ever question my orders again, you're dead! There will be no insubordination while I'm in charge!"

The threat sent a chill racing down Mary's spine realising McWilliams was a cold, calculating killer. He would kill in a heartbeat to protect his criminal empire."

"We're coming back, Glen," whispered Mary, sliding back into open air. Outside the gates, they jogged to the car and climbed in just as the heavens opened.

Torrential rain hammered the car for a solid ten minutes before it began to ease off. Using the break as a signal, Glen moved away and headed for Mary's home.

Mike was the first to break the silence. "Glen, that bastard McWilliams is a nasty piece of work. Dangerous is a gross understatement. Bloody psychotic is a description that fits him well."

"Narcissistic is a far better word, Mike, to describe the mongrel," said Glen, slowing down for a red light.

"Reynolds' mine!" said Mary, burning in anger. "Calling Mira a scraggly old crow. He does not insult my friends. I am going to kick the crap out of him."

Mike went to poke fun until he saw Glen slowing shaking his head as if warning him. He closed his mouth and remained silent; he'd ask him later.

The car alongside moved ahead. Glen noticed the plate number. "Mike, isn't that Joshua Harvey's car.?"

"I think it is. Wait." Mike checked his notebook. "That's him all right."

"I wonder where Harvey is off to. His home's in the opposite direction."

"It's early. Let's play a hunch and follow the man. We may uncover a new lead or another member of this group," suggested Glen feeling it was the right course of action. "Any objections?"

"Is there a possibility that if we applied pressure, the man might turn state evidence, to avoid going to jail or for a lighter sentence?" asked Mary.

"It's the right kind of idea, but there's one drawback. If we approach Harvey and he refuses to cooperate, our whole set up is in jeopardy. We need more information on him or another advantage of some description," replied Glen.

"Boss, our man might have a mistress. That would interest his ex-wife, from what was bandied about, she is a vindictive bitch. There could be other dark secrets we could exploit to our advantage," suggested Mike.

"That's not ethical," protested Mary strenuously.

"Neither is a billion dollars of ice sold on the streets, ruining people's lives. Killing innocent people or murdering a police officer. When it comes to scum, I'll use any method to bring them down. They play by their rules, why the hell shouldn't I?" demanded Glen, anger burning deep in his eyes. Mentally seeing Laura and Alice in the morgue and nursing Neil as he died.

"I'm sorry, Glen. That was thoughtless of me. I do know where you're coming from, and how you feel. Believe me, I do," replied Mary softly.

"It may be unethical, Mary, but I want to stop this bunch from contaminating our country. If I have to break or bend a few rules to achieve that aim, I will. If leaning on weak-minded people will gain us an advantage, I'll do it. Everybody is responsible for his or her life choices. If they choose to stick their necks out and break the law, they know what the penalties are."

Glen's car slowed as the car ahead turned into a busy road and halted at a block of flats. Driving on by, Glen stopped at a fast-food outlet.

"Mike, follow him into the flats. See what you can find out. Don't make it look obvious; this may be entirely innocent," instructed Glen.

"Right, boss, on my way." He started walking towards the flats when the sound of gunfire erupted from the unit block. Seconds later,

Joshua Harvey, staggered from the building, shot several times and collapsed on the sidewalk.

Hearing the shots Mary and Glen exited the car and raced towards the flats, fearing Mike had run into trouble. They found him kneeling over the severely injured Harvey.

"What happened?" demanded Glen.

"I don't know, boss. I was approaching the building when I heard the shots. He came staggering out and collapsed. Shot several times in the chest. It looks like a small calibre weapon. Possibly a twenty-two."

Mary returned breathlessly. "The ambulance is coming. I rang Pat. Is he still alive?" she asked.

"Barely. It's touch and goes at the moment," said Glen looking up at her.

Mike had stripped his shirt off and was holding it tightly against Harvey's chest, trying to stem the blood flow. He looked up at Glen. "I hope that ambulance gets here fast. This bloke won't survive much longer."

The sound of a Claxton siren in the distance answered his question. Joshua Harvey's eyes fluttered open, looking at Mike. "Who are you?" he asked in a weak voice.

"Don't try to talk, mate," said Mike, ignoring the question. "Someone shot you several times in the chest. Do you know who did this to you?"

Harvey shook his head gently. "Just a blur in the shadows."

"What's your name?" asked Mike as the ambulance screeched to a halt alongside them.

"Joshua Harvey."

"I'll leave you with the paramedics, mate. They'll care for you," said Mike, standing up and walking over to Pat who had arrived and was talking to Glen and Mary.

"Pat, keep him under wraps for as long as you can. His name is Joshua Harvey. Place a twenty-four-hour guard on him. Someone wants him dead. I'm not sure if it's drug-related or personal. Pat, whatever happens, keep McWilliams and Reynolds away from him. This could involve them," said Glen.

"Our friend, has he any links to McWilliams and Reynolds?" asked Pat, looking them all in the eye.

Honestly, I have no idea. Nothing surprises me these days," replied Glen, avoiding giving a straight answer. Glen wanted no entanglements with the shooting or the state police investigations.

"Last question: why are you here?" asked Pat, knowing he was going to get the runaround.

"That's easily explained, Pat," answered Mary. "We stopped at the fast-food outlet to get a feed when we heard the shots. You can ask around. You'll find we're telling the truth. We heard the shooting, ran towards the building, he staggered out and collapsed on the sidewalk. Now, Pat, would I lie to you?"

"Bloody oath you would, Mary! In a heartbeat! Go before I run you in for loitering," growled Pat with a roguish grin.

Piling into the car, they headed off, just in time to avoid McWilliams' arrival.

"Manage to gain any Intel from our wounded friend, Mike? Perhaps, who shot him?" asked Glen wheeling into the driveway.

"All he saw was a blurry shadow. Then he felt the bullets hitting him. He staggered outside where I found him."

"There's a possibility that McWilliams changed his mind and decided to get rid of a weak link. Perhaps he had a contract placed on him?" suggested Mary.

"It was bloody sudden. No, this shooting was for a different reason. Once we know why Harvey was visiting the flats, then the truth will emerge. If he has a mistress, it may be a former lover, ex-husband or the bloody woman herself. Who knows?" theorised Glen. "All I know is it's inconvenient to our investigation. I was hoping we might have turned him to our side."

"That's still possible, boss. I think he'll become state evidence given the right encouragement. Do I have your permission to try?" asked Mike.

"Go for it, Mike. Just be careful. McWilliams is one of his mates," said Glen, "and he knows you by sight."

Chapter Seven

Where's Mike?

"This shooting of Harvey, what do you make of it, Mary? I need a woman's view. Forget he's a drug dealer for a moment. Someone who acted in anger - a crime of passion? You once stated, a long time ago, that a woman sees different qualities in men. Harvey is not film star quality. He has a wife, possibly a mistress. What other qualities would women find in him?"

Mary looked at Glen for a moment, gathering her thoughts before answering. "Money, good in bed, kind, considerate, loving and trustworthy. There's a long list of possibilities."

"Suppose he broke that trust. How would women react to it?' asked Glen.

"I'd kill him without a moment's hesitation if there were kids. Without kids, I'm not sure how I would react. I know I'd be hurt, angry, and hateful."

At that moment, the phone rang. "Yes. Thank you," said Mary, hanging up the phone. "Pat. Harvey was visiting his daughter. That's confirmed. He thought it might interest you."

"Wow! That throws a new slant on the shooting," said Mike.

"It sure does. Possibly the daughter's ex-boyfriend thinking Harvey is a new suitor? Decided to attack him in a jealous rage?" suggested Glen.

"I think it boils down to three possible reasons. The daughter's ex-boyfriend's involved. McWilliams ordered a hit or a third person holding a grudge against Harvey for a sour drug deal. Whatever it is, we are no wiser and time is becoming shorter," stated Mary. "Glen, Pat said your ex-boss turned up moments after we'd left."

"What the hell!" exploded Glen, "That bastard has his nose in everyone's business?"

"Also, Harvey wanted nothing to do with McWilliams and told him to his face. He asked Pat to keep him away," finished Mary.

"Boss, here's our chance. If Harvey thinks McWilliams ordered a hit on him, we may be able to turn him, gain Intel and put McWilliams away permanently," stressed Mike.

"I think you're right, mate," agreed Glen. "We'll never get a better chance. Mary, see if you can get Pat to let Mike talk to Harvey."

"There's no guarantee he'll help after that line of bull you gave him earlier on," said Mary, looking forward to talking to Pat again.

"Do it in the morning. It's getting late, and I don't want anything happening to you, deliberate or accidental. Mary, keep Sam with you." ordered Glen, taking stronger security measures. "Mike and I will sleep in the lounge room, just in case we have any unexpected guests."

The night passed uneventfully, Glen waking to the smell of bacon cooking. His left arm ached where he had rolled onto it through the evening. He found Mike busy in the kitchen. "Mary still in bed?" asked Glen, heading for the bathroom.

"No, mate. Mary's next door ringing Pat, trying to arrange a visit for me to speak to Harvey."

Mary arrived in time for breakfast with some disturbing news. "Mike can see Harvey anytime he wants. The sad news; one of the Dalcas' men managed to worm his way out of jail last night and has gone to ground. Pat said that this bloke was Dalca's, right-hand man. He's also known to carry a gun and isn't afraid of using it."

"Well, now we're aware who tried to take Harvey out. Weasel was to report to Harvey and tell him the others were in jail and let him know where Dalca was," reasoned Glen. "They think Harvey has double-crossed them. They are assuming Weasel had passed the message on and that Harvey double-crossed them and left them in jail to rot."

"That makes it a revenge shooting, payback for not helping them," added Mike. "This's the information I needed to use as leverage on Harvey. This question just came to mind; how did the shooter know where Harvey would be?"

"Harvey strikes me as a creature of habit," said Glen. "If this reasoning's valid, the others knew as well. They used prior knowledge to set an ambush."

"Why inside the building?" asked Mary, coming into the conversation.

"Several reasons, Mary. For that time of night, the Street's always busy. Too many witnesses. Harvey wouldn't see his assailant until it was too late. Our shooter disappeared through the rear entrance. Did any of us see someone running from the building, acting suspiciously?" said Glen, continuing.

"No. This was a straightforward and well-carried out plan. I believe Harvey knows who shot him, which is why he refused to speak to McWilliams. He thinks McWilliams set him up."

"I don't blame Harvey for believing that," said Mary. "Not after the threat, McWilliams made against him."

"If I'm to make the most of this opportunity I need to visit Harvey," said Mike.

"Mary's received the green light for your stay, Mike. Get the most out of it. Don't use my name, Mike," said Glen, wiping his brow.

"I'm off, boss," said Mike, grabbing his keys and heading for the door.

"Mike, watch your arse, mate. McWilliams will kill Harvey in an instant if he thinks Harvey is selling out. Do not underestimate him. The man is dangerous," stressed Glen, watching him disappear.

"You're worrying about him?" said Mary, looking at Glen's furrowed brow and the perspiration forming on it. "I think your fever has returned," she said, feeling his forehead. "You stay seated. I'll make coffee and get tablets to help lower your temperature. Then I'll change the dressing on your arm."

"Thanks, Mary, I appreciate your efforts, the way you take care of Mike and me," said Glen, watching her apply the dressing.

"Your wound looks good. Has it been giving you much pain?"

"When I knock it," replied Glen, sliding his shirt back on.

"How do you think Mike's going?" asked Mary. "Do you believe he can get Joshua Harvey to turn state's evidence?"

"I don't know. It would help a great deal," said Glen, checking his watch.

"Look, Glen, it's clear to me you're worried about Mike. Shall we go for a drive and take a peek. That way he'll have us watching his back if anything arises."

Twenty minutes later, they were entering the hospital, heading for Harvey's room when the sound of Mike's voice caught their attention.

"Stop, police!"

Moving out of the line of vision, Glen and Mary watched as Mike crash tackled the running figure, bringing him to the ground. Swiftly, Mike, had his hands cuffed behind his back. Jerking him to his feet, he frog-marched the man back down the hall and handed him over to the state police.

They heard Mike ask a doctor near Joshua Harvey's room, "How's your patient, Doc. Will he make it?"

"It'll be touch and go. We'll know in a few hours if Mr Harvey is going to survive."

"I only left him for a couple of minutes to go to the toilet. When I returned, I caught the offender with a pillow over your patient's face trying to smother him. Someone has a grudge against the poor bastard."

"That's a strong possibility, officer. Someone pumped five bullets into him then tried to smother him. I'd say that's a definite fact," said the doctor sarcastically. Resentful at the way Mike had expressed himself, the doctor turned and walked back into his patient's room.

"Let's go! I can't wait to hear Mike's version of this. It'll be a dilly," chuckled Glen as he turned to leave.

Grabbing him by the collar, Mary jerked him backwards whispering, "McWilliams' coming in the main entrance." Slipping into the hospital coffee shop, they managed to avoid him.

Watching him from a distance, they waited for McWilliams to erupt when told he couldn't visit the patient because of serious medical complications. He stormed from the hospital like a rabid dog frothing at the mouth. From what they could gather, nobody had tried to explain to McWilliams that someone had tried to murder Harvey minutes earlier.

Arriving back at Mary's, they were chatting over coffee when Mike returned wearing a long face.

"What's up, mate?" asked Glen. "Why the long face?"

"I was this close," said Mike, indicating with his thumb and finger, "in convincing Harvey into turning state's evidence - this close. I left to go to the bathroom. When I returned, I sprung this bloke smothering him. I challenged him, and he bolted. Giving chase, I had to tackle him in the passage, cuff him and hand him over to the state boys. Just after this, McWilliams turned up wanting to see Harvey. He became angry, then stormed out."

"Did he see you?" asked Mary.

"Not bloody likely but I'd caught a glimpse of him entering the hospital, so I made myself scarce," finished Mike.

"Joshua Harvey, is he alive?" asked Glen.

"Barely – the doctor reckons it's a close race. At the moment he's hanging in there, fighting," said Mike "I was so near to an agreement, so damn close."

"How did he react to your proposal?" asked Mary, placing a coffee cup in front of him.

"Better than I'd expected. Harvey remembered me helping him last night. We discussed the shooting in some detail. He's insistent it was too dark to recognise the shooter, suggesting it was a deliberate attempt on his life."

"As I was asking him who he thought it was, a doctor entered wanting to examine him. I went for a walk to the bathroom and, returning, I caught him smothering Harvey. It turns out he was Dalca's second in command," said Mike, continuing. "It wasn't long after that that McWilliams turned up, giving an Oscar performance of a right proper bastard."

"You tried, mate, that what counts," praised Glen. "At least you caught that other mongrel."

"That's not the point; I failed my mission."

"I don't see it that way, Mike. If you were a minute or two later, the man would surely have died. You've given him a fighting chance. If he survives, you'll get another crack. I promise you that," said Glen, concerned about Mike's lapse of confidence.

"Come on, you pair. While you've talked the morning away, I made lunch for us. A hot meal will do us good particularly you Mike. You look a little down," said Mary, judging his mood right.

"Tonight could be interesting, to put it mildly," said Mary. "That office will be overworked. Their little group is close to splintering. They're pulling in all directions. It's surprising what idle conversation may be floating around. We could pick up enough Intel to bust this case wide open. Besides we have to replace parts or lose our only source of information."

"You're right, Mary. There's a job to complete," said Glen. "A hot meal won't hurt."

After eating, they sat around talking and bringing files up-to-date. Planning their next move against McWilliams, they knew from his behaviour earlier that day that his nerves were stretched tight and frayed around the edges.

"What do you think is going through McWilliams' mind at the moment?" asked Mary, clearing the table with Mike's help.

"I honestly don't know. The man is hard to fathom at times. At the moment, McWilliams is concerned about Harvey's shooting. He'd issued no order. Is another drug cartel trying to muscle in on his business? A possibility, but unlikely," replied Glen, giving the matter much thought.

"Imagine what his reaction would be to find his men are creating havoc in the ranks because of a misunderstanding," added Mike.

"There's one definite positive advantage in this," said Glen, summarising the facts.

"What in the hell is that?" asked Mike in surprise.

"It's taken his mind away from us. Outside events have changed beyond his control, and they're rattling his superior intellect," said Glen summing up.

"That should make him prone to mistakes," suggested Mary, sitting down at the table. "So, do we return tonight as usual?"

"I don't think we have any choice. We've come this far. Let's complete it," chimed in Mike, a smile on his face.

"You know what's gnawing at me the most, Mary? The initials E.T.B. I have no bloody clue what they stand for," said Glen, agreeing with the others.

"Don't worry, Glen," said Mary. "We'll discover their meaning. Neil knew what he was doing when he hid that letter. But I admit, at the moment the clue has us stumped. Yet I feel its right under our noses. It'll turn up, I know it."

"If McWilliams is prepared to go extreme lengths to recover the letter, the information must be explosive," replied Glen. "Perhaps enough to lock them up for life. Once we've exposed McWilliams and other corrupt police, they'll be facing the loss of their careers and several years jail time ahead of them. Then we'll have completed our job to the highest possible standard."

"I'm certain McWilliams will fight and kill to protect his illegal empire," said Mary. "But I'm equally determined to get justice for Neil. Glen may have taken out his killer but, as far as I'm concerned, McWilliams is the one giving the orders, and he should pay for Neil's death."

"We feel like that, too, Mary. I have two damn good reasons to have that bastard locked up. They're both lying in Rookwood Cemetery turning to dust well before their time because of this drug, ice, McWilliams is peddling," said Glen angrily, walking from the room to hide the tears welling up in his eyes. Mike looked at Mary, mystified at Glen emotional outburst and not understanding the anger.

"Give me a hand to make afternoon tea and coffee, Mike, and we can talk about events that happened not that long ago," said Mary, walking into the kitchen with Mike in tow. She quickly explained to

Mike of the death of Glen's family and the emotional hold it had on him. "With Neil's death, it nearly pushed him over the edge."

"What about you Mary, how are you coping with the loss of your husband?"

"I have my kids, and I must be strong for them. Don't make any mistake; I miss my man, my lover and the father of my children. Not like Glen; he lost everything precious to him," said Mary, a sad look on her face. "Glen's slowly bouncing back. Lord help McWilliams when Glen's fit and alert! That's the day I am waiting for."

"So, does Glen takes unnecessary risks because of his lost family or is something else driving him?" asked Mike quietly.

"His loss is possibly a part of it; I know responsibility for our safety and well-being weighs heavy on his mind. With his injury, he's made the decision to let us go into danger. He's not comfortable with that; it's eating away at him," finished Mary, carrying the sandwiches and walking into the lounge room before calling, "Smoko, mate."

Heeding her call, Glen sat on the couch, munching on a sandwich, his mind still in turmoil. He'd overheard Mary explaining to Mike. At first, he was angry and then the realisation hit him that not telling Mike was unfair to him and placing his life in danger.

"The routine tonight is exactly as last night. Remember, if trouble occurs, stay within two kilometres of the car. That enables me to track you, and I'll pick you up," ordered Glen, wiping the sweat from his forehead.

Noticing this movement, Mary quietly stood up walked to the kitchen. She grabbed some tablets and a glass of water and made him take them. "Have a rest, mate. I'll wake you when it's time."

Glen knew it was useless to argue with her when she was in this frame of mind.

Glen returned to the bedroom and slept until Mary woke him after dark.

Rising from bed, the black fog which had clouded his mind for the past six weeks lifted. The effects of the alcohol had gone, his mind was sharp and clear. For the first time in weeks, he felt rejuvenated, fresh and wanting to work.

"You are a bloody miracle worker, you redheaded beauty," said Glen kissing Mary on the cheek. "I'm ready to tackle McWilliams' thugs at their own game."

"About time," replied Mary, touching her cheek in astonishment, "I was getting sick of carrying you."

"Mary, you and Neil helped me climb from a deep, dark, cold abyss. I was tottering on edge, ready to fall either way. Laura and Alison wouldn't want me to sacrifice myself needlessly. My job is to stop drugs entering the country," said Glen.

"Welcome back, mate!" said Mary, giving him a hug. "I've been waiting a long time for this day to occur."

Later that night, Glen let Mary and Mike out beside the warehouse and parked in the usual spot, waiting for the others to move into position. Mike and Mary crept cautiously towards the office and managed to slip under the building before the first car arrived. Minutes later, three other vehicles had filled up the parking space. Their occupants trooped inside, closing the door behind them.

They could hear McWilliams' voice clearly as he angrily turned on the group. "Which one of you bright bastards shot Harvey?" demanded McWilliams, "Do you know what problems you've caused? Without Harvey, getting that container released has become a whole lot harder," thundered McWilliams.

"We didn't shoot him, boss, we had no reason to."

"If none of you blasted him, who the hell did?" bellowed McWilliams angrily, confused by the shooting and the strenuous denials coming from the group which was at a loss to explain.

"Maybe the coppers shot him and are trying to cover their mistake," suggested one of the group.

"Don't be so bloody stupid!" snarled McWilliams turning on the man in question. "The police had no idea of his existence until one of you bastards pumped him full of lead and left him for dead. Now they're asking him all sorts of questions. I've tried to see him, but the doctor told me he'd had a severe relapse and may not make it. If Harvey dies, getting to the container will become harder, and it will take longer to recover. He may not want to help us."

"Why? Joshua's fully committed," said one of the men. "We didn't shoot him."

"He was getting cold feet, so I leaned on him the other night to ensure his cooperation. Then some fool went and wounded him outside his daughter's unit. I'm confident he thinks I ordered the hit."

"What about Dalca and his mates?" asked another member. "He's become twisted and vicious since Nicky death. He's homicidal. He kills for the sake of killing. He wants to shoot the woman and her children because of his brother's death at the hands of that uncover cop."

"Who gives a damn about that smart-arse little bitch and her snotty nosed brats. They're just a waste of space. Anyhow, I told Dalca to go after her to stop Johnson from closing in on us. If he's protecting her, he has less time to check our movements," snarled McWilliams in a sadistic tone.

Hearing the threats made against her children and herself, Mary muttered softly, a hardness in her voice Mike had never heard before, "That's what you think, you sadistic bastard. This smart arse little bitch is going to play havoc with you and your plans and will have you locked away for a long time. If I can't, I'll kill you myself."

Even in the darkness, Mike recognised a thinly veiled threat when he heard one. He knew Mary meant every word and would shoot the man if the opportunity presented itself. The saying the female of the species was deadlier than the male. In this case, the adage could be right. Reaching out, he touched her gently on the shoulder and, feeling her tense, whispered, "Relax, we'll get him or die in the attempt."

They lay beside each other listening to the conversation, hearing McWilliams make plans to involve Harvey's daughter and force her to act as their go-between. He'd hold her child hostage and threaten to harm the child if she didn't comply with their demands.

"The bastard!" growled Mike. "I'd love to wrap my hands around that prick's neck. Better still, meet him in a dark alley then kick the crap out of him."

After the meeting had broken up, the place was left in darkness. Having completed their tasks, Mary slipped out from beneath the building and wiped herself down. As she stared around the edge of the building, a voice challenged her presence.

"Hey, kid what are you doing here? Get out of here. This is no playground."

Aware she'd been mistaken for a kid, Mary bolted, running up a lane between two buildings heading for the main street at the other end.

Mike heard the shout and froze as the security guard lumbered past him in pursuit of Mary. Mike heard him call out over his shoulder, "Go the other way, Frank. We'll cut him off at the other end."

"Glen, Mary's in trouble. She's heading for the main entrance. She'll need help."

Hearing the car start, Mike quickly left the complex and made his way to a phone box and waited, hoping that Glen could get to Mary in time.

Mary outdistanced the guard and kept giving Glen her position so he could pick her up at the first opportunity. She rounded the corner only to find the other guard closing in on her. She didn't want to hurt them nor did she want them seeing her, so she concealed herself in the thick shadow of a doorway.

Moments later, she was lifted off her feet and dragged through the door. Struggling violently, she halted abruptly as she recognised Glen's voice. "Stop, or they'll capture both of us." Glen locked the door behind them. Waiting in the dark Mary felt her heart pounding as she clung tightly to him.

The two guards rounded the corner together crashed heavily into each other and falling to the ground in a tangled mess. As they struggled to their feet, Glen heard one of them say, "Where's that kid?"

"How in the hell do I know?"

They heard the guards try the locked door "No way has he gone in there," one said. They searched the immediate vicinity before moving on.

Mary and Glen breathed a sigh of relief, waiting in the darkness, still clinging to each other. Thirty minutes passed before they ventured out and headed for the car. Once or twice they darted into the shadows to avoid the prowling guards. Several times, they backtracked to get around them.

It was taking them longer than they expected because some guards were moving around, hunting for the fugitive.

"What do we do now?" asked Mary. "Mike will be worrying about us, wondering where we are."

"We wait until we can get a clear exit," answered Glen. "Mike is going to wait as long as it takes. They're hunting for a kid. Let's leave them with that impression."

They'd waited several more minutes before Mary suggested a possible way out. "We could go among the containers to the wharf, slip into the water and leave that way."

"It's worth a try if nothing else," agreed Glen, his left arm throbbing where Mary had clung to him. He'd decided to go with the suggestion to keep her mind occupied and off other problems.

Leading the way Glen carefully picked his way among the containers until he came to a poorly lit space between the wharf and the water.

Taking Mary by the hand, Glen dashed across the open space. Reaching the edge of the dock, they lowered themselves into the icy water below, their energy sucked from their bodies, attacking their resolve. They scrambled to escape the clutches of the freezing ocean.

Dragging themselves to safety, they managed to make their way to where Glen had left the car. They towelled one another dry with a blanket then drove around to the phone box looking for Mike. He was nowhere in sight. Cruising the vicinity for over an hour, they failed to find him. Worried by his unexpected absence and his failure to meet them, Glen drove back to Mary's place, hoping to find him there; nothing.

After showering and changing clothes and with a hot drink in their hands, Mary and Glen, sat and discussed Mike's disappearance and McWilliams' plans for Joshua Harvey's daughter and grandson.

"What are we going to do about Mike?" asked Mary, concerned over his mysterious disappearance.

"Why wasn't he at the phone box?" added Glen. "What's happened to him? We have a more pressing engagement - the welfare of Harvey's daughter and grandson. As for Mike, we know nothing. We have to get to Harvey's daughter and grandson before McWilliams and his men otherwise Harvey won't risk their lives for immunity against prosecution." Unexpectedly his train of thought was interrupted by a knock at the door. "Visitors? Now?" said Glen getting swiftly to his feet and drawing his pistol. Silently he walked to the door. Standing to one side, he nodded to Mary to answer.

"Who's there?" asked Mary, "Do you know what time it is?"

"It's Pat Murphy; I need to talk to you and Glen urgently. It's about Mike."

Recognizing the voice, Glen opened the door letting the burly detective sergeant enter.

"Boy, I am glad to find both of you here. Mike's in jail."

"What's he in the lockup for!" exclaimed Mary and Glen.

"A couple of uniformed constables picked him up near a telephone box at the abandoned warehouse in Reagan Street. They were patrolling the block looking for a teenager who had slipped illegally onto government property. Spotted by two security guards the kid bolted when challenged and was able to elude them."

"What's Mike been picked up for?" asked Glen, puzzled at Mike's arrest.

"They thought he was involved in some way."

"In fact, Pat, Mike was waiting for us to arrive," said Mary, cleverly switching the topic. "Would you like a cup of coffee, Pat?"

"Yes please, Mary," replied Pat, not falling for her ploy. "I thought as much. He rang and asked if I could let you know he was safe and well. As they have nothing concrete to hold him on, he'll return later this morning."

"That's a relief," said Mary, handing Pat a mug of coffee. "We've been worrying about his welfare, fearing he'd trouble or been in an accident."

"What job was he doing?" asked Pat, waiting for the run-around.

"We've been keeping an eye on McWilliams. He's spent many hours at the warehouse. I thought it wise to keep a watch on his movements, find out what he's up to," cut in Glen. "Mary was to drop me off, pick up Mike and return. When we arrived, Mike was not at the appointed meeting place. We cruised the immediate vicinity looking for him. Having no luck, we came back here hoping he'd returned."

"He didn't want to break his cover just in case McWilliams received word he was snooping around the docks. If that happens, it could interfere with your continuing investigation. Mike's adamant nothing should interfere with your case."

"Thanks for letting us know. It was decent of you to call in," said Glen, relieved his junior partner was okay and pleased that Mike had used his head and played along. With his identity safe, there was a slim chance he may pick up intelligence about the drug trade around the docks.

"I'd better be going," said Pat finishing his coffee. "Glen, I'll make sure Mike's release is the first cab off the rank."

"Thanks, Pat. We'll catch you later. Take care, old man," said Mary, a devilish twinkle in her eyes.

Pat gave her a roguish smile and left.

"At least we know what happened to Mike," continued Mary closing the door behind Pat.

"What I find funny is that they're searching for you. And the police picked Mike up for being in the wrong place at the wrong time, thinking he's loitering with intent to commit a crime. When in reality, he's carrying out a valid assignment. His release is assured if he chooses to reveal his identity. But it will be McWilliams who is the ranking officer contacted to confirm his identity. If that occurs, McWilliams will know or suspect we're on to him or someone working for him," grimaced Glen. "That's the reason he's taken this course of action."

Three hours later Mike turned up, opened the door and called out.

"Honey, I'm home. Did you miss me? Sorry, I'm late."

Mary strolled from her bedroom and looked him up and down. "I don't know, Mike. There's something different about you. I just can't place it at the moment. What do you reckon Glen?" she asked as he strolled from his room.

"I think I know what it is, Mary. The prison parlour he's developed, locked up with all those hardened criminals. There's more. I know, it's the stench of the jail. It's oozing from his pores and contaminating the surrounding air."

"Funny, bloody funny," growled Mike, a beaming smile encompassing his features. "The both of you missed me. I'm touched."

"You can bloody count on that," commented Glen, a greedy glint in his eyes. "After what you put both of us through I think you owe us at least a three-course meal... With all the trimmings. What do you reckon, Mary?"

"That's the least he can do, worrying us half to death. Running around, carousing with his mates in jail, making crude remarks about women. What is this world coming to letting riff-raff like Mike out on the street to corrupt the morals of real Australians!" added Mary, laughing at Mike's reaction.

"Cut it out. The police thought I had some involvement with some brat of a teenager who'd broken into the secured area. I was waiting near the phone box for you to pick me up. Didn't Pat tell you?"

"Yeah, mate, he did. The teenager they were looking for was Mary. They had guards looking everywhere for her. In the end, we swam out."

"Hell, that water is freezing at this time of year!" commented Mike.

"No bloody kidding Sherlock, tell us about it." Said Mary sarcastically.

Switching subjects, Glen cut back in. "At the moment, more important matters need attention. For example, Harvey's daughter and grandchild - McWilliams has unpleasant plans about their future or lack of it."

Chapter Eight

Dacla runs amuck

After a brief breakfast, all three headed out to Harvey's daughter's unit.

"How are you going to approach her, Glen?" asked Mary looking at him, wondering how he would approach her.

"I'm not sure now, Mary. I think you should take the lead in this. She may respond better to a woman if approached correctly. Regardless, she must be convinced that there's a credible threat to her and the child's safety."

"I'll do the best I can," replied Mary, relishing the freedom Glen was giving her to help this young woman.

"That's all anyone can do, Mary." Switching his attention to Mike, he said, "Mike, I want you to stay with the car, acting as our security. Keep a sharp lookout for our friends. They may turn up. If they do arrive, rev the car to let us know. Then follow them in."

"Right, boss," replied Mike, happy to have an active role in the proceedings.

"Mike, don't be too casual or off-handed towards this lot. Take no chances whatever. These bastards are playing for big money and will kill you to protect their shipment," warned Glen, worried about Mike's cavalier ways and inexperience.

As they made their way towards unit six, Glen sixth sense kicked in, warning against impending danger. Mary looked at him sharply, sensing a change in his demeanour.

"What's wrong?" she asked.

"I don't know. Something is out of place. There's danger about. I know, I can sense it," related Glen moving to one side as a man, young woman and child came down the stairs towards them.

The distressed look on the woman's face told him all he needed to know. As the man went to push past him, Glen rammed him into the wall, yelling to Mary, "Get them out of here!" and, at the same time, driving his right fist into the male's solar plexus, doubling him up and leaving him gasping for breath.

The scruffy individual grabbed for his coat pocket as if to pull out a weapon. Glen hit him on the point of the chin, knocking him unconscious. He cuffed him and searched his pockets. Finding a small calibre automatic pistol, Glen slipped it into his own pocket then jerked the prisoner to his feet and half marched, half dragged him down the stairs to the waiting car. He thrust the prisoner into the rear seat alongside Mike and climbed in beside him, saying, "You drive, Mary and, Miss Harvey, you and your child sit in the front with Mary. You're safe now."

"How do you know my name? Was I in trouble?" she asked, tears rolling down her face and onto the child.

"We received an intelligence report suggesting a possible kidnapping of you and your baby. We were on our way up to see you, when I spotted the distressed look on your face. We acted to free you and remove you from danger," answered Glen.

"Who are you? Does this have anything to do with my father's shooting?"

"We're Australian Federal Police, and yes; it has a lot to do with your dad's shooting," replied Glen showing her his badge.

"Shut your mouth bitch or…" began the prisoner before Glen's elbow caught the side of his head, stunning him and abruptly closing his mouth.

"Mary, locate the nearest phone and let Pat know we have a new prisoner for him," said Glen, his mind racing, hoping to exploit the situation to their advantage.

"My mobile, would that help?" said the girl, producing it from her coat.

"Thanks, that will be a great help," replied Glen, thankful to the young woman's foresight for keeping her phone hidden.

Reaching Pat, Glen quickly explained their immediate problem and the need to rid themselves of a prisoner. Agreeing to meet him at an appointed place, Glen hung up and handed the phone back. "Thank you, said Glen, searching for words, realising he didn't know her first name.

"Julia," came the quick response. "Can you explain to me what my father is involved in, that has created this problem? Who shot him?"

"Once we get rid of this unpleasant character," replied Glen, looking at the young woman and the anguish in her face. "Then I'll explain the whole story. I must warn you, it's not a pleasant picture."

She faced the front again and nodded mutely. Glen felt sorry for the kid, knowing she was crying silently, her shoulders shaking. They drove in silence the rest of the way. When he met with Pat and handed his prisoner over, he received a rude shock; the prisoner was one of Dalca's men. He'd been freed the night before on bail, but no one had bothered to tell Pat, placing his life in danger and theirs as well.

"I think McWilliams found out and somehow managed to manipulate their release. Either that or someone has made a monumental blunder by accidentally releasing them without checking with you first," said Glen, concern mounting over their safety. "By the way, Pat, this weapon belongs to your prisoner. He tried to use it on me when I arrested him."

Pat pocketed the weapon. "That gives me several serious charges to lodge against him, kidnapping, resisting arrest, carrying a concealed, weapon attempted murder plus several more I can think of." Pat grimaced, not looking forward to the rest of the day.

"Pat, there is one possibility you missed - bribery. Remember that germ - the one with the funny name who tried to kill Mary for ten thousand dollars? Don't be too quick to rule it out."

"Thanks for reminding me of that. I'll check into several people who were on duty. Two come to mind. I hope you're wrong."

"For your sake, I hope I am," said Glen. "Take care, Pat. This Dalca character is on the warpath. He won't care if he shoots either of us in the back."

Walking back to the car Glen climbed in and said, "Dalca's loose. Released without Pat being told. During this investigation be aware of your surroundings and people around you who are also on heightened alert. He's a mean bastard with a motley crew around him. Our prisoner was one of his."

"I don't know this man. What has it to do with me?" asked Julia Harvey.

"It's a means to an end," said Glen. "They're after your father; they think he has betrayed them. You and your child were to be used to force your dad out into the open. They're unaware that one of their members shot him then tried to smother him while he was in the hospital. Luckily for your dad, Mike here saw him trying to murder your father. He intervened and captured the man responsible. That man's locked in a cell alone set apart from the prison population. Communication's impossible because of a continuing investigation," finished Glen.

"What am I to do?" asked Julia Harvey. "I have nothing for my daughter Skye. I take it that I cannot return to my unit?"

"Let Mary know what's needed, and she'll arrange for the delivery of the items," said Glen. "You okay with that, Mary?"

"I'll arrange it shortly. First, let me look at that left shoulder," ordered Mary. "After all that strenuous exercise this morning, I'm concerned about you ripping the stitches out."

Glen looked at her defiantly for a few seconds. Then he growled, "Aw, what the hell!" and stripped down to his trousers.

She unravelled the bandage, looked at the wound and commented, "I don't think that dip in the harbour this morning did you any favours. It looks infected. The good news is, the stitches are still intact."

"Does that mean I don't have to go to the hospital or stay in bed for a month?" said Glen sarcastically, knowing Mary would respond.

"Glen Johnson, any more of that crap and I'll kick you where it hurts. You know I can do it!" she said, pulling the bandage tighter than necessary.

Glen gritted his teeth as pain coursed along his arm forcing an involuntary tear to roll down his cheek. Glen looked up at her and murmured, "You can be a real bitch when you want to be."

"I know, and you love it," smiled Mary, in a devilish manner, loosening the bandage slightly as Mike and Julia watched on in astonishment.

Leaning across, Julia whispered to Mike, "Are they married?"

"No, it's a game they play." Said Mike, "They've been friends for years. Glen's wife and young daughter died in a car accident when a hyped up drug addict ran a red light and slammed into their vehicle. Mary's husband has murdered a week or so ago. She's become a Special Constable. I came on the scene last week."

"She's fiery? Does she have any kids?" asked Julia.

"Yes, three. The kids are with her husband's parents. She can be very fiery. But she's also kind, considerate, intelligent and as game as Ned Kelly. So never underestimate her. Most importantly, don't piss her off. She can be deadly," said Mike accepting Skye as Julia stood up.

"Need to go to the powder room."

Mike pointed the way as the baby bounced up and down on his knees, smiling and pulling at his nose.

"You look like you've done that before," said Glen standing up, free of Mary's tender ministrations.

"I have an older sister with a couple of kids who like to harass their old uncle every time they see him," replied Mike as Julia returned.

"Julia, if you'll come with me, I'll order whatever you need for the baby, and some new clothes for you and they'll be here within the hour.

"I can't afford to buy a new wardrobe," protested Julia, alarm spreading across her face.

"You won't have to. The department's picking up the tab," replied Mary, looking at the young woman.

"What do I have to do to earn this gift?" asked Julia cautiously, fearing a trap of some description.

"All we want is your help to get your father to turn state's evidence. In return, he could be granted immunity from prosecution," replied Glen coming into the conversation

"How do I know you'll keep your word?" she asked.

"Julia, if you want, we can arrange for the presence of a lawyer of your choosing as a witness. An agreement would be drawn up in his presence," offered Glen, desperately wanting the young woman to co-operate."

"If you want to help your dad, this is the best way of going about it. If you don't want to become involved, perhaps your mother would help," suggested Glen.

"Ah, that'll be the day. That bitch chucked me out of the house when I fell pregnant. When dad supported me, she walked out, and we haven't seen her since," replied Julia Harvey angrily, a distressed look on her face.

"I'm sorry to hear that, Julia," said Mary, feeling for the young woman's plight.

"Since then my father's business has suffered due to the court cases lodged against him. She came from a wealthy family. She inherited a vast fortune when her parents died. Now she's causing him financial grief because of me," cried Julia, tears streaming down her face, miserable at the treatment her father was receiving from her mother.

Mary pulled the young woman to her and held her tight. "Come on, darling, let's get to work and order what's needed before your daughter starts yelling for a feed or a nappy change."

As the women left the house, Glen turned to Mike. "Now we know why Harvey's mixed up in this mess. Money; his ex-wife is deliberately bleeding him dry. She's trying to destroy him because he supported his daughter. At least he wants to help her. Regardless of whether his method's unlawful, it has the potential to work in our favour if she convinces him into becoming a state witness."

"I take it that's where I come into the picture. You promised me another crack at Harvey. If Julia agrees, we may just achieve our goal," replied Mike, thinking of the young woman who had gone next door with Mary, whose baby he was still nursing.

"If Julia's satisfied with the arrangement, I'll have Mary contact Pat and see if it's possible to visit him today. Of course, that's if he's able to receive visitors."

"Boss, tell me something. What do you have against mobile phones? How come we aren't using them?" asked Mike.

Glen looked at him for a moment before answering. "I'm not against them, Mike. With the house phone tapped, don't you think McWilliams is also checking the mobiles? Though he's acted stupidly on a couple of occasions, it does not mean he is. The man is brilliant. Otherwise, he wouldn't have reached the rank he has Mike, for your sake, don't underestimate him or anyone else."

"Sorry, I hadn't thought of that," answered Mike, receiving the explanation he was seeking.

"They looked up as the women entered the house, chatting away as if they were old friends. "Good news, Glen. Julia has decided to try to talk her father into turning state's evidence," said Mary. "Isn't that beautiful?"

"It's great. Now we need Pat's permission to see him. Do you think it could be arranged for today, Mary?" asked Glen, feeling happy about the progress they'd made and the weight it would add to the prosecutor's case.

As Mary went next door, Julia went to take Skye from Mike only to find she had fallen asleep in his arms, content with him nursing her.

"Look!" Julia exclaimed. "Goes to sleep with the first man that comes along!"

"What about her father?" asked Mike, without thinking looking up at her, he realised he'd blundered. "I'm sorry, Julia. I didn't mean to pry into your personal affairs."

"It's okay. Skye's father cleared out when I told him I was pregnant and he hasn't surfaced since. Dad helped me when he was able. It becomes frustrating and lonely living alone, raising a child. Apart from her grandfather, you are the only male she's met and accepted," said Julia, amazed at her daughter's reaction to Mike.

They all looked up as Mary walked in and said, "Pat has arranged for extra guards for your father's protection and a lawyer to act on his behalf and to protect your dad's legal rights. He said three o'clock sharp."

"I have an extra request. I'd like Mike to come with me as well," asked Julia, pleading to Glen with her eyes.

"How do you feel, Mike? Are you prepared to go with Julia and protect her if trouble arises?" said Glen, looking at Mike, a smile on his lips.

"That'll be all right with me. It would be a personal pleasure," responded Mike without a moment hesitation, a sparkle in his eyes.

They were sitting having coffee when a knock came at the door. Taking Julia and the baby with her, Mary waited a few seconds while Glen and Mike took up positions then called out, "Who is there?"

I have packages for a Mrs Henderson from the pharmacy and the clothing store," came a female voice.

"I'm coming," replied Mary, breathing a sigh of relief. She walked to the door. She collected the parcels, thanked the driver, watched her walk back to the van; climb in and drive off.

Later that afternoon the group worked out a plan to get Julia and Skye safely into the hospital.

With Mike driving and Glen riding shotgun, the women hidden in the back as they headed for the hospital. They cruised around several times before stopping near the Main door of the hospital. After letting Glen and Mary out, Mike drove swiftly to the rear entrance Mary allowed the others in, while Glen checked that the surrounding areas to ensure security was tight and free from prying eyes.

The all-clear sign was given, Mary escorted the others through to Harvey's room.

As Pat had already arrived, Mary ushered the others into the private room. Seeing her father, Julia rushed to his side, tears streaming down her cheeks.

Leaving Mike to take the lead, Glen stepped back beside the door, silently alert for any sudden interruptions. From this position, he could hear the conversation quite clearly and gave a slight nod to Mike.

"Hi, Joshua. How are you?" asked Mike. "I have Julia and Skye with me. Your daughter's worried about you. She needs to know if you're okay."

Joshua Harvey's eyes fluttered open. "Julia," he croaked, his voice barely recognisable as he fumbled for her hand.

"Daddy! Oh, Daddy, who has done this to you?" she cried, tears now flowing in a continuous stream.

"Julia, you must leave Sydney. They will hurt you. They are ruthless men who will kill to protect their identities and drugs."

"No one is going to hurt your daughter or grandchild while I'm around," vowed Mike. "We need you to turn state's evidence. That way we can protect all of you. We'll grant you immunity from prosecution."

Harvey peered up at Mike, his eyes struggling to focus. "You are the one that came to my aid when someone shot me. Are you a police officer?"

"Yes, Joshua, I am," answered Mike, feeling sorry for the injured man and the situation overall.

"No way can you protect us. McWilliams will find out and come after us."

"We know all about McWilliams and the Dalca family. We are aware one of them shot you," said Mike. "Julia is with us now to ensure she's protected."

"How do I know I can trust you?"

"Daddy, listen to him. Skye and I wouldn't be here if it hadn't been for Mike and his friends. They saved us from kidnapping or worse," sobbed Julia clutching her father's hand tightly. Skye reached for her grandfather, not understanding his reluctance to hold her.

"But Julia."

"No, Dad. Mike and his friends have helped us. I'm not going to let you throw away your freedom and our happiness because of misplaced loyalty to your so-called friends. They shot you, not us," pleaded Julia, determined to help her father out of his current difficulties.

At that moment, Skye reached out to Mike who accepted her without hesitation as she snuggled into his right shoulder.

"If my granddaughter likes you, that's okay by me. She always had a good sense about people. I'll do it," croaked Harvey, tears welling in his eyes.

Kneeling, Mike lowered Skye gently to her grandfather so that she could hug him.

Happy that everything was under control, Pat and Glen left the room and walked outside. They found the proceedings depressing and confining.

"I hope that will help your case against McWilliams," said Pat opening the rear exit door. As they walked out into the sunlight, several shots rang out. One round hit Pat high in the shoulder, driving the big man back into the wall. "Bloody hell, its Dalca and his men," cried Pat sliding down the wall of the hospital, blood pumping from his wound.

With lightning reflexes, Glen pulled Pat into cover. Returning fire, he forced the three oncoming men to duck for shelter. The rear door burst open. Two of Pat's people rushed outside, adding firepower to the raging gun battle. Dalca and his men refused to retreat and continued to pour gunfire at Glen and his reinforcements' position.

Suddenly, Mary was by his side. He yelled at her. "Pat's wounded, Mary. Get him inside. He needs medical attention urgently. Tell Mike - no one is allowed into that room. You stay and protect Harvey and his daughter. Mary; makes sure they don't try to slip in a bogus doctor. No one, Mary, not even Jesus Christ himself is to enter that room. Understand?" Mary nodded her acknowledgement.

Helping Pat to his feet, she had started to move, when Glen yelled, "Not yet. We'll give you cover. Suppressive fire – now!"

Hearing the command, Mary help Pat back into the hospital as bullets struck the brickwork around them, sending chips of masonry flying in all directions. Once inside and Pat in safe hands, Mary raced to Harvey's room to warn Mike of the impending danger. She stopped briefly to give the guards details on the shooting occurring outside. As well, she gave them instructions that anyone entering the room was at risk of a 'shoot to kill' order. With this dire warning ringing in their ears, Mary hurried to the ward to give Mike Glen's instructions.

"I'm coming in, Mike," she called making sure Mike didn't shoot her by mistake.

"It's okay Mira, come in." Mary halted in her tracks. Mike had given her a clear warning of danger. Tucking her pistol into the rear of her skirt and pulling her top over it, she entered the room.

Walking in, she found a man in a white coat aiming a gun at her.

"What do you want?" challenged the armed killer.

"I've come to check on my patient," replied Mary, walking up to Harvey and taking his pulse without a flicker of emotion on her face.

"I wouldn't bother if I were you. Our friend Harvey is going to die in a few minutes."

"Are you a doctor?" asked Mary, in an arrogant tone, trying to stir him up. "No, you're too stupid-looking to be a doctor. More like a cowardly punk with no brains." taunted Mary.

"You dumb, redheaded bitch," snarled the gunman stepping forward to hit her in the head with the heavy automatic clasped in his fist. Reacting with lightning reflexes, Mary ducked under the swinging arm and kneed him in the groin. As he doubled up, she grabbed him by the hair and drove her knee into his face, splattering his nose across his face and rendering him unconscious. Removing the weapon from his hand, she looked up saying, "Cuff him, Mike. And thanks for the warning. Well carried out."

"He arrived a couple of minutes before you. The only way I could warn you about our security breach was to call you Mira," replied Mike, still in awe of her performance. "Glen told me to never underestimate you. Now I know why."

Having cuffed the man, Mike dragged him to his feet, marched him to the door and handed him over to Pat's people. Hearing about Pat's wound, Mike spent a few minutes with him making sure he was okay. "Pat, make sure your boys take the credit if anyone should ask." Mike left as one of Pat's men entered.

Returning to the room, he found Glen talking to Mary and Julia. "Everything okay, boss?" asked Mike.

"No, mate. Dalca managed to escape, and he's on the run. That makes him dangerous to us, Mary in particular," replied Glen, fearing the results.

"That's no good, boss. It hampers our movements," said Mike, worried about Julia and Skye. "What about his men? Did they get away?"

"No thank God. Both wounded, taken prisoners. Also, the one You and Mary captured. You were a bit rough on him," commented Glen, with a cheeky smile.

"Not I, boss. Our friend made the mistake of calling Mary a dumb, redheaded bitch. She exploded into action. The poor bastard didn't stand a chance," protested Mike. "Beautiful to watch. Poetry in motion."

"Yeah, bad mistake using bitch and dumb in the same sentence. That would have done it," said Glen, a smile on his face. "She's a dynamo when she gets going. I keep forgetting how terrible and deadly she can be in a tight corner."

"There is another problem, boss; Julia and her family. We need protection for her and Joshua. We can't watch her twenty-four hours a day, as much as I want to," said Mike, looking at the young woman and child who had brought joy into his life.

Signalling the two women to join them, Glen said, "Mary, do you think Neil's parents would mind a couple of houseguests for a few days?

"Who – Julia and Skye?"

"Yeah. We need to get Julia and Skye out of danger and into a safe environment," replied Glen.

"I'm not leaving my father," protested Julia, frightened for her father's safety.

"Julia, from four thirty pm today your dad died from his wounds. If anyone comes looking for him, he no longer exists. We'll transport him to a new location where he'll receive the best of care and is in a controlled and safe environment," said Glen, wanting to simplify several pressing problems.

"Julia, I'll keep in contact with you daily and report your dad's progress, so you'll know how he's going," promised Mike, squeezing her hand. "I'd feel happier if I knew you were out of danger."

"Okay, I'll go and stay for long as necessary providing you ring me every day," said Julia.

"I can't promise the same time each day," returned Mike, "because of investigation demands."

"Now that's settled, Mary, I want you to go with Julia for protection and introduce her to Neil's parents. It'll also give you a chance to see your kids. Take two days off; come back in the third, the same way as last time. Keep your wits about you. Dalca is crazy, so take no chances." said Glen, looking directly at her and waiting for an argument.

"If that's what you want, when?" asked Mary quietly, refusing to fall into the trap he'd laid.

"Preferably unknown to McWilliams and co. If you can find the time, check on Pat. I've taken a liking to that big Mick," said Glen deliberately, waiting for Mary to explode at the use of the word.

Again, Mary's reaction seemed muted. She smiled and nodded her head. Taking Julia with her, she disappeared next door to make all the arrangements.

"You did well today, Mike. It was quick thinking on your part to warn Mary. Getting Julia onside will work in our favour. Let's have the paperwork drawn up and get Joshua Harvey's solicitor to okay it. Then have Joshua sign it," said Glen. "Once it's signed, hand it to the Department of Prosecution as evidence. Pray they can use it to our advantage," said Glen. "But at the moment, that's secondary. I'm worried about Dalca and his next move. From what I understand about him, he's the attack type. After today's effort, I'm positive he'll come after Mary."

"Where – here?" asked Mike, looking sharply at Glen.

"Yes, sometime in the next forty-eight hours, possibly earlier," replied Glen.

"A logical reason for escorting Julia to Queensland," suggested Mike. "It gives her a chance to see her kids and keep her out of danger without her knowing it while giving Julia a capable bodyguard."

"That's it in a nutshell," smiled Glen stiffly, concerned about his young companion's welfare.

Their conversation was interrupted by the women returning, chatting loudly as they came through the door.

"Could you arrange a flight?" asked Glen, happy that Mary had diverted Julia's mind from her immediate worries.

"Yes, we fly out at eight tonight. Neil's dad will pick us up at the airport. Pat's okay, and he's taking care of Harvey's transfer as we speak." answered Mary, smiling and sidling up to Glen. She whispered, "You are a sneaky bastard, Glen Johnson. If you think I don't know what you are up to, think again. But I love you for it."

"You were the logical choice," said Glen, looking at her and realising she could read him like an open book.

"I know, that's why I went with it. I also know our colleague has a soft spot for a particular young woman."

"Even blind Freddy could see that," answered Glen, looking at the others sitting in the lounge softly talking.

"I can assure, you, it's returned. Julia has it bad," said Mary following his line of sight, a smile widening on her face. "I'll do my best to protect her, mate. Don't worry."

"I know you will. That's why I selected you for the job, with other considerations in mind."

"I'll get a meal ready then pack. We don't have much time. Let's spend some of it on a decent meal and good company," suggested Mary with a smile.

With the women preparing the meal, Glen had Mike join him and ran through a plan to stop Dalca carrying out his murderous plan.

"Once the women are aboard the plane we'll return here and set a trap to nail this bastard."

"Boss, what happens if he doesn't try?" asked Mike. "Do you really think he'll risk capture or death just to take her out?"

"We'll face that hurdle if we ever come to it, mate. To Dalca, it's a blood feud. It is essential he carries out his threat. We'd look rather stupid not taking precautions. If Dalca turns up here unexpectedly, both of us could end up dead."

"It's your call, boss. I'll go along with anything you say."

"I'm pleased to hear that, mate. Both of us should still be alive at the end of this case provided we don't underestimate our opposition," said Glen, trying to impress the danger on Mike.

The call to eat interrupted their discussion and they walked into the kitchen and sat down. Time had passed before they were aware it. They quickly ready themselves to leave.

With the women on board and the aircraft safely airborne, they headed back to the house to prepare for any eventuality.

Entering the house, they discovered the lights failed to work, Glen quickly pulled Mike to the floor, whispering, "We have a visitor. Our friend Dalca is here. Be bloody careful. Don't move from here. I have no wish to shoot you accidentally."

Without another word, Glen wormed his way into the bedroom, fitted an infrared lens to a camera and wriggled back out into the lounge room. Slowly and methodically, he scanned the room looking for his foe. Glen expected light to flood the room at any second and a bullet to hit his body. Finding nothing, he scanned to the right. Seeing Mike was still in place, Glen whispered to him, "Shut the door." Next moment, the door shut with a bang and Mike rolled behind the lounge. Still nothing. Had someone entered the house or had a fuse blown? A wrong decision could be deadly.

Chapter Nine

Deadly Warning

They lay there for several minutes without speaking, scanning the room for a hint of movement. Silently Glen wormed his way across to Mike before whispering, "Can you see or hear anyone?"

"Not a damn trace. It's blacker than hell!" came the response. "I can barely see you, and you're only half a body length away."

"Keep your wits about you, mate. Could be a blown a fuse or someone has pulled one and is waiting for someone to step outside," said Glen, his mind racing. He had no sense of immediate danger, but he wasn't willing to test that theory by standing up. Caution was the keyword now. "Stay here and cover me. I'm going to scout around."

Inching his way forward, Glen headed towards the back door, every nerve in his body stretched to breaking point. Every movement was slow, painful and deliberate; Glen didn't want to draw attention to himself. He could hear his heart pounding in his ears as blood coursed through his body. As he entered the most visible part of the room, his adrenalin kicked in.

Reaching the door, he checked the lock. Finding it secure, Glen found the flap for the dog, moved to one side and called, "Sammy! Here, boy!" Seconds later, the flap pushed open, and Sam came rushing inside. "Good boy, Sammy," said Glen, patting the dog, pleased to find him fit and well.

Standing up, he called out to Mike. "I'm coming across, mate, so don't shoot. Sam's in the house with us. So hold your fire."

"Okay boss."

Using a flashlight, Glen found the fuse box and checked the fuses. He replaced the blown one, he returned inside and switched on the lights. Cautiously Glen checked each room. Finding the house secure, he breathed a sigh of relief and turned just as a bullet smashed the window pane and struck the wall alongside his head. He dived for the floor as the quick-thinking Mike flicked off the lights and joined him.

"Boss, I have the distinct impression someone dislikes you intensely," commented Mike. "It's becoming unhealthy standing near you. Mrs Lord didn't raise her little boy just for someone to drill him full of holes. I'm allergic to bullets."

"No shit, Sherlock. That makes two of us. If you hang around long enough, I'll personally introduce you to him," returned Glen coldly, slithering across the floor to another window. Peering cautiously out, he could see the faint outline of a man leaning across a car aiming a weapon at the house.

"Mike, come here. Our friend's outside pointing a gun this way. I want you to keep him covered while I slip out the back door and approach him from the side. If shooting starts, nail the bastard!" ordered Glen, heading out the back door, sick of being a target for trigger-happy hoods. "Oh, Mike. Be bloody careful where you point that damn weapon. I don't want to be a casualty of friendly fire."

"Boss, don't you trust my shooting?" protested Mike, innocently. "I haven't shot anyone yet, bad guys included."

"That does nothing to boost my confidence, not one bloody iota," replied Glen's fading voice, knowing deep in his heart, Mike's shooting would be acceptable.

Sticking to the dark shadows, Glen worked his way around to the right of the house, to the side gate. Easing it open, he slipped through it and inched forward towards the front of the house. Using what shadows were available, he managed to manoeuvre himself into position to take a shot from behind a large gum tree.

With the shooter in his sights, Glen yelled out a challenge. "Police! Lay down your weapon and come out with your hands up." The man turned and fired several times in one swift movement. Rounds hit the tree in front of Glen, who returned two shots in rapid succession. He heard the bullets strike home. Two more shots rang out from the house as Mike opened fire bringing the man to his knees. He knelt there for several seconds before falling forward on his face, dead, the gun clutched in his outstretched hand.

The porch light came on as Glen made his way to the body.

"Careful, boss, he might be playing possum," called Mike from the porch.

Kicking the weapon from the man's hand, Glen rolled him over as Mike joined him.

"It's Stephan Dalca, and he has four holes in him," said Glen coldly. "He was given a chance to surrender, but he made the wrong decision, and paid for it with his life."

"He had no intention of surrendering peacefully, boss. I heard you call out for him to surrender his weapon. He had a death wish, Glen." replied Mike, looking down at the dead body.

A minute or two later a police car screeched to a halt alongside them. Pat Murphy emerged, his shoulder strapped up and looking worse for wear. "I should have known you two were involved," he said, looking down. "Dalca! After Mary?'

"Yes, as far as we can figure out," replied Glen, looking at Pat's pallid features.

"Where's that redheaded spitfire?" Pat asked, looking around.

"Babysitting Julia Harvey and her daughter in Queensland," said Glen. "Pat, why aren't you in the hospital?"

"I wanted this bastard. Dacula's the one that gave me this, and I wanted to return the favour."

"I'm afraid we did that, Pat. Think of it as payment for the times you have helped us," said Glen.

"We have no problem if you and your boys want to take the credit for this," continued Glen. "We don't want any involvement with the media at the moment because of current undercover work."

"If that's the case," suggested Pat, "You pair had better disappear inside before they arrive and leave the rest to us."

Taking their leave from Pat, they went inside the house with only minutes to spare. When the media arrived, the house was dark and empty, and the cars were gone.

Glen, with Mike in tow, returned to his unit for the first time in days. They parked the cars and went upstairs. Opening the door, Mike stopped dead in his tracks. "Are they bullet holes?" he remarked, poking his finger through one. "When did that happen?"

"Just before you joined us," replied Glen, nonchalantly.

"Hell, boss, you have a winning way about you. Every evil bastard in the district is trying to drill you full of holes. What did you do to draw all this attention?" asked Mike, his curiosity aroused.

"Offhand, I'd say – drank myself into oblivion and had friends visit me," came the curt reply.

"The bloke responsible for this mess?" asked Mike pointing his finger at the door.

"I gave chase, and we fought it out in the stairwell. He lost."

"Hell, boss, death comes calling when they tangle with you."

"An unfortunate fact of life, mate. When it comes right down to it, it's either them or you," said Glen, closing the door behind them.

Early next morning they returned to Mary's house. On the way, Glen arranged for the repairs to the front window then checked the computer for messages from Mary.

Mike played with Sam for several minutes before feeding him. He returned inside to see what progress Glen had achieved. "Any news, boss?" he asked.

"Yeah, mate, the strike on the docks has escalated, buying our investigation more time. Time is the one item we need but can't control."

"Great, what's next?"

"I've finished here. We'd better go and check on Joshua Harvey and see how he's coming along. Scooping up the keys, Glen tossed them to Mike saying, "You can drive, and keep an eye on our rear in case we pick up a tail. When it comes to McWilliams, I don't trust that bastard at all."

"Shall I head straight to the hospital or drive around for a while?" asked Mike.

"Play it safe. Turn in the opposite direction and enjoy the sunshine for a while. Let's see if anyone is interested in our movements," replied Glen, stretching back in the seat.

After a few minutes, Mike said, "Glen, look in the side mirror. See that white vehicle about six cars back. It's been behind us ever since we left the house."

"Take the next right, then the next left then plants your foot and come back to their rear. We'll soon find out for sure," said Glen, sitting upright.

As Mike turned the corner, he flattened the accelerator. The car surged forward, picking up speed. Two hundred meters later, he turned sharply left before the other vehicle had entered the street. Moments later he was back on the main road. Slowing down, he approached the turn off with caution. The white car was sitting at the intersection, its driver pondering which way to go. Moments later, with both of them watching it turned right and headed back onto the main road.

Keeping their distance, Mike followed as discretely as possible. Several minutes elapsed before the car turned off and pulled up in front of a block of units. A tall blonde woman, dressed in a police uniform alighted from the vehicle and entered the complex

Mike grabbed the binoculars, read the registration plates and wrote down the number, make and model of the car. An hour had passed before she returned, accompanied by a man. They stood by the car for several minutes talking, before the woman kissed him, climbed into the car and drove off.

"Mike, follow him. Find out what unit number he goes into and their name if possible," ordered Glen. He watched as Mike sprinted down the road, slowing to a walk as the man entered the building.

Ten minutes ticked by before Mike reappeared. He stopped at the mailboxes. Glen watched as Mike removed a letter, read it, then returned it to the postbox. Mike walked back to the car saying, "Their names are H & M Welsley, and the unit number is seven."

"Well done, Mike. Head for Harvey now. After that, we'll follow up on why we were being tailed," said Glen. "I'm curious to know if Pat had anything to do with it or if she is freelancing for another group."

Calling into the private hospital, Glen and Mike found Harvey well guarded and his health improving gradually. They spoke to him briefly, explaining that Julia was safe in Queensland and that she wouldn't be back until it was safe to return. As far as the rest of the world was concerned, he had died from his wounds. Purchasing several magazines for him, they left him in high spirits.

Speaking to one of the guards, Glen asked, "Is Pat around? I need to talk to him urgently."

"No, he's across the road at the motel, catching up on some sleep," came the reply.

"We'll catch up with him at the motel."

Leaving the hospital, Glen and Mike caught up with Pat, who was in the motel café having a coffee.

"What are you pair con merchants doing, roaming the suburbs at this time of day?" he asked, taking a sip of coffee.

"Looking for you. I have a question that needs answering," said Glen, looking him straight in the eyes.

"Sounds like you have a problem. Shoot."

"Do you have surveillance on us?' asked Glen bluntly.

"No, why?' asked Pat, his interest peaking.

"Do you remember the other day when I said you might have a mole in your group?" said Glen.

"Yes, what happened?" Pat asked.

"We picked up a white car following us this morning when we were about to visit Joshua Harvey. Lucky for us, Mike spotted the car straight away, so we were able to lead it away from Harvey,"

"Any idea who the driver was?" asked Pat, alarm spreading across his rugged features.

At this stage Mike broke in, ripping a page from his notebook. "Here's the name and address of the woman involved and the registration of the vehicle," said Mike, handing the paper to Pat.

Pat looked at it briefly, pulled out his phone and made a quick call. "She'll be here shortly, and we will get to the bottom of this immediately," said Pat, replacing his mobile in his top pocket.

"We weren't sure if she was acting under your orders, or if she was freelancing on her own initiative or something more sinister. That's why we've drawn your attention to it," said Glen. "It's not the first time McWilliams has tried to use the organisation against us."

"What do you know about her Pat?' asked Mike.

"Unfortunately, not a great deal. The constable transferred to me a few days ago under a cloud. No explanation was given. Now I'm beginning to suspect she may be internal affairs or one of McWilliams' stooges. Either way, we could be in for some heavy flak. We've bent several rules over the past few days and kept certain individual prisoners isolated, trying to protect your investigation. It may have just blown up in our faces. All we can do now is wait and see," finished Pat, looking up as a policewoman walked through the door.

"Did you send for me Pat?" she asked in a direct and straight forward manner.

"Yes, constable. These two gentlemen said you were following them this morning after they'd left their quarters. Is that right?"

"Yes, Pat. I was given orders by Sergeant Wilson to go to that address and shadow them wherever they went."

"Was any reason given for this operation?" asked Pat, an angry look appearing on his face at the victimisation of the constable.

"Yes," she replied.

"What was that reason, may I ask?" said Pat.

"That they were drug dealers and I had to follow them wherever they went, then report back to him daily on their movements."

"Both these men are Federal police officers working undercover. Show her your badges. The other day, We had a security breach in this squad, putting both these men's lives in danger. Up until now I haven't been able trace the source. Thanks to you, that leak has been discovered. Next question, why were you transferred to my squad, if it's not too personal?" asked Pat.

"I stepped on the toes of a Federal police commander after he made some crude suggestions and I told him where to go. Next thing, I was transferred to you. No explanation or reason was given," said the woman.

"Let me take a stab at that commander's name: McWilliams. Is that right?" asked Glen.

"How do you know that?" asked the constable, a dumbstruck look on her face.

"He is the most disliked officer you'll ever find," said Glen. "He had you transferred to Pat because he must know Pat and I are working together. Wilson is working for McWilliams. That way they can make your life a misery if you don't comply with their wishes."

"That wouldn't surprise me at all. Wilson has a big mouth at the best of times. Now we know who the leak is, we can use it to our advantage," said Pat, his blood boiling at the mere thought of the young constable receiving that sort of treatment from one of his team.

"What will I do? I can't go back and tell him that I lost track of you," she said.

"You won't have to," replied Glen. "We'll work out a schedule for you to submit each day. It'll be necessary for you to travel that distance every day, by following the route we would have taken. Make sure you describe the places in detail, so if it's checked they know you have been there."

"What happens if they decide to follow me or doubt the reports I submit?"

"That should cover you for a few days. If you run into problems, contact Pat and let him sort it out. He knows how to communicate with us in an emergency if we have to cover for you," replied Glen, trying to foresee any problems arising.

Sitting down at a table, Glen quickly worked out several possible avenues of investigation he might take trying to find the information he might be seeking. Then he handed it to the constable. "This should keep you out of trouble for the next few days. If you need more, tell Pat, and he will get word to us. Remember what I said. Do it by the book."

"Thank you very much," said the young constable. "Thanks for believing in me." With that, she turned and left.

The three men watched her drive away before returning to their conversation. "Well Pat, what are your thoughts on her?" asked Glen.

"Personally, I think she's okay," replied Pat, tentatively moving his injured shoulder. "When it comes to Wilson, that is a different story. The woman knew nothing about our operation. Wilson did. He had ample opportunity to inform McWilliams about us. As you said yourself, Glen, McWilliams is known to use the organisation to keep tags on people. Less suspicious that way."

"It's your call, Pat," said Glen. "Your word's good enough for me."

"What are you going to do about Wilson, Pat?" asked Mike, interested in the man, and his brand of persuasion.

"He's been the main reason I haven't taken leave," replied Pat.

"How come?" asked Glen. "What has he got to do with you taking leave?"

"He'd lead the squad while I'm off," replied Pat. "With what we've just learned, it would place both your lives in extreme danger, and I wouldn't like that at all. Besides I like you, three oddballs."

"Pat, what sort of car does Wilson drive?" asked Glen. "If we're right, he might meet up with someone to pass on the information. I, for one, would like to know who."

"I can soon find out, said Pat."

"Also, his address. It could be interesting," said Glen, a plan formulating in his mind.

Pat made a couple of phone calls and was able to obtain the information he required. He scribbled it down and handed it to Glen.

"Thanks, Pat, we owe you one," said Glen. "We'd better be off. Mike has a phone call to make, and I have some serious planning to do."

Taking their leave, they headed back to the house just in time to let the glaziers in. Making a cup of coffee, Mike handed one to Glen who was watching the window being replaced.

"What do you think of the morning's efforts, Mike?" asked Glen, taking a sip from his mug.

"It could work out well if that constable is to be believed. If not, we could be in a ton of trouble, especially if McWilliams finds out about Harvey," stated Mike.

"We'll check out Wilson tonight and see what we come up with." Replied Glen. "Meanwhile, you have a phone call to make. While you're at it, check to make sure Mary and the kids are okay. Also, tell her that we may need her back here earlier if things start to develop. Tell her I'll send her an email."

Leaving Mike to handle the messages gave him time to work out how he was going to use Wilson. Glen knew he had to make contact with McWilliams, but how. McWilliams was too smart to use the phone. He'd use a quiet out of the way place with no witnesses, isolating himself from the surrounding community. The question was, where?

At that moment, he heard a vehicle pull up in the drive. Peering through a crack in the curtains, he was surprised to see Pat walking up the path. Opening the door, he watched the burly man approach.

"This is a surprise, Pat?" said Glen, letting the man into the house. "What's up?"

"Wilson," came the reply. "He's dead. Struck by a hit and run driver about an hour or so ago."

"Damn," growled Glen, "I was in the process of making plans involving him, hoping he might lead us back to McWilliams."

"I'm sorry, Glen. I had a feeling you may have been thinking along those lines. I thought you should know straight away."

"Thanks, Pat. Would you like a coffee?" asked Glen.

"No, mate," replied Pat, "I have too much work to do." With that, Pat left.

Minutes later, Mike returned, a broad smile on his face as he entered the house.

"I can see the call went well," said Glen, looking at Mike's beaming face

"Everything's ok, Boss," said Mike. "Mary's chafing at the bit to return, and she wants to bring down McWilliams as soon as possible so she can bring her kids back home."

"That's great," answered Glen. "And how is the fair Julia and Skye?"

"Great, boss, great," replied Mike. "She's pleased her father is recovering from his wounds, and Mary's kids are spoiling Skye rotten."

"I received some news while you were away. Our jaunt for tonight is off," said Glen.

"What in the hell happened?" asked Mike, looking sharply at Glen.

"Pat called in while you were away. Wilson dead, a vehicle accident about two hours ago. The driver didn't stop so we don't know if it's an accident or deliberate. Pat will pass on more details when they come to hand."

"That sucks, boss," said Mike. "I was looking forward to tonight's little adventure. Now, what do we do?"

"Follow up on the only lead we have. We'll go back to the dock area and nose around, see if we can find out anything of value. Besides, we need to renew several items while we're there."

"Won't that be risky, boss, after the close call Mary had the other night?" asked Mike.

"Possibly, but we need intel, and we won't get it sitting on our butts back here. Besides, that wharfies' strike won't last much longer. We have to be ready at a moment's notice. The problem is going to be coordinating the departments involved. Like Border force, Customs, State and Federal police," said Glen. "Come to think of it, Mary can handle that side of things. She's a damn good coordinator."

Scooping up the keys, Glen said, "Come on, Mike, I want to have a look at the accident scene, to see if we can pick up any evidence the state police might have missed. The more I think about it, the more I believe it was murder. I have nothing concrete to go on, just a feeling really. I want to satisfy myself." Seconds later, they were on the move, weaving their way through the traffic.

"What makes you think it wasn't an accident, Boss?" asked Mike.

"It's nothing I can place my finger on. Just a gut feeling. It just seems so convenient that the only decent lead we get ends up dead.

Here's a thought, Mike. After we left that constable's place, did you keep checking our rear to see if another vehicle was following?"

"No boss, I didn't think it was necessary," replied Mike. "A double tail?"

"It's possible, I have heard of them, but never seen one in action," said Glen. "If it was, Joshua Harvey could be in danger. We may have led them right to him." Slamming the car into one eighty degree turn, Glen planted his foot and raced back to the hospital. Screeching to a halt outside, they ran into the private room, just in time to see a man preparing a hypodermic needle.

"Hold it right there, sport," yelled Mike, his pistol aimed at the man's chest. "Now move away nice and slow before I drop you where you stand." As the man backed away, Glen checked Harvey to make sure he was still alive.

"Guards, come here!" bellowed Glen. Both men rushed in with weapons drawn. "I thought you were supposed to be defending this injured man. Who assigned you to this duty?"

Sergeant Wilson, this afternoon, just before he was killed."

"You ring Pat, and you, get a doctor. Move!" roared Glen, realising how close they'd come to losing their star witness.

A doctor rushed in. "What's the problem?" he asked, breathlessly.

"Check this vial, I need to know what it contains. Also, this syringe, as fast as possible."

The doctor checked the bottle then said, "This looks like it's a homemade substance. I'll have to get the lab onto it."

"Good – get it done now. If it's what I think it is, a poison of some sort, we need the answer as soon as possible. Doc, can you check Mr Harvey before you go?"

The pale-faced doctor examined Harvey thoroughly before giving him a clean bill of health.

"He seems to be fine. Heart, respiration, pulse are all standard. Earlier on, he complained of pain, so he was given a shot to ease it, plus a pill to help him sleep."

"That explains why he hasn't roused during this crisis," said Glen, relieved that the drug had not been administered.

After the doctor had left, Glen turned on the guards. "Where in the hell were you pair?" demanded Glen. "Your job was to protect this man. There were no guards in this room when we came in. This man came within a heartbeat of dying from some form of poisoning because you two couldn't do your job. What is your excuse."

"There was a disturbance in the hall, and we were called to break it up."

At this point in the conversation, Pat arrived, wondering what in the hell was going on.

"What's up Glen, what in the hell has happened?" asked Pat.

"We were outmanoeuvred, Pat. That young constable this morning was set up to act as a decoy. Unbeknown to her and us, there was another car involved. Mike and I are both at fault here. Neither of us checked to see if there was another tail. We led them straight to Harvey. To make matters worse, Wilson pulled the old guards and replaced them with two green officers. When a disturbance started, they both went to investigate," said Glen bluntly, "leaving Harvey unprotected for a few minutes."

"Lucky for all of us, Glen wasn't convinced that Wilson's death wasn't an accident. We were on our way to check the crash site when Glen remembered the double tail ploy," said Mike, cutting in. "This bastard here was about to eject him full of some crap when we arrived. Wilson's death was deliberate. They were tying up loose ends."

"If everything had gone to plan, there would be no witnesses left to point the finger," finished Glen. "Mike get on the phone. Let Mary know what's gone down and warn her that there could be an attempt to grab Julia and her daughter once they find out their plan has failed."

"Do you think McWilliams knows where Julia is?" asked Mike, alarm spreading across his face.

"That's a strong possibility, mate. Why take a chance?' stated Glen, emphatically.

Without further hesitation, Mike took off to place the call. He wanted to make sure Glen's warning was received as quickly as possible.

"Pat, we can't leave Harvey here, not after what has happened. We're going to need to move him somewhere safe with experienced men to guard him. The main question is, where?" said Glen, a worried look creasing his face.

"Leave it with me, mate," said Pat. "I'll have a chat to the powers to be and see what I can come up with."

Leaving the arrangements in Pat's capable hands, Glen went searching for Mike. He found him just as he was hanging up the phone.

"What did Mary say?' asked Glen when he'd reached him.

"She was placing a call through to our big boss, asking for additional resources to be allocated from the Federal force for guard duty from the Queensland command," said Mike. "She stated that everything possible will be done to protect Julia and her child from this bunch of bastards. Also, she told me to tell you, that McWilliams is no longer safe from her."

"That doesn't surprise me one little bloody bit," said Glen, nodding his head with understanding. "He's caused Mary lots of grief over the past week or so. She'll go after him if anyone tries to endanger her kids or Julia. Make no mistake, Mike, she will kill him, just for the sheer pleasure of it."

"Boss, we'd better extract our digits and get to him before she does. I don't want to see that lady end up in jail, for killing a prick like McWilliams," stated Mike with lots of passion.

"Neither do I, Mike. Neither do I. So, mate, as you so eloquently phrased it, we'd better extract our collective digits and move our arses if we're going to save that woman from herself," said Glen. He, better than anyone, understood Mary's bitter hatred of McWilliams.

They were about to leave the hospital when the doctor who had taken the sample away for testing, came up to them. "That vial you asked the lab to test? Here's the toxicology report. It was 98 percent pure ricin. Whoever did it, knew what they were about? I'd say a trained chemist or someone along that line. Two milligrams is more than enough to kill a human. That needle had six milligrams in it."

"More than ample to take Harvey out," said Glen.

'Yes, it would have been a horrific death. It can kill within three days. With this amount injected, and in his weakened state, it could have been a lot less."

"Thanks, doc," said Glen. "Give that report to Pat Murphy. He's the man in charge of the guard detail. Tell him you have already shown it to us. Thanks again, doc, for the speed with which this report was pushed through. I really appreciate it."

Leaving the hospital and strolling back to the car, Mike asked, "What is this Ricin shit you and the doctor were discussing?"

"It's a poison derived from the castor oil plant. The seeds can be refined, making the liquid highly toxic. I don't know if you remember, a few years ago, no - 1978 from memory. A Bulgarian writer Gregori Markov was injected with a pellet filled with Ricin fired from an umbrella. He died three days later. His murder was supposed to have been carried out by the Bulgarian secret police in London," Glen informed Mike.

"Hell, boss, in broad daylight!" exclaimed Mike, the rest of his sentence lost in a loud explosion, as their car erupted in flames. The powerful blast knocking both men to the ground stunning them for several seconds.

Pat, the first to emerge from the building, rushed up to them yelling, "Glen, Mike, are you both okay?"

"I think so Pat," answered Glen shakily, rising to his feet. "What about you Mike?"

"I'm not bloody sure. What in the hell happened?" asked Mike, regaining his feet.

"From the look of your car, someone just tried to assassinate the pair of you in one fell swoop. I would say, without hesitation, that both of you boys have trodden on some big shot's toes once too often," stated Pat, concerned about the welfare of his friends.

"No, Pat. That is a clear sign of desperation. They think we are too close for comfort," said Glen, an ugly look spreading across his face. "This was a warning to us, Pat: back off or else!"

Chapter Ten

Attack on Sam

"What makes you think this was a signal telling us to back off, boss?" asked Mike, watching Pat's car disappear down the road.

"It has to be, Mike. Otherwise, why not wait until we were in the car or closer before tripping the bomb. That way, they could have killed us both or injured us severely enough to slow down the investigation. If they kill both of us, both the State and Federal police would be all over the place. Besides, the Commissioner receives a daily update on our progress."

"He's not a man to let the death of two of his officers go unpunished," cut in Mike, thinking through the issues. "He'd take direct and drastic action. McWilliams is smart enough to know that."

"Still, all this is distracting us from our primary task. It's about buying time. Time for McWilliams to move the container to a safer location, so they can dispose of its contents in comparative safety," said Glen, opening the front door.

Entering the premises, they both stopped dead in their tracks. "Gas!" yelled Glen, "Open all the windows and doors, Mike. Hurry!"

Once the room had cleared, Glen found the source of the gas leak. All the burners on the stove had been turned on.

"Hell, that was the close, boss. I'm beginning to think somebody doesn't like Mrs Lord's little boy, not to mention you, boss. That's twice in one day, someone has tried to barbecue us, and I don't like the idea that we are the meat on the grill," said Mike, annoyed.

Glen, now in a highly alerted mental state, raised his finger to his lips and walked outside. Mike followed.

"That gas was meant to distract us. It's obvious someone has been in the place, but I don't think it was, as you articulated, to barbecue us. Though it could have had that effect plus burning the house down and eliminating any evidence," said Glen. "Our arrival back here was unexpected. The gas was turned on to delay us. The question is why?

"Maybe they were still in the house when we arrived and needed a diversion to get clear," reasoned Mike.

"I think your spot on there, mate. When we go back inside, don't say a word. If what I'm thinking is correct, the place has been bugged again. I have a little device under the bed which will help us locate them."

They both re-entered. Glen went to the bedroom, reached under the bed and pulled out a bag. Reaching in, he grabbed an electronic device which he switched on before beginning a thorough search of the house. They located eight concealed listening devices spread throughout the rooms.

Walking back outside, Mike asked, in a matter-of-fact tone, "What are we going to do about these bugs?"

"I've been thinking about that, Mike. If we isolate them or remove them, they'll know we've found them and decide to cause more grief for us. By leaving them in place, we can feed them misleading information, thus buying us the time we need to wrap this whole case up, McWilliams included," replied Glen.

"You know, boss, you are a devious old bastard when it comes to turning the tables," stated Mike.

"Hey, enough of that old shit! I'm only thirty-eight," growled Glen, a smile on his face.

"Sorry, boss. It must be all those colourful people you know that have aged you," quipped Mike.

"When we go back inside, I want you to react in opposition to what I say as if we're arguing," said Glen.

149

Entering the house again, Glen yelled at Mike. "How can you be so bloody stupid, forgetting to turn the gas off? You could have killed both of us? To make matters worse, the whole house could have gone up in smoke. If that happened, there would be hell to pay with Mary."

"Don't blame me. We rushed out of here so quick this morning, I hardly had time to do what I had to do," Mike bellowed back.

"I don't care! You have to keep your wits about you all the time, or it could cost one of us our lives."

They argued for another five minutes before walking out into the back garden and away from the house.

"Do you think they believed it?" asked Mike, looking back at the house, a curious look on his face.

"I'm not sure, Mike," said Glen, "Let's make out that we're going out for a meal to see if we picked up a tail. We'll drive down to the restaurant and have a feed. If nothing happens, we'll check out Harvey's office to see if there's any action going down there."

"Sounds like a plan to me," agreed Mike, happy to be on the move, not practising being a sitting duck.

Walking back into the house, they made some small talk before leaving Mary's home to go to the restaurant. Once outside, Glen checked both inside and outside of his car, to ensure they had no tracking or listening bugs. Satisfied, they drove slowly towards their destination, keeping a close eye out for any form of surveillance.

Glen parked where he could watch the car while they ate, making sure no one could tamper with it. After their meal, they cruised around for a while, both on the lookout for a tail. Finding none, they headed for the docks and Harvey's office. Here they hoped to find something more tangible to work on.

The dock area was like a morgue that night, silent and forbidding as if telling them to be on guard. Sensing the danger, Glen moved with extreme caution. Mike following his lead. As they slipped beneath the building, Mike heard a slight scuffle on the floor above. Grabbing Glen, he raised his thumb in the air, indicating that there was someone in the office. Nodding in reply, Glen quickly replaced the batteries and cards, then motioned for Mike to move out. Once clear of the building, they promptly returned to the car and sat listening. The longer they waited, the louder the men became.

"Boss, let's get to hell out of here," hissed Mike. "They knew we were coming. But how?"

"I don't know, Mike," replied Glen, his mind working overtime on the problem. "Not unless they planted bugs in the backyard."

"How was that possible?" asked Mike. "Sam was in the backyard. He would have gone off his trolley, not to say take an enormous chunk out of them in the process."

"Mike, do you remember where Sam was when we came home and found the gas on?" inquired Glen.

"Vaguely. Sam was lying in his kennel, asleep. He barely looked up when I opened the back door and windows. Wait a minute!" exclaimed Mike. "He usually runs up to us when we get back. He missed this afternoon. He stayed where he was."

"Sam was drugged; that's why he didn't respond the way he normally does. We didn't pick up on it, because of the gas and the planted bugs. Even when we went into the back garden, Sam never moved, he was still full of drugs," replied Glen.

"But how?" asked Mike, "He would have ripped them apart."

"Tranquillizer gun. They have a range of about eighty meters. Sam's kennel is at least twenty meters from the side of the fence," reasoned Glen. "On average, a male Siberian Husky cross weighs between thirty-five and forty kilos. It wouldn't be hard to find these facts on the internet. However, Sam's not a purebred. He's a cross between a German Shepherd and a Siberian Husky. That's what makes him a good guard dog."

"Do you mean to tell me, they shot him from the fence, waited for the drug to work, then just walked in?" asked Mike, horrified at the thought of Sam being shot.

"I'm afraid that's about it, Mike," replied Glen, grim-faced. "One good result came out of this fiasco. They were expecting us to break into the office. Not crawl under it. Hopefully, they're no wiser to our visit."

The first thing they did when reaching the house, was to deactivate the bugs, then call Sam inside. He was still unsteady on his feet. Glen checked him carefully, parting the fur until he found a puncture mark on his upper right rear leg. "That's how they did it," said Glen, showing it to Mike.

"I wonder how much of that shit they pumped into Sam?" asked Mike.

"More than enough. Those mongrels could have killed Sam. Lucky for him, he's a big bloody dog."

Glen decided to keep Sam inside from then on, to give him more protection and keep him safe from any intruder wielding a tranquilliser gun.

Leaving Mike to take care of Sam, Glen, then switched on the computer, looking for any emails from Mary. He found one, brief and straight to the point. "Thanks for the timely warning. Rats caught in a trap, singing like birds. Guards in place, coming back tomorrow. Mary"

"Hey, Mike, looks like Mary had some unwanted visitors," said Glen.

"Everybody all right?" asked Mike coming to the computer with a rush.

"See for yourself, mate," said Glen, smiling.

"The message is a bit cryptic, but I get the gist of it. I'd love to be a fly on the wall in that interrogation room," commented Mike.

"McWilliams name won't even be mentioned. He'll be so far removed from that attempted kidnapping, you wouldn't see the connection with the Hubble telescope," said Glen. "There would have been that much money offered or paid, nobody will know where it came from. McWilliams is too crafty to leave a trail back to himself."

"Do you mean the letter we're looking for will implicate him?"

"That's my guess, Mike. Otherwise, why go after it in such an uncoordinated and amateurish way. The man panicked. He's convinced that the letter is our hands and that it will incriminate him to such an extent that he's prepared to take whatever measures are necessary to protect himself from prosecution."

"What in the hell are we going to do about it, boss?" asked Mike, frustrated and angry at the continuing drama surrounding them.

"The perfect solution is to find that damn letter and fast. We've looked everywhere, and yet we're no wiser to its location. We've searched the house and found nothing. Mary is convinced Neil would have hidden it in plain sight. Knowing the importance and the explosive material it must contain, I'm going along with that thinking," said Glen, at his wit's end trying to solve the mystery.

"I think all of us should be here, applying ourselves, boss. I'm sure we'll find some solution."

"Mary's due back tomorrow. We'll put all the evidence we have to the boss, but without that letter, I don't think we have enough to put McWilliams and his cronies away for good. We need to catch them red-handed at the container with the drugs."

"Boss, I think we should go back and just listen in to any idle conversation that might take place. After what they did to Sam, I'm prepared to break a few bones," growled Mike angrily, for he'd grown quite attached to the big dog.

"I'm inclined to agree with you, Mike," said Glen. "We might pick up some type of intel."

After preparing flasks full of coffee and some sandwiches, they threw some blankets into the car and headed back to the docks. They parked in the usual spot. Turning on the scanner, they wrapped themselves in blankets and waited for signs of movement or chatter from Harvey's office.

An hour passed, without a sound and, several cups of coffee later, Glen was beginning to think they were wasting their time when the phone rang in the office. Mike and Glen sat upright as someone answered the phone.

"Yep. No, nothing. It's as dead as a tomb. What? You want us to go to the domestic airport, grab this redhead and take her to the meeting place." The phone went dead.

"Hell boss, they're going after Mary!" exclaimed Mike.

"That's not the question – how did they know Mary was coming back tomorrow. Somehow they have tapped into the computer or have planted a bug nearby or on it. Somehow we had missed it when we scanned the house."

"But boss, they are going to kidnap Mary."

"That's what they think," said Glen. "That will happen only over our dead bodies. Come on, let's get back to the house."

The following morning, they were up early. The first order of business was to check the back garden. Glen found several concealed listening devices and two on the front porch and one under the printer. Satisfied that the property was completely free of bugs, they prepared to pick up Mary from the airport, wanting to make sure they arrived on time so that Mary wouldn't receive any nasty surprises from unexpected people.

Arriving at the airport with time to spare, Glen went straight to the airline concerned, showed his badge and wrote a message to be sent to her. "Indians are hostile – be on guard."

They watched as Mary cleared security and made her way towards them.

"Hi, what's up?" she asked on reaching them. "What was that strange message about?"

"Two of the men from Harvey's office was ordered to kidnap you last night. We're here to make sure that doesn't occur," replied Glen, pleased to see Mary back safely.

"How's Julia and Skye?" asked Mike, "Are they okay?"

"Yes, Mike, both are fine. Thanks for your timely warning. We set a trap, and they walked right into it," smiled Mary. "Do you know who gave the order last night?"

"No, it was a new voice, one I hadn't heard before," said Glen.

"How do you want to play this?" asked Mary.

"You walk in front of us by about five meters carrying a bag. We'll follow close behind carrying the other two, making out we've just arrived as well, and see what happens," replied Glen.

Walking towards the car park, Mary hesitated briefly, then turned right, after receiving a slight nod from Glen. She continued slowly as a black sedan entered the parking area and headed towards her. The vehicle sped up as it drew closer. Sensing the danger, Mary ran between two cars, then turned to defend herself against the attack.

A massive set man jumped from the car to grab her, only to find there was insufficient room to manoeuvre. As he squeezed between the vehicles, Mary took full advantage of his lack of mobility. She leapt high into the air and delivered a side kick to the assailant's face, flattening his nose and driving him backwards.

Stung by the sudden viciousness of her attack and the sound of running feet, he clambered back into the car. As the driver accelerated towards the running men, Glen and Mike dived sideways, Glen landing heavily on his left shoulder. He felt the stitches rip out and pain sear through his body. Fighting the darkness that threatened to engulf him, Glen struggled to sit upright. Mike, seeing Glen's slow recovery, raced to his aid, calling, "Are you all right?"

"No, mate, I think I've ripped the stitches in the shoulder, and it hurts like bloody hell," uttered Glen in a raw voice. He fought to stay upright as Mike helped him to his feet.

Mary, summing up the situation, raced across to them, telling Mike to get the car. Slipping under his arm, Mary struggled to hold Glen upright as the black sedan reappeared, driving straight for them. Snatching Glen's pistol from its holster, Mary shoved Glen between a couple of parked vehicles, cocked the weapon and fired twice. Both bullets punctured the windscreen, missing the driver's head by a hair's breadth, causing him to flinch in shock, swerve away and drive off.

Mike heard the shots, whipped his pistol out, but held his fire, as the vehicle headed away from him towards the exit.

Seeing Mary struggling with Glen, he jumped into the car and drove to them. Opening the back door, Mary shoved Glen in and climbed in beside him.

"Let go, before people start asking questions," she ordered, ripping the shirt sleeve from Glen's injured shoulder. "Is there a first aid kit in the car?"

"Under the front passenger seat. It's not very big."

"It will have to do. Hell!" exclaimed Mary, looking at the wound. "You've ripped all the damn stitches out, and it's bleeding like a stuck pig."

Bandaging his shoulder to stem the flow of blood, Mary said, "Take him straight to the hospital so that we can get this wound tended to straight away. He's losing too much blood, and I'm having trouble controlling the flow."

Feeling Glen's forehead, Mary recoiled in surprise. Glen was feverish to the touch. "How do you feel?" asked Mary, a worried look spreading across her face.

"Lousy." came the reply, as he passed out, falling against Mary who held him tightly to her body to prevent him tumbling onto the floor.

Several minutes later, they pulled up at a private hospital. Mike raced into Emergency and came out with a gurney and a couple of male orderlies. Gently, but firmly, they lifted Glen onto the trolley and rushed him inside to the Emergency room.

Sitting in the waiting room, Mike looked at Mary's tracksuit, exclaiming. "My God, look at your clothes! You weren't kidding when you said Glen was bleeding badly!"

Mary, looking at her bloodstained clothing, stood up, saying, "I'll go to the car and get a suitcase so that I can change."

"Not bloody likely," retorted Mike. "After what happened today, I am not letting you out of my sight. Glen will kill me if anything happens to you. I can go out. You cover me from the entrance."

Mary nodded her approval, and they walked to the door. Mary watched Mike as he ran to the car and grabbed a blue case.

"No, the other one."

Swapping cases, Mike returned, glancing around looking for any threat. Finding none, he breathed a sigh of relief as he handed her the suitcase.

"I felt like a sitting duck out there," said Mike, with increasing concern about Mary's and his safety.

Mike stood guard while Mary showered and changed. Then they returned to the waiting room in time to speak to the doctor. "Your friend is a stubborn man. He's refusing to stay in the hospital to give that injury a chance to heal. He gave me some hogwash about diving out of the way as a vehicle tried to run him down."

"That's not hogwash, doc, that's a fact. If we hadn't dived out of the way, both of us would have ended up here. Some bastard tried to run us down as we were leaving the airport," stated Mike, bending the truth slightly.

"Tell me what's required and I'll ensure he will be well looked after. I used to be a nurse before I was married," said Mary.

Taking Mary at her word, the doctor explained how he wanted the wound treated and what medication she had to use. Then he supplied her with enough drugs and bandages to keep her going for several days.

"I want to see him back here in three days, understand?"

"Yes doctor, in three days."

Half an hour later they were on the move and heading for Mary's place. Glen sat in the front, his head leaning against the door frame. Looking into the side mirror, he noticed a black sedan about four cars back. "I think our friends from the airport are back. Take a look Mike, about four cars back."

"Yep, boss, it looks like them. I can see the bullet holes in the windscreen. What do you want to do boss?"

"Mary, we have to break a security rule. Ring Pat on your mobile. We'll lead these bastards into a trap."

"No need, mate," replied Mary. "I purchased a new phone in Queensland, under Neil's mother's name. I'm sending a text through to Pat now." Minutes ticked by before Mary received an answer.

"Turn left at the next street, travel about five clicks, then turn right."

Mike drove at a steady pace, not wanting to alert the vehicle behind. As they turned, two cars followed.

"There's a cul-de-sac ahead on your right-hand side, turn into it, go to the end then head back out. Pat's people are in place ready to shut the gate as soon as they enter," instructed Mary.

"Mary, hand me my weapon," said Glen. "If any shooting starts, it's better if I return fire. That way, if anyone is injured or if they complain about you shooting at the airport, it was me. Are you okay with that, Mike?"

"Yeah, no worries, boss," came the reply.

"Well, I'm not!" protested Mary. "Why should you take the blame for something I did?"

"You are only a special constable. You're not allowed to carry arms. If the truth comes out, you could have all of us up on charges, which includes the Commissioner as well."

"This is not just to protect you, it's all of us. I have the injury to prove those mongrels tried to run us down. That gives me the legitimate right to defend myself," argued Glen.

"Besides, Mary," said Mike cutting in, "These blokes won't be too anxious to tell people they were driven off by a little short arse female with an attitude." Mike's mouth slammed shut abruptly, realising what he had just said.

Mary's emerald green eyes blazed in anger at Mike's description of her. The tiny hands were forming into fists, ready to belt Mike.

"I'm sorry Mary. I didn't mean it the way it sounded. It sort of slipped out. It was supposed to sound like high praise," pleaded Mike in self-defence.

"You can go on bread and water for the next week or so," threatened Mary as she passed the pistol to Glen, a faint smile creasing her face.

"No time for this crap now. When these mongrels get closer, Mike, turn in front of them," instructed Glen.

"No, wait. Pat said to do nothing. They've got it under control," said Mary.

They sat and watched as four unmarked vehicles closed in on the black sedan. Both men were hauled from the car, slammed up against it and searched. Protesting that they had not broken the law until concealed weapons were removed from their clothing. They were handcuffed and pushed into a police car.

Pat, walking across to Glen asked, "What's going on with these two?"

"Try attempted murder of two Federal Police officers and attempted kidnapping of Mary. That should be enough to charge them," said Glen.

"Where and when did this happen?" asked Pat, taking the details down.

"At the domestic terminal. Those men tried to kidnap Mary. Then turning their attention on to us as we ran to her assistance, they tried to run both of us down. I fired two shots, hitting the windscreen, scaring them off," stated Glen.

"I take it was the big fellow that tried to grab you, Mary?" asked Pat switching his attention to her.

"Whatever made you come to that conclusion?" asked Mary, looking at Pat with astonishment.

"You left your usual trademark," replied Pat with a broad smile.

"What?"

"A broken head," said Pat.

"I'll have to watch that Pat, I'm becoming predictable," replied Mary, meekly.

"Also," said Pat, carrying on, "I'll need a statement from all of you, concerning your involvement and complaints."

"Can you call around to the house later on," said Mary. "I need to get Glen home. His left shoulder split wide open again when he dived out of the way of the car."

"The hell you say!" exclaimed Pat, looking closely at Glen's pallid features. "He doesn't look any uglier than before."

"Get stuffed, Pat," said Glen, as he removed the jacket covering his shoulder, exposing his damaged and blood-soaked shirt and the bandages stained red.

"Shit, mate, that looks bad," said Pat, as he examined the shoulder. "I'll catch up with you at Mary's place."

Leaving Pat and his men to clean up the situation, they headed back to Mary's, this time Mike keeping his eyes on the rear, looking for anymore uninvited guests.

After Glen had showered, changed, and propped himself up on the lounge with blankets and pillows, all three sat discussing the overall situation and what action was needed to bring the case to its conclusion.

"Let's examine the facts we have," said Mary. "One - we know McWilliams, Reynolds and maybe one or two others from within the A.F.P. are involved. Two – they've been killing off anyone that can connect them directly."

"Three," said Glen, "they think we have a letter linking them to the shipment of drugs. Until recently we had no knowledge of its existence. The only clue to its whereabouts is the initials E.T.B, and we have no idea what they mean."

"Four," added Mike, "we know they're getting desperate and nasty with the attempted murders of Joshua Harvey and Mary. Then, there are the three attempted kidnappings of Julia and Mary plus the blowing up of the car, trying to warn us off."

"Five," continued Glen, "The tranquilising of Sam and the planting of electronic surveillance equipment for the second time." Glen halted mid-thought, leaned over and whispered something to Mike.

Leaving the room for several seconds, Mike returned with the scanner and swept the house again. Finding it clear, he nodded to Glen to continue.

"At the moment, McWilliams is noticeable by his absence. The other night a new voice started issuing orders. Who? I don't know."

"Seven," cut in Mary, "the hostage crisis at Glen's in-laws. And what's this about Sam being injected with a tranquilliser the other day?"

"Sorry about that. Everything has been happening so fast we haven't been able to keep you up to date," said Glen. He quickly explained what had taken place and the reason Sam was inside.

"So you have Sam inside for his own safety?" asked Mary.

"Mike and I thought that it was a good idea. That way he can let us know if any danger arises and he's protected from people with nasty habits," said Glen. "Plus, people will be less inclined to break in if Sam is inside ready to tear strips off them the moment they enter."

"I'm glad the pair of you had Sam's welfare at heart. The kids and I are very fond of Sam."

"Now that that's settled, let's run through the facts again, in chronological order," said Glen. "One – this lot was onto Neil about ten days before his murder. We know this because Ken Reynold's took up with Mira about that time. Two - because Mary and Neil were helping me, McWilliams assumed Neil had passed on to me the letter they are so desperately searching for. Neither Mary nor I knew of the letter's existence until Ken Reynold's used Mira and her mother to try to get it."

"That is why McWilliams was so desperate to get Neil's notebook and file and plant a bug," cut in Mary. "When that fell through, they sent someone to steal it. Glen made up a dummy one, and we handed it over to Mcwilliams, thinking this would get him off of our backs. We did not know that McWilliams was looking for that damn letter. However, we managed to get McWilliams on tape signing for the file and the copy of the receipt, thus documenting his involvement."

"A great deal of the information we gained was by using illegal methods," said Glen. "We need to gather sufficient evidence with all the legal documentation to back up the evidence we have."

"How are we going to do that?" asked Mike, who had been listening intently to the conversation.

"That's a good point, Mike. This is where Mary comes into her own," stated Glen, looking at her. "I need you to coordinate all the information and send it to the Commissioner to see if there is any way he can obtain the legal paperwork to make what we have, stand up in a court of law."

"What, send it from here?" asked Mary.

"No, download it onto a USB stick, take it to the local library and send it from there," said Glen. "Once you've sent the information, ring him from your new phone and give him that number so he can contact us directly if the need arises. Mary, when you go, you will not be alone. Both Mike and I will escort you."

"You're placing a tremendous amount of faith in me, Glen. I hope I can live up to it."

"If I thought you couldn't do it, I wouldn't have given it to you," answered Glen, lying back down as a wave of pain coursed through his body causing him to feel sick.

Mike, noticing the change in colour grabbed a bucket from the laundry, while Mary asked, "You are in lots of pain, aren't you?" Glen looked at her, then nodded before sticking his head in the bucket.

Using one of the syringes supplied by the doctor she gave him a quick shot of morphine, then stood back and waited for the drug to take effect.

As the pain eased, Glen fell asleep. On awakening hours later, he asked Mary to switch on the television so he could watch the local news. What he feared most had happened. The waterfront strike had finished, and the workers would be returning to work the next morning. "Great, that's just bloody great! The wharfies' strike has ended, and I'm as helpless as a newborn child," he groaned, unhappy at his limited movement.

"What are you grumbling about now?" asked Mary, walking back into the room with a mug of steaming coffee in her hand. She sat it on the table. "What's the problem now? she asked.

"That damn strike has ended. We've run out of time. The ships will start unloading tomorrow."

"Relax, mate," said Mary. "While you've been snoring your head off, I've been in touch with the boss. He's put in place several measures to slow down the unloading process as well as alerting the other relative departments. Our friend Mr McWilliams and his cronies are in for one hell of a surprise."

"Where's Mike?" Glen asked, looking around the room.

"He's gone to check on Joshua Harvey, then to ring Julia on his condition," said Mary. "She's very concerned about her father. Plus, she wanted to talk to Mike."

"That poor bastard's already under the thumb only he doesn't realise it," smiled Glen, looking at Mary.

Mary looked at him for a moment, then said, "It will do that young man a world of good. A wife, a child, and responsibilities."

"How long has he been away?" asked Glen, looking at his watch and changing the subject away from Mary's matchmaking.

"A while, about an hour or so," said Mary. "I hope he hasn't run into any trouble. I don't want to see him injured."

"That makes two of us," answered Glen, concern creeping into his voice. Mike had become a critical part of the team. His loss would be devastating.

Chapter Eleven

Post Office Incident

Several hours had passed when they heard a car stop outside and a car door slam. They looked up as the door opened and Mike walked in, his head bandaged, his clothes ripped as if he had been in a fight.

"What in the hell happened to you?" asked Glen, staring at his dishevelled appearance and battered body.

"I ran into a slight hitch when I left the post office after withdrawing some money. A couple of dimwits tried to manhandle me and force me into a car. When I strenuously objected, the fun began. I ended up laying both of them out. Unfortunately, not before the local police arrived and dragged us down to the police station."

"Why didn't you contact us? We could have come and bailed you out," said Mary, unwrapping the bandage and looking at the nasty wound on his forehead. Deciding it needs more attention, she walked into the kitchen looking for a medical kit, a bowl, and a towel.

"Do you think it was an attempted kidnapping related to the job or something unique?" asked Glen, looking at Mike and his battered features.

"At first, I thought it was job-related. Then, later on, the local boys discovered that my attackers were seeking to roll someone for their money. I'm still not convinced about that. The bloke in front of me pulled out a thousand dollars, and he was a lot older than me.

I'd only withdrawn a hundred dollars. The other bloke walked out counting his money, that's the part I don't understand. I decided to contact Pat and let him straighten everything out."

"How come you didn't ring us to help you out?" asked Glen, mirroring Mary's earlier question.

"I knew you were in a bad way, and I didn't want Mary out on her own in case somebody was watching the house, someone who might try to grab her again. I wanted to play it safe for everyone concerned."

"That was very considerate of you, Mike, but we're a team Now sit down and let me treat your wounds before you end up flat on your back," said Mary, re-entering the room. "By the way, who bandaged your head?"

"Pat did. He said it was only a scratch and it wasn't worth dressing. As I was losing blood, I thought it would be prudent to strap it up."

"Good thing you did! This wound needs four or five stitches in it. I have some strips here that will close the cut until you see a doctor tomorrow," said Mary.

"That'll be all right, Mary. Go ahead, let's get it out of the way."

Glen winced at the casual way Mike agreed to Mary's suggestion. He knew from past experience how gentle she could be.

Quickly and expertly Mary taped up the five cm wound then applied the bandage. "That should suffice for the time being. Make sure you have it checked by a doctor."

The sound of a car stopping and a door slamming caught the attention of them all. Sam stood up, his tail wagging. That made Mary walk to the window and peer out. "It's okay, Pat's coming up the path. Most probably he's after our statements," said Mary opening the door. "Come on in, Pat, and take a load off those big flat feet," continued Mary, an impish grin on her face.

"Thank you, my darling, for your concern," countered Pat. "Yes – I would love coffee."

"You'll keep, Pat Murphy," replied Mary walking into the kitchen.

"Come for the statements, Pat?" asked Glen sitting upright.

"Not exactly. I have learned from the friends Mike made today that Joshua Harvey has a silent partner. A new bloke has taken over for McWilliams while he's in Western Australia. He's running the show at the moment. This bloke is pretty high up in Border Force and is well placed to sink your whole operation if he learns of it."

"Do you have a name to go with this character?" asked Glen.

"Unfortunately, no. The prisoners realising they'd said too much, both clammed up, and we haven't been able to get any more."

"How come they attacked me?" asked Mike. "Don't give me any crap about money. They had a different motive to that."

"True, Mike. You're absolutely right. They wanted you so they could force Glen to hand a letter over to them. Do you know what they're talking about?" asked Pat.

"Yes. We are aware of it. Unfortunately, we don't have the letter. The first we knew of its existence was when we had the hostage situation. We've looked everywhere but haven't been able to locate it," replied Glen.

"The problem is that my husband hid it too well, leaving only three letters from the alphabet as clues," said Mary, cutting in. "We haven't been able to decipher the meaning of them."

"From what we can gather, this letter must incriminate all of those involved, including McWilliams, Harvey and his partner," added Glen.

"Well, if I learn anything else, I'll let you know," said Pat standing up. "Do you three misfits understand how much paperwork is piling up on my desk because of your shenanigans and forays out into the real world. Bloody heaps."

"Sorry about that, mate. It isn't intentional, believe me," said Glen, grateful for Pat's help and understanding.

"You three, have created a year's work in less than three weeks. If you lot keep this up, I'll have to hire secretaries just to do the bloody paperwork," said Pat with a smile. "I have to go. Catch you later for those statements."

After Pat had left, Mike looked at the others and said, "If we don't act quickly, this bloke in Border Force could cause us a lot of grief, especially if we don't uncover his identity."

"You're right on that point, Mike," said Glen, turning to Mary. "Mary, contact the boss and pass that snippet of information onto him. Explain to him that it's essential he plays his cards close to his chest until we're able to uncover the culprit or at least get a lead on him."

Nodding her acknowledgement, Mary moved into the kitchen to make the phone call.

Glen sent Mike into the room he was occupying to bring back a little blue bag. Opening it, he pulled out Neil's notebook and thumbed through the pages until he came across a list written in code. Glen asked Mike to find Neil's dictionary, then - using it, worked his way through the numbered groups. When he'd finished, he had a list of five names. Four Glen already knew. The fifth he'd never heard mentioned. Was this the man from Border Force or was he someone else entirely?

"Mike, I want you to go through the Sydney phone book to see if you can match this name with these initials. If you can, go through the electoral rolls for those areas and see what you can come up with. It's a long shot, but it may pay off. If you find nothing, try matching the name to any Customs or Border Force employee. If that doesn't work, we'll have to ask Harvey himself," said Glen. "However, at the moment that's an avenue I don't want to take if I can help it."

"This could take sometime boss," said Mike, picking up the telephone directory and flicking through the pages.

"I'm well aware of that, mate. Just do the best you can. We need to uncover this character as soon as possible, so we know what we are up against. Time is crucial at this stage."

Mary re-entered the room as Glen finished speaking. "I've been talking to the Commissioner. He was alarmed by the news. He understands why you've made the request and will do as you've asked. He said to give him a name as quickly as possible. Until this character's identity is known, the Commissioner's actions are limited."

"Yeah, that's the sort of reaction I was expecting. That why I have Mike checking out a name that's written in code in Neil's notebook. I am hoping we can turn up a suspect or lead. Surely to

God, there cannot be that many names in the phone book called Chessingham and with the initials P. R." said Glen.

"You're right on that score," commented Mike. "None listed nationally."

"None whatsoever!" exclaimed Glen, a look of disbelief on his face.

"It could be an unlisted or silent number," said Mary, after giving the subject some serious thought.

"If that's the case, it could take several days to get the paperwork through," said Glen, "Time we don't have."

"What if we put the name to the commissioner? In his position he may know someone by that name or something similar," suggested Mary. "We have nothing to lose and everything to gain."

"Do it. Let's use what time we have constructively," instructed Glen, wanting to come to grips immediately with the new threat.

"I'm on it," said Mary, walking back into the kitchen.

"What are we going to do if we can't uncover this bloke's name in time, boss?" asked Mike.

"I suppose we proceed with extreme caution, hoping not to alert the character involved."

"The boss hasn't heard of the name either," said Mary walking back into the room. "He's going to make a few discrete inquiries and get back to us."

"Great, that leaves us with nothing!" growled Glen, irritated by the pain in his shoulder and the lack of progress.

"Hang on, boss, I may have something. I have a list of all of the Australian Border Force employees. One sticks out like a sore thumb; Peter Graham Chessingham transferred from the Australian Federal Police to the Australian Border Force when it was established in August 2015."

"What is his rank, is he in a senior position? That means he knows McWilliams. Any chance they're friends?" asked Glen.

"There's always that chance. Instead of jumping to conclusions, why don't we find out for sure? I'll ring the boss, give him a name and a possible connection to McWilliams and see what turns up," suggested Mary, dialling the commissioner once again.

"I have a question, boss," said Mike, cutting back in. "If this bloke Chessingham was in the A.F.P before joining the Border Force, how come the Commissioner doesn't remember him, or know of him?"

"The reason for that is two-fold. The commissioner was enlisted from the British Police and has only been employed in the job for less than two years. Since he's been Commissioner, he's promoted better men over McWilliams. That's why McWilliams despises him.

""Hell, I didn't know that, boss," said Mike.

"Our new Commissioner is far more preferable to McWilliams. Many of the current officers threatened to resign if McWilliams received the job. This action forced the Federal Government to search overseas for a suitable replacement."

"That's how McWilliams missed out," said Mary, hanging up the phone. "You should have heard what Glen and my husband had to say about the whole affair. It was enough to make an elegant lady like me blush."

"Forget that, it's ancient history. What did the Commissioner have to say about Chessingham?" asked Glen.

"He's still making inquiries and will let us know as soon as he can."

"Injury or no injury, we can't sit around here all day wondering. We have to check this bloke out for ourselves," said Glen, pulling himself upright. "Unfortunately, all the legwork will have to be done by the two of you. Is there an address listed?"

"Yeah."

"Okay, let's check him out and see what we can uncover," said Glen, wincing as he stood.

"Do you want a painkiller before we leave?" asked Mary, noting his reaction as he stood up.

"No, not yet. The pain will help keep me awake and alert. That way I'll be able to help to some degree. Mike, you drive. Mary, sit in the front and navigate," said Glen as they walked out the door.

Moments later they were on the move, looking for Chessingham's address. Glen noticed that Mary had dressed in a hooded tracksuit and sneakers. He thought it suited her and was quite practical. She would be able to cover her flaming red hair and jog past the house without drawing attention to herself. However, these plans changed as Mike approached the sizeable house. Glen spotted a car pulling into the drive. "Stop, Mike!" called Glen urgently. "Back up slowly. That car belongs to Dave Reynolds."

"What in the hell is he doing here?" asked Mike, slowly reversing.

"I don't know. But there's one thing I am sure of. This bloke Chessingham is mixed up in this business somehow."

The three of them watched in silence as Reynolds left the car and walked up the path to the front door. A woman answered his knock, then disappeared back inside. What happened next surprised the lot of them. Reynolds pulled a gun and forced the tall man who came to the door back into the house, his hands raised above his head.

"What's this all about?" said Mary who'd sat silently observing the proceedings. "Falling out amongst thieves?"

"Maybe, whatever is going down is to our advantage. There's more to Chessingham than meets the eye," said Glen, "and we need to find out quick."

"What do you suggest, boss?" asked Mike, checking his weapon." "Intervention; that could be bloody dangerous."

"That's putting it mildly," said Glen, his mind racing to formulate a plan of action. They needed Chessingham alive to answer some vital questions. Before he was able to craft one, the front door opened and three people left. The tall man and a woman who initially answered the door, both in handcuffs and Reynolds, still holding the gun.

"Mary, switch on that scanner to see if that bug is still active in his car. If it is, we should be able to track them from a distance."

"Yes, it's still picking up a strong signal," said Mary, watching Reynolds drive off with his two reluctant passengers.

"Follow them, Mike. Let's see where Reynolds is off to. I have a bad feeling it's not to our headquarters. Stay well behind them, Mate. I want to keep Reynolds completely oblivious to our presence."

"Right, boss."

"What do you think is going to happen, Glen?" asked Mary, alarmed at the recent course of events.

"I'm not really sure. But I have a funny feeling Chessingham is not an active player. As they believe Joshua Harvey is dead, someone has to front for the company. If he is a silent partner, they may need his signature to have the container released. Who knows? What I am certain of, the moment he signs the paperwork, Chessingham and the woman will disappear, never to be seen again. They cannot afford to leave any witnesses alive to testify. Once that container is out of the terminal, we could lose it permanently."

"Looks as if they're heading out of the city, most probably to private property where they can't be disturbed."

"Stay with them, Mike. Regardless of what goes down, we may have to intercede although I hope not. Reynolds must remain totally oblivious to our interest in his movements. That way, we may catch all of them with their hands in the cookie jar," said Glen hopefully, as Mike skillfully manoeuvred the car in and out of traffic, just keeping their quarry in scanning distance.

After about an hour and a half, the traffic had thinned out. "Looks like we're heading out towards the Warragamba Dam area. There are numerous properties concealed in that district. Just the place you would want to unload a container full of illicit drugs," commented Mary.

"Or a place to dispose of bodies without being interrupted," added Mike, stating the worst case scenario.

"Slow down, Mike, I believe that they're turning into a property. Yep – they've turned off to the right. Now they've stopped," said Mary.

Mike eased the car to a standstill. "What now, boss?" he asked, turning to Glen.

"How far ahead are they?" asked Glen.

"About half a kilometre, maybe a fraction more," said Mary.

"This is close enough," said Glen. "Find a place to conceal the car, so it's invisible to prying eyes, We don't want certain people to know that we're around."

Mike found an old fire trail, drove along it for a hundred meters or so until he found a well concealed area and parked.

"Mary, take the lead," said Glen. "Bring the scanner and hone in on the signal to keep us headed in the right direction. I'll come next. Mike, you bring up the six."

Mary worked her way through the undergrowth, past grass trees, wattle trees, and with tall eucalypts trees standing as sentinels.

At any other time, Glen would have enjoyed the walk through the bushland. But not today. His shoulder ached like hell, two people's lives were counting on their help, and it was starting to become overcast and the light beginning to fade.

Gradually the bush began to thin until they reached a six strand wire fence. An old, dilapidated weatherboard farmhouse became visible. On seeing it, Mary knelt down and waited for the others to join her. "How do you want to tackle this, Glen?" asked Mary.

"It's too open this side, we'll have to work our way to the rear of the house and use what trees there are for cover," said Glen kneeling beside her, perspiration beading on his forehead from the physical effort and the temperature that racked his body.

Without speaking, Mary pulled a couple of white tables from her pocket and handed them to Glen. He looked at her in surprise for a moment, accepted the tablets and swallowed them. He nodded his head in thanks then said, "Let's get moving; time is growing short."

Staying in the cover of the bush, they worked their way along the fence line until Mary found a place where the fencing had fallen down, allowing easy access to the farmhouse.

"Mary, use that big peppercorn as cover. Work your way to it. If everything is clear, wave us on," said Glen softly.

Acknowledging his instructions with a nod, she covered the fifty metres swiftly before coming to a stop. As Glen watched, as she peered cautiously around the old tree. Finding the way clear, she waved them on. Huffing and puffing like an early steam train, Glen arrived at the tree closely followed by Mike.

"I'm getting too old for these kinds of antics," said Glen, still trying to catch his breath.

"Hard liquor has that effect on your wind," said Mary, feeling sorry for him.

"Work your way slowly forward into a safe position, then let us know," said Glen,

Ignoring Mary's comments, knowing deep down she was right.

Glen and Mike watched in silence as she crawled the next twenty meters on her stomach.

Arriving safely at the back of the shed, Glen and Mike quickly joined her. From this position, they could hear the murmur of voices from within the house. Glen whispered,

"Sounds like Reynolds has a couple of mates in the house with him."

"That is going to make things rather difficult. What the hell!" exclaimed Mike, as he heard Mary's phone vibrates in her pocket.

Quickly she checked it, finding a text message had been left. "Container will be unloaded tonight. What is your location?" She showed the text message to Glen.

He read it, then whispered. "Give coordinates, expect the container to be unloaded here. Also, have a hostage situation. Chesshingham and a woman. I believe it's his wife, held against their will."

After showing the text to Mike, she sent Glen's message, then waited. "Received and understood. Stay on site. Help hostages if possible. Reinforcements are being dispatched. Should be on site within two hours. Pat Murphy will contact you."

Seeing the text, Glen nodded, "Okay."

Minutes later, a phone rang in the house. They heard Reynolds answer.

"That's great news! We'll leave right now. I have Chessingham. He'll cooperate, he has no choice; we have his wife. Okay, we're on our way." He hung up and said, "That was McWilliams. The container is being unloaded tonight. He needs Chessingham to sign for it, so we have to take him with us to the docks. Make sure you bind her tight. A few hours or so on her own will give them both time to reflect on their future, or what's left of it," laughed Reynolds

173

sadistically. "Your fate depends on your husband's behaviour and my generous nature. That's right, I don't have any."

"Well, there's one thing we know for sure," said Mike, watching as the four men left the house, climbed into the car and drove off. "McWilliams is back running their agenda."

"I'm pleased about that," said Glen, "I don't want that animalistic bastard escaping his date with destiny."

They waited a full twenty minutes, before checking the interior of the house. They found a middle-aged woman bound tightly to an old wooden chair. Her eyes widened as they slipped into the room. Glen indicated to Mary to free her while Mike and he checked out the rest of the building. Finding conditions for the remainder of the house entirely spartan, they return to the kitchen.

"Glen, Mike, this is Mrs Joyce Chessingham. She has an amazing story to tell in regards to today's events, so I'll let her tell it," said Mary.

"Well, it started this afternoon, about two o'clock," cried Joyce Chessingham, wiping tears from her face. "This man, Reynolds, came to the front door and asked to see my husband. So Peter went to see what he wanted. That's when he pulled a gun and demanded that we go with him. On the way here, he told us that he knew Peter was a silent partner to a man called Joshua Harvey and that he had the authority to sign on this man Harvey's behalf. At first, Peter denied it, but when they threatened to harm me, Peter relented and agreed to do it on the proviso that no harm came to me. All he had to do was sign some paperwork, and we could go home. Once we arrived here, we found out this Reynolds character was a crooked cop and had no intentions of letting us go. You see, my husband works undercover for the Border Force. Trying to expose a drug cartel. He was working with a Federal Police officer until the man was murdered about a week or so ago."

"Do you know the name of this murdered police officer?" asked Glen, noticing Mike was writing down every word the woman was saying.

"My husband said his name was Neil Henderson," answered Joyce Chessingham. "Since then, my husband has been terribly afraid for our safety. Peter didn't know who to trust. Apparently, Neil warned Peter that several high-ranking Federal policemen and a Border Force officer were involved. Do you know Mr Henderson?"

"Yes," said Mary, in a dull voice. "He was my husband."

"You poor thing. I'm so sorry."

"Mrs Chessingham," asked Glen, trying to obtain every last bit of information he could, "did your husband or Neil ever speak about a letter that would incriminate any of these men?"

"No – nothing at all like that. I would have remembered."

"When did your husband, or you, last see Neil Henderson alive?" asked Mike, cutting in for the first time.

"The night before he died," came the swift response from Joyce Chessingham.

"Do you know what is going on now or where they've gone?" asked Mary, setting a trap, hoping to catch the woman lying.

"Back to the docks, so that Peter can sign for a container they're expecting," replied Joyce Chessingham.

"What then?" said Mary.

"They're planning to bring the container back here. Reynolds bragged about having a truck standing by to move it away from the terminal as soon as it was cleared."

"Reynolds didn't mention a time he would be back?" asked Glen, trying to formulate some workable plan, once the container and McWilliams and his cronies had arrived. His train of thought was interrupted by the vibrating of Mary's phone.

She moved away from her colleagues and Mrs Chessingham, speaking softly so no-one else could hear. She then hung up and asked Glen to talk with her outside.

"What's up?' he asked once outside.

"Pat and his men are moving into position."

"Put this in writing. Make sure all vehicles are concealed well away from the road. These mongrels must be allowed to unload and take possession of the drugs before we move in and arrest them. No one is to act until I say so."

Mary nodded, then sent the message. "Anything else?"

"Yeah, if Reynolds gets past me, take him out. He was the one that ordered Neil's death. I recognised his voice the day they called around to collect the file. Believe me, I was close enough to hear but not to see. Also, ask Pat if he can spare a couple of men to re-enforce us here."

Leaving Mary to send the message and sifting through the information he had just given her, Glen re-entered the house to see how Mike was getting on with Mrs. Chessingham.

On entering, Glen found Mike alone. "Where's Mrs Chessingham?" Glen asked. "What's going on?"

"She had to go to the bathroom, or what serves as one. But I have some vital information. Three weeks ago, Neil knew nothing about the Border Force having a bent officer. He was sharing information with Peter Chessingham. Unbeknown to Neil, Chessingham was reporting his daily progress and details of his liaison with Neil to a superior officer. After this report had been submitted, everything started to go wrong. That's when they knew someone inside Border Force was on the take. By then it was too late, the damage had been done," said Mike.

"So that's how his cover was blown and why their attention was transferred to Mira and me. They believed Neil had passed the letter and other information onto me. And as Mira was my sister-in-law they sought to use her to get to me."

"Assuming that you knew about the letter and its contents. That's where they made a monumental mistake. By going after the file, they drew attention to themselves, thus making Mary and you suspicious," concluded Mike, just as the woman returned.

"Mrs Chessingham, can I ask you a direct question?" said Glen.

"Ask me anything you like? It doesn't mean I know the answer?'

"Who was the high ranking officer your husband submitted his reports to?" asked Glen, hoping he may get the information required.

"To be honest, Peter never told me. Only that he was third highest ranking Border Force officer in the state."

"That may be enough to prevent a disaster occurring tonight. Thank you," said Glen, turning and walking back outside to Mary.

He gave her the information, telling her to send it by text so that it was in writing.

Just then, two figures approached them from out of the dense fog that had developed. "Glen!" one called, "Pat sent us."

"Come on in, this could be a long wait," said Glen ushering them into the house, explaining what would be required of them in the pending proceedings. "The most important thing is that we need to catch all of them with the drugs in their possession. Remember, there are some members of the Australian Federal Police and the Border Force involved in this cartel, and they're on the take. So watch yourselves. I don't want any lives lost due to stupidity or rashness on our part."

"We need to get Mrs Chessingham out of the line of fire and into more comfortable surroundings," interjected Mike, knowing it would be easier for them to manoeuvre and shoot if the situation arose.

"Good thinking, Mike. Have one of Pat's men escort her out and make sure she doesn't communicate with anyone until this business is completed. What about you, Mary? Do you want to go with her or stay?" asked Glen, knowing in his heart she would stay to the bitter end.

"I'll stay. I've come this far, and I intend to see it through to the end," replied Mary thoughtfully, looking at Glen. She knew he was giving her a way out if she was willing to take it.

"Okay, that's settled. Let's see if there's any coffee or tea around this dump and any means of making it," said Glen, suddenly feeling tired and worn out.

"Yeah, I found a small gas stove and cylinder hooked up, with several tin mugs and a billy in the lounge," advised Mike. "There are sugar and coffee, but it'll have to be black, boss."

"That'll do, just make it strong and sweet. I need all the strength I can muster to get through the rest of tonight," replied Glen, slumping in a chair.

"Coming right up, boss."

"You'd better make it for five," called Mary, seeing the other officer returning.

"Five it is."

Glen felt the hot coffee warm his body and lift his spirits at the same time. Meanwhile, it was drizzling with rain, and the thick fog made it almost impossible to see more than a few metres in front of them.

He was hoping nothing would go wrong. He didn't want to be responsible for any more deaths.

The feeling of gloom was starting to invade his thoughts when Mary spoke.

"Glen, give yourself a chance. We're all over twenty-one, footloose and fancy-free. Let's get this job done and go home. These conditions are enough to get anyone down."

Glen looked up at her and nodded. "You're right, Mary. Brooding over the past isn't going to help. Let's get this job done and move on. I have an old mother-in-law who needs some love and consideration. Maybe between us, we can give her some joy in her life. Or what's left of it."

"That's the spirit, mate," said Mary, softly. "I know you're hurting and you've been wrong-footed from the start, shot at, stabbed and numerous other things. But you've hung in there. Let's see this through together."

The sound of Mary's phone vibrating on the table interrupted her. "Yes, sir, everything's in place. We're waiting ready to act. Yeah, he's right beside me," said Mary, handing the phone to Glen.

"Sir," said Glen, "I've already given those instructions - no action until after the container is unloaded and no shooting unless it is essential." Glen handed the phone back to Mary, saying "Let everyone know it's nearly showtime. The truck's about ten kilometres away."

Chapter Twelve

Loss of Memory

As they waited in the dark, Glen could feel the tension build within. His adrenaline rising in anticipation of physical action. He knew that Mcwilliams and his cronies wouldn't give up a billion dollars without a fight. Death would be calling tonight, the question was for who?

Glen saw the head lights cast their dull light through the swirling fog as the vehicles approached the property. He heard the truck change gears as it slowed to a crawl and entered the gate and drive up to the house. The slamming of doors and the motor rev, as a hydraulic crane mounted on the truck lifted the container and lower it to the ground.

"Let's get this crap out so we can get to our haul," said a voice.

Glen smiled coldly, he knew it was McWilliams' voice. "Got you," muttered Glen, watching, as the men worked feverishly in the harsh glare of the headlights. He felt Mary's hand grab him and give a slight squeeze as if reassuring him that he wasn't alone, or was it to steady her own nerves. Whatever the case, it helped ease the tension as they stood there in the dark, waiting.

As the last of the floor was lifted, Glen heard Mcwilliams give an order. "Take that bastard Chessingham and tie him up with his wife, we'll deal with them later. He watched as one of the men pushed Chessingham in front of him and headed for the house.

"It's near showtime. Mike take that bastard out as soon he enters the room." Said Glen.

Standing behind the door as Chessingham was shoved inside, the gunman entering after him grunted as Mike pistol-whipped him from behind and slumped to the floor. Closing it, Mike quickly cuffed him and tied a gag in his mouth and used the man's boot laces to bound his feet.

"Peter - are you okay, "asked Glen, helping the man to his feet.

"Yes – who are you - where is my wife?" asked Chessingham in a confused state.

"We are the police and your wife is safe and out of danger." Answered Glen.

"Thank God for that," said Chessingham, "I knew Mcwilliams was a nutcase when I worked for the Federal Police now I am sure."

"I want you to stay here, we are about to break up this little party," said Glen.

"Not on your bloody nelly. I've had that mongrel Reynolds goading me all day. Now it's my turn to howl."

"If you insist," said Glen, "Give Peter the weapon you took off of your new friend, Mike."

Outside Glen heard Mcwilliams crowing. "Look at that; one billion dollars in drugs. It's party time."

"Give Pat the signal Mary."

"Go."

All of them rushed out from the house, while other closed in from outside.

"Police," yelled Glen, "You are all under arrest. Put your hands in the air."

Total confusion reigned, men ran in all direction, only to be met by more police.

Reynolds darted around the front of the truck, his features highlighted by the headlights.

"That's far enough Reynolds," yelled Mary. "Your days of treachery are over."

"Shut your stupid mouth, you stupid little bitch," snarled Reynolds, who swung around and fired.

Mary, anticipating the move, dropped to the ground and squeezed the trigger. A red mushroom appeared on Reynolds' forehead, a look of disbelief on his face as his eyes glazed over - dead.

Glen heard the shot, looked over and caught sight of Reynolds and Mary, watched as he tumbled to the ground, nodded in grim satisfaction as he carried on after Mcwilliams.

"That's far enough Mcwilliams, stop, or I will drop you where you stand." Shouted Glen Mcwilliams halted and turned around, a pistol hanging loosely in his hand. Staring at Glen, hate filling his eyes. "You," yelled Mcwilliams in defiance. "You should be dead. Interfering in my private business."

"The moment you crossed over and when you ordered the death of Neil Henderson, you made it my business," continued Glen. "The moment you had Dalca and his men go after Mary and her kids to try and divert my attention from you and your little band of cutthroats in the office on the wharf. It was your stupidity and pigheadedness that brought you undone. However, the biggest mistake you made was going after my mother and sister in law. For that alone, I like to put a hole in you, not to kill. To kneecap you, leaving you in pain, unable to walk, your body wracked with pain for the rest of your life. Pleading for mercy. No, I rather see you locked up for the rest of your life, fighting for survival with some of the men you have put away."

"Don't you call me stupid – you-you bastard." Stammered Mcwilliams, enraged at the slur. "If that dumb wife of yours should have listened to reason. I offered to pay for the film, but no; she wouldn't sell it."

Glen's features hardened, at the mention of his wife, what did she have to do with all this? He had no idea what Mcwilliams was raving about. But at this stage of the game, he was willing to learn. So he let Mcwilliams continue to run-off at the mouth, hoping he would convict himself.

"She had you pegged right from the beginning. What were the words she uses? That's right. A whacko and a nut job. A poor excuse for a man." Said Glen, making up lies, goading McWilliams ego into verbal retaliation. Looking for some answers about his wife involvement and what roll of film was Mcwilliams was referring too.

"My wife only used digital cameras, not film. She could have downloaded the file at any time, from any place." Taunted Glen, trying to push McWilliams over the edge.

"How dare she defame me like that," spat Mcwilliams, hatred burning in his eyes. "The pathetic creature deserved everything that happens to her. She tried to contact you, but Reynolds fobbed her off and convinced her you could not be reached. That he could take a message and pass it on."

"Which I never received?" said Glen, keeping tight control of his emotions, as anger built inside him.

"Unbeknown to us, she somehow palmed the film to Henderson. We found out after the arranged accident," boasted Mcwilliams, getting carried away with his own self-importance" "So you had my wife and daughter killed to protect your dirty little empire?" said Glen, as the flames to kill Mcwilliams raged within him. "You need to be fitted for a straight jacket

"When we searched the car she never had it on her. It was missing." Continued Mcwilliams, throwing caution to the wind.

After checking around, we found out later, that Henderson had what we wanted. He must have beaten us to the crash site. Your wife may have given it to him before she died. As his wife and he were always around at your place, we assumed he passed it to you. The only trouble was you never left your unit."

"So you had my family killed and my home burgled, just like the cheap narcissistic hood you are." Said Glen, feeling his handshake, as he fought desperately to control the urge to kill Mcwilliams where he stood.

The vision of his wife and daughter lying side by side in their coffins flashed into his mind, how it had torn the heart out of him as he gazed at their dead bodies with tears rolling down his face.

Instead of squeezing the trigger, he manages to control the impulse, deciding to provoke Mcwilliams even further, trying to get him to crack wide open and give him the answers he had been seeking.

Mcwilliams exploded into verbal abuse at being called names that belittled him. "There is nothing cheap about me. If it hadn't been for Henderson subversive activities, I would be commissioner by now, but for that damn partition you pair organised."

'You are unfit to command an ice cream stand, let alone the Australian Federal Police," stated Glen bluntly, feeling the anger raging inside him. "Mcwilliams, you are nothing but a power-hungry thug. A user of innocent people, whose lives are expendable as far as you are a concern."

"Lies – all lies, I am a businessman going about his business." Screamed Mcwilliams, losing total control. "I was born for greatness, and I will stand on anyone who gets in my way."

"Bullshit; you are a drug dealer, murderer, blackmailer and a stand over merchant." Countered Glen with equal passion. "You are not fit to lick my wife's boots or mentioned in the same breath as her."

"I will kill you for that slur Johnson."

"You are full of shit," growled Glen, savagely. "There was no film, no letter. Just a small memory card."

"Lies – lies," screamed Mcwilliams.

"I doubt that Mcwilliams," said a voice behind Glen, "I've come across your sort before. Full of self-importance, use your power to bully and manipulate people into cooperating with you. Just like the person on my own staff, you blackmailed. I have a sign confession from the individual implicating you. After what we just heard, you are responsible for the death of this man's family, caught red-handed importing a billion dollars worth of drugs into this country. Numerous other crimes. You are nothing but a sick and deranged man who is going to spend the rest of your life in jail or a mental asylum." Said the commissioner, stepping forward level with Glen.

"Sir;" cried out Glen, "He is armed." Throwing himself at the commissioner, knock him off his feet as Mcwilliams raised the pistol and fired. Glen felt his gun recoil in his hand, then a screaming pain as a bullet grazed his head. He hit the ground hard and laid there looking up as figures gather around him. Glen could hear Mary talking to him but was able to respond to her. Later - he felt himself being loaded onto a stretcher and then into an ambulance. He felt Mary holding his hand and talking to him, while the paramedic worked on his wound. The wailing of the siren, burnt deep in his memory, then blackness engulfed him.

Three days later he awoke to find himself in the hospital with a nurse sitting beside him. "Where am I?" he asked.

"In the hospital," came the reply. "Helen, get the doctor, Mr Johnson is awake."

A middle-aged man, dressed in a white coat rush into the room, grabbed his wrist and checked his pulse. Satisfied, he said, "You are a fortunate man Mr Johnson, a centimetre the other way and you could have been dancing with the devil's handmaidens."

"What happen?" Glen asked, his memory fuzzy about his injury.

"You have been shot in the head. More accurately, a bullet left a furrow along the side of your head. You're fortunate not to have suffered brain damage. There may be short-term memory loss, hopefully, in time, it should return to normal."

"When did this happen, why was I shot?" asked Glen, not recalling getting injured or what led up to it."

"Three days ago. When you arrived, we received no response. For three days you lay in limbo as if fighting a war deep inside, a war between life and death."

"Okay, you answered when. Now, why?"

"I know that you are a police officer, I would say something to do with your job." Said the doctor.

"Doc, I need water, my mouth feels like the bottom of a bird's cage." Asked Glen.

"Only a sip, but you can suck on some ice."

"Thanks, Doc, I appreciate it."

As he lay in bed, Glen's felt as if he had been kicked in the head by a mule. "Nurse can I get something for this damn headache."

"You poor thing, I will check with the doctor to see if it is okay." She said walking away. She returned a few moments later, with water and a couple of tablets. Glen promptly swallowed them, then handed her the empty small plastic cup.

"Now; lay back in bed and try and rest."

Glen must have dozed off, for when he awoke, Mary was sitting by his bed, holding his hand.

"Welcome back stranger," she said, "You had us all worried."

"Hi," replied Glen, "Do I know you," he said, looking at her flaming red hair. The colour triggering something within his brain.

"Yes, the doctor said you had some short-term memory loss and with a bit of luck should regain it fully." Said Mary gently. "My name is Mary."

"I have heard that name before. "It's not Mary - Mary quite contrary and you have a garden."

"No, I'm not that Mary, that is a rhyme from your childhood." She smiled at his attempts to remember.

"How silly of me, getting it confused. You have a little lamb, and its fleece is white as snow."

"No, wrong Mary again."

"How stupid of me, I can't remember you," said Glen, confusion on his face.

"I'm Neil's Henderson wife."

"You can't be, Neil died in Afghanistan. No - a car accident. That's not right either."

"You are on the right track, keep trying," urged Mary, "Some of your memory is returning.

It's only a matter of time."

"I feel so helpless, lying in bed not remembering." Said Glen, frustrated.

"Give it time, mate." Said Mary, tears rolling down her cheeks. "Do you remember Laura and Alison?"

"I knew a Laura in Afganistan, she was a photojournalist. But I can't remember seeing her lately.

"Alison, I don't remember Alison."

"You will mate, believe me, you will." Answered Mary, standing up, tears rolling down her face as she pictured Alison long flowing blonde hair, her beautiful, angelic face, and the undying love she had for her father.

"Did I say something to upset you?" asked Glen, puzzled at Mary's tearful reaction.

"No – you will understand as your memory returns." Replied Mary, wiping her her eyes. "I have to go I have a job to complete, I will return later."

"Okay, I'm not planning to go anywhere soon." Answered Glen, watching Mary walk away. *"What did I do wrong?"* He thought as she disappeared from sight.

As he laid back in bed, he felt his left shoulder beginning to ache., wondering what had caused it to be strapped up tightly. He closed his eyes, thinking about his talk with Mary, particularly the mention of Laura and Alison, and why their names seem to be significant. He fell asleep, their names burrowing deep into his subconscious. He was awoken several hours later, by the medical staff, covered in perspiration, calling out. "Laura – Alice."

Glen looked up as the doctor spoke to him. "Mr Johnson, it's only a nightmare."

"No; it's not. My wife and daughter, they are dead. Murdered!" exclaimed Glen, as blurry images came flowing back, filling him with anguish and heartbreak. Tears streamed down his cheeks, remembering the painful past and all that it entailed.

"That is one of the dreadful parts of regaining one's memory, it doesn't filter out all unpleasant memories. Sometimes you have to face them again." Said the doctor, having been acquainted with the facts by Mary.

"That's unfair Doc," said Glen, "So unfair."

"Yes it's unfair, but that's life." Said the doctor, with finality.

Glen looked up at the man, his words ringing in his ears.

Afterward, he lay watching the ceiling, random images flashing through his mind as he tried to piece together parts of the puzzle that eluded him. Essential particles of information Glen needed to remember to make sense of the situation. The woman that claimed to be Neils wife, what part did she play in his wounding. His thoughts were interrupted by a voice alongside him.

"How are you, boss, how are you feeling?"

Glen stared at the young man standing by his bed, his face seems familiar and friendly, but he was unable to place him amongst the revolving images playing out in his head.

"Good day," – said Glen, "I'm sorry I can't remember your name."

"That's okay boss, you have taken one hell of a clout to the side of the head, it's enough to scramble anyone's brains. "My name is Mike Lord, I'm a part of your team, along with Mary."

"If I seem vague; everything is messed up in my head, Mike. I am having trouble placing you and Mary, and the events leading up to now."

"Don't worry mate," said Mike, "The doctor thinks your memory will ultimately return, but he can't tell when."

"Mike can you fill me in on the details when I was shot, and what led up to it." Asked Glen.

"No worries, boss. We had just completed a drug raid, against McWilliams and his cronies. You challenged the man, the commissioner came up beside you to arrest him personally when McWilliams produced a weapon and fired at the big boss. But for your quick action, the commissioner would be dead. You knocked him over, firing at McWilliams. Either by chance or design, you knocked the gun from his hand, slicing off two of his fingers in the process. His bullet sliced down the side of your head, putting you in here." Finished Mike, distressed to see his colleague in a state of confusion.

"So I didn't kill this McWilliams. Was I trying to?" asked Glen.

"We don't know for sure; after what he said about your family, none of us would blame you if you had." Answered Mike truthfully.

"This is where I lose the story, I cannot remember McWilliams or what he said. I remember my wife and daughter now and that they were murdered, but by who or why is a complete mystery to me." Said Glen.

"Mind you, we didn't hear all of the conversation you were having with McWilliams, just enough to confirm he and his cronies ordered a hit on your wife's car. Apparently, she had taken some photographs that he objected to. He wanted to buy the roll of film, and she refused. That's what we have been searching for, but nothing was found." Said Mike, "That bloke who forced his way into the house, mouth off that a letter was taken from an office. We know

now that it was bullshit. It's a series of photographs your wife shot, somehow could be incriminating evidence against McWilliams and other high-profile figures."

"Mike, Is it possible that Laura shot the photos in complete innocence, not realising this crowd was in the background, say; a busy café or restaurant situation. She would be concentrating on the main subject, whatever that was and not notice these men sitting at the table in the background." Suggested Glen, trying to remember details that may help them.

"It's possible. If that is the case, why would McWilliams draw attention to himself by approaching Laura, trying to buy the film or photos, whatever?" said Mike scratching his head, "It just doesn't make sense."

"Whatever the reason, it cost my wife and daughter their lives. I owe it to them to find out why if nothing else." Said Glen, his body trembling with emotion.

Noticing Glen's reactions to the conversation said. "Look mate rest for a while Mary, and I will return later, to see if we can help you work out some of these things."

Glen watched as Mike left the room, he sat up with his legs dangling over the side of the bed, His mind clouded by fuzzy images, lost his balance, falling onto the floor with a thud. Moments later, two nurses were by his side helping him back into bed.

"I need to have a hot shower," said Glen in an angry tone. "I have to clear my head. It is terribly important."

"Mr Johnson, the doctors believe you have retrograde amnesia, how is a hot shower going to help that," demanded one of the nurses.

"I don't know, but I need a hot shower." Said Glen, frustrated by the nurse's defiance.

"Okay, I will speak to the doctor, if he gives his permission, we will arrange it for you. Stay in bed until the physician agrees." Said the nurse walking away.

Minutes later, Glen was in a bathchair, under a hot shower, letting the water cascade over him. The hot water seems to wash away his frustrations and ease the tension that had racked his body since he started to regain his memory. He felt the heat working miracles upon him the battered frame. Defying the nurse's orders, Glen stood up, feeling his strength returning to his limbs. Turning, he lost his footing, fell, giving his head a glancing blow on the tiles, then slipping into darkness.

He awoke about an hour later, tucked up in bed, with Mary sitting by his side.

"I wish to hell you would obey orders, Glen Johnson. You scared the damn daylights out of the nurses," growled Mary harshly, happy to see him awake and alert.

"Hi Mary, what are you doing here?" asked Glen, grinning impishly. "Where is Mike, wasn't he suppose to be coming with you?"

"Mike had an urgent mission, he had to get some papers signed for the case."

"I see. Has Mike made any headway with Joshua Harvey?"

"Actually — that's where he is at the moment. Joshua turned state evidence. He is signing it today." Said Mary, looking at Glen strangely before continuing. "Have you worked out what the initials E.T.B stand for yet?"

"No for some reason I completely forgot about them. I do know that it's not a letter we are looking for, its photos. Laura never used films in most of her cameras. It is a memory card."

"How do you know that?" asked Mary, excitement rising in her, realising Glen was talking about past events in clear and concise terms.

"Laura very seldom used film, unless it was for portraits. She was extremely professional when it came to her work. We need to find that memory card and quick. The information on it must be highly incriminating, to say the least."

"You know how hard we tried to find it." Said Mary, shaking her head in disbelief at Glen's total recall of the past events. Not wanting to break his train of thought, she let him continue.

"If what McWilliams said is true, and I have no reason to doubt him. Laura stumbled across a clandestine meeting and accidentally caught it in the background of her photographs." Said Glen thoughtfully, looking up as Mike entered the room. "How did you get on?"

"Great–" replied Mike. "However we don't have all of the parties involved under lock and key."

"What do you mean?" asked Glen sharply.

"According to Harvey, there were two other people at that meeting. Joshua didn't know their names, only that one is a member of parliament, the other has something to do with a drug cartel."

"If that's true, it explains a lot. And why they were so desperate to lay their hands on Laura's photos, and why they always hounded us." Said Mary coming into the conversation.

"McWilliams balls it up. When he approached Laura and became aggressive, made her suspicious of his motives and actions. So she tried to contact me. A message I didn't receive." Said Glen, a picture of Laura's desperation flashing through his mind.

"So she did the next best thing, contacted Neil and managed to pass him the card. How or when we have no idea." Said Mary, tears forming in her eyes.

"The question on my mind at the moment?" said Mike, "How did McWilliams find out about Neil having the card?"

"Maybe – just maybe, Neil mentioned it to Chessingham, and he placed it in his daily report." Suggested Mary.

"That is a strong possibility," said Glen, "Mike we need to find out for sure. Can you follow that up?"

"I'm on it boss," replied Mike walking away.

"I need to get out of here Mary, can you see what you can do?" asked Glen.

"Not bloody likely mate," protested Mary.

"Why?'

"You have been shot in the head, had temporary memory loss. Then to top it off, fell while you had a shower. Most probably hit your head on the tiles. Scaring the hell out of everybody because you failed to obey the nurse's instructions. On top of all that, you sat up in bed and started talking to me as if nothing had happened."

Glen looked dumbfounded, then said. "There is nothing wrong with my memory."

"Not now - you idiot. That smack on the head may have returned your memory. It has been known to happen. Until the doctors are a hundred percent sure it is safe for you to leave here, you are not." If you try, I will have the boss handcuff you to the bed."

Glen stared at her in disbelief, willing to argue with her. But unable to gather his thoughts in his own defence. "Don't you understand we have two people still unknown to us. That they may get away if we don't act." Said Glen - stumbling over the words, angry she was challenging him.

"Of course we know. But your health is important as well." Said Mary forcibly. "There are details Mike, and I can check, while you concern yourself on recovery. If you want something to do, employ your intellect on solving the meaning of E.T.B. I'm still convinced it's something simple. So simple we have overlooked it."

Glen looked up at her, knowing her argument was sound. It still burnt him up, that he was confined to bed, letting the others assemble the outstanding details. "Okay, have it your way." Said Glen, conceding defeat.

At that moment, Mike returned with some news regarding the memory card. "I spoke to Peter Chessingham – boss. He can't remember if he had added that bit of information to this report. He will check on his copy once he gets home. That will be in a couple of hours or so."

"That's a great help," growled Glen irritably, "But I suppose it can't be helped. Mike what if you go back to Joshua Harvey and see if he can remember any information or detail, however slight that may help us get a line on these two blokes."

"I'll try boss, but don't hold your breath?"

"Don't interrogate him, just sit down and chat, talk about his daughter and his granddaughter. Try and get to know the man. You never know what may turn up." Said Glen, desperate to glean what information he could.

"Okay boss, I will give it a whirl. Besides, I will be talking about one of my favourite subjects. Julia. I'm off."

Glen smiled as he watched Mike disappear from sight. "It sounds like it's getting quite serious?" he commented, relaxing slightly.

"It is," said Mary, noticing the smile. "By the way, Emily asked me to give you a message."

"Yeah – what is it?" said Glen, picturing the little girl with hair of copper and a cheeky grin.

"She said get well soon, and she will come and visit you as soon as she gets back."

"I hope to be out of here before that happens," said Glen.

"I doubt it, mate, I have to pick up Julia and the kids up from the airport in a couple of hours time." Smiled Mary. "Besides Julia wants to see her father, she still worried about him."

"Bloody hell," growled Glen, "I'll be surrounded by ankle biters."

Mary looked sharply at him for a moment, then smiled. "Yes – and you will love every bit of it. Now, you concentrate on solving the riddle of the initials while I pick up Julia and the kids." Said Mary handing Glen his notebook and pen.

Glen watched Mary vanish from sight, before turning his attention to the task at hand. Flicking through the pages, he scrutinised each notation, trying to understand what he might have missed. Writing down specific facts as they appeared. "We know now that we are looking for a digital camera memory card, not a letter and it is small enough to be hidden in plain sight. The question is – in what?" he muttered, scratching his head. "What begins with E?"

Several hours passed and no closer to a solution when Mary returned with Emily.

"Hello Uncle Glen, what are you doing?" asked Emily, climbing up on the bed beside him.

Shocked at their sudden appearance, Glen looked at the little girl beside him, then at her mother, later commented. "That was quick?"

"I have been away three hours." Answered Mary, looking at the notebook in his hand. "How did you get on – any progress?"

"None what so ever."

Emily look at the letters on the page, giggled, then asked. "Why do you have my teddy bear's name written down? Uncle Glen." Asked Emily.

"Glen looked at Emily in total disbelief, trying to comprehend what the girl was saying. "What do you mean your teddy bear name?"

"Daddy bought me a new teddy bear, just before he went to heaven, and told me he had given it a name. Emily teddy bear. I wanted to call him Gus, but daddy said he had to be E.T.B until you asked me about him. But you never did."

"No darling, I never did," said Glen, became conscious at that moment that Mary had picked it up in their search, but they dismissed it because it wasn't big enough to conceal a letter. "Besides - I never knew you had a new bear. Did your mother?"

"No – daddy told me not to let mummy know, because he would get into trouble from her for not buying the boys anything and that she would find out soon enough."

Glen looked up at Mary shattered look and said quickly. "Don't take it to heart. It was Neil way of protecting you and the kids. Remember I suggested to send the kids to his parents and I never saw them at all before they left. So, Emily couldn't tell me what her father said."

"But if I had known, we could have located the information quicker," answered Mary, tears streaming down her face.

"Mary – at that stage we knew nothing about this information. Now we have it, I need you to get the card and check out the photos. Remember to sift through the background, I believe what we are looking for is there. I'm pretty sure Laura was unaware she had photographed anything suspicious or incriminating. McWilliams saw her, panicked, drawing attention to himself by trying to purchase the photos."

"There could be another reason?" interrupted Mary, wiping her eyes. "He may have thought she had been sent to collect evidence, assuming his organisation cover had been exposed."

"That is a possibility, a slim one." Said Glen. "However, we must concentrate on recovering the memory card. If Neil has hidden it in the bear, you should be able to find it by checking the stitching."

"I'll do that as soon as we get back." Replied Mary. "I have spoken to the doctor, he said I can take you home, only if you are careful over the next couple of days. He is concerned you may have dizzy spells when you least expect it."

"That's bloody great, grab my clothes and let me get dress."

A quarter of an hour later, he left the hospital, taking his time as they walked to the car. Emily opened the door for Glen, then closed it behind him. As they drove back to the house, Emily said. "Uncle Glen, can I call my bear Gus now?"

"I don't see why not — as long as it's okay with your mother."

Emily looked at her mother with pleading eyes, "Can I mummy?'

"If that is what you want darling."

They drove the rest of the way in silence, as they swung into the drive, they noticed Mike car parked at the curb.

"Looks like you have a full house." Said Glen.

"It seems so."

Chapter Thirteen

The Brazilian Connection

Entering the house, the first thing Mary did was ask Emily to get her teddy bear. Then sent her children to play in the backyard. Taking it, she examined it thoroughly. After a few moments, she turned to Glen saying. "I think this is the spot," showing it to him.

"Yeah – that looks like the place," said Glen, checking it. Handing it back, he watched on as Mary unpicked the stitching. Probing the stuffing with her slender fingers, she withdrew the memory card and gave it to Glen.

Going to the computer, Glen switched it on and inserted the card., bringing the photos up, he scrutinised each one scrupulously. Selecting four photographs, he made copies and transferred them to Photoshop. He enlarged the backgrounds until he could see four people sitting at a table inside a café. Happy with the results, Glen printed off the photographs and walked back into the lounge. Handing one each to Mary and Mike. "Do you know any of the faces?" asked Glen.

"One is McWilliams." Replied Mary, "But none of the others."

"The Border Force officer is one, he's sitting on the left-hand side of McWilliams. How I know that - I was at the station when they arrived with him. He had been arrested. The other two I have no idea." Said Mike.

Julia who had been looking over Mike's shoulder said, "The one sitting at the end of the table is a Member of state Parliament. I don't know his name."

"That's great Julia – that fits in with what your father told me. Said Mike giving her hand a squeeze.

"That means the other one must be from the drug cartel. All we have to do is find out the character's name," added Glen. "First, let's concentrate on the MP. With a bit of luck, we should be able to locate him fairly quickly."

"Go online," suggested Julia, "All the state members should be listed along with their photographs."

"Great idea Julia," said Mary, "It could save you two lots of legwork." Indicating to Glen and Mike.

Taking the initiative, Mike walk to the computer, did a quick search. A minute or two later Mike exclaimed! "I found him – his name and address."

"Does he hold any cabinet positions Mike?" asked Glen cautiously. Thinking of the complications that were going to confront them

"None that I can find."

"We better let the boss know, this will have to be handled delicately. Let's see what the boss wants to do. Can you get onto that Mary?"

"I'm on it," came her reply, as she walked into the kitchen, her mobile to her ear.

"Boss - how do you think the commissioner will react to this news?" asked Mike.

"I don't know mate?" replied Glen. "All I know we will have to do this by the book, otherwise there will be a severe backlash."

At that moment, Mary entered the room saying, "Jack told me to proceed with caution. That all we have is guilt by association and nothing much to back it up."

"Feel like taking a ride Mike?" asked Glen, "We will check this character out, and see what reaction we get."

"How are we going to do that boss?"

"Show him the bloody photograph of course."

Twenty minutes later, they pulled up near the MP's house Leaving the car they strolled up the path and knocked on the front door. Receiving no answer, Glen called out. "Anyone home?"

Still no response, They walked around to the back door. Finding it open, Glen called out again. "Hello – anyone home?" Silence greeted his call. The hair on the back of his neck, stood up, warning him of impending danger. "Trouble." Muttered Glen.

Unholstering their weapons, they covertly proceeded inside. Their eyes searching for signs of movement. Covering each room one at a time, they found a man, laying on the bed with a gunshot wound to the forehead. Checking for a pulse, Glen found none and his body was cold to the touch. He's been dead for some time.

"Suicide Boss?" asked Mike, looking down at the dead man. Glancing at the photograph in his hand. "This is our suspect. There is no doubt about that."

"Maybe. Sometimes things are not as they appear." Getting on his hands and knees, Glen checked under the bed. Finding nothing. Examined the entry wound, noting the size of the hole. "Contact Pat, let him know where we are and what has happened."

Leaving Mike to follow his instruction, Glen checked the house thoroughly, looking for evidence of any kind. Finding no note or explanation, Glen kept his mind open until he was proven wrong. Certain things about the scene did not sit right with him. He didn't know what. It was just too neat – to pat. Letting these thoughts run through his mind he searched the rest of the house. Finding nothing of interest returned to Mike.

"Pat's on his way," said Mike as Glen entered the room.

"You asked me a moment ago if it was suicide. In my opinion, it was a professional hit. There is no note. A small calibre weapon was used. Most probably .22. There are powder burns on the entry wound and no exit wound. At one stage, his wrists were bounded, you can see the indentation marks on his skin. Especially notable by its absence - no gun."

"Killed to prevent him talking or identifying any of his associates?" said Mike, looking closely at the wound and wrists again.

"That's my guess," said Glen, "Tying up any loose ends I'd say."

"If that's the case, what about McWilliams and the Border Force officer. Their lives could be in danger as well." Said Mike, alarmed at the prospect.

"Bloody good point!" exclaimed Glen, "Get hold of Mary and have her to contact the commissioner and have them placed in protective custody. I just hope we are not too late. Mike while you are at it. Have that other character in the photograph run through all the law enforcement data banks and Interpol to see if we can get a hit."

While Mike was carrying out his orders, Glen checks the bedroom once again, looking for any clues they might have missed. He was growing impatient, he knew time was of the essences.

As he walked from the bedroom, he heard a car arrive. Going to the front door, he saw Pat and walked over to him. "We have a body of a man. He was in a photo along with McWilliam and the Border Force officer. By the looks of it, he has been eliminated to stop him talking. Mike and I came to interview him. He has been dead for several hours."

"Any idea who he is?" asked Pat, shaking Glen's hand, pleased to see he had recovered from his injury.

"Yeah – he's a bloody state politician by the name of Ian Moses. From the company, he has been keeping, he could be bent big time." Said Glen, showing Pat the photograph.

"I hate to do this Pat, we have to run, there is another suspect we need to collar before he disappears or before other people meet with a fatal accident."

"I take it you haven't heard about McWilliams. He died abruptly last night. We suspect poisoning. We are waiting on an autopsy report."

"Hell:" exploded Glen, "Just what I was afraid of. Time is running out. If we don't track this bloke down, we will have no principles left to point the finger at him."

Glen look up as a plainclothes officer approached and whispered in Pat's ear. Pat nodded then look at Glen. "Sorry mate, I have just been informed we have lost another prisoner, the bloke from the Border Force. He was found dead in his cell a couple of hours ago."

"Bloody hell – that's all we needed. We have no direct link to this character. Only that photograph. There is no way we can convict him on guilt by association. From what has happened, this bloke must have plenty of influence to be able to get to prisoners behind bars. To be honest Pat we thought McWilliams was the mastermind behind this operation. Clearly, that's not the case, someone was else was the brains in planning this importation."

"Who do you think may be behind it?" asked Pat, feeling Glen's frustration.

"I don't know, perhaps a large South American drug cartel or possibly the Mafia. Who in the hell knows. My wife and daughter were murdered because of some innocent photographs. I'm not going to let this go until this murderous bastard is behind bars or dead. Preferably the latter if I have a choice."

Pat looked at the nasty expression on Glen's face and knew he meant every word of it.

"Take care, my friend, I don't want you to end up like McWilliams or on the wrong side of the law."

"I will mate – I will." Replied Glen as Mike returned. "We have one slim lead left to investigate and little time. So we will be on our way."

Leaving Pat and his team to handle the inquiry into Ian Moses death, they headed back to their headquarters to follow up on their request. They were still several minutes away from their destination when Mike's mobile phone rang.

"Yeah – what's up?" asked Mike. He listens intently, to Mary's words then hung up.

"We have learned who the other bloke in the photo is. His name Eberardo Fermandes, thirty-seven years old and he is a Brazilian national. He has no priors, it's rumoured he is a hitman for a well known Brazilian drug lord."

"Bloody hell – We don't have evidence to apply for an extradition warrant. And even if we did, it's highly unlikely they would extradite one of their own citizens."

"The funny thing is, according to records he has never left Brazil." Said Mike, looking at Glen's face as he spoke.

"That means this bastard is in the country on a false passport if we can nail him before he leaves. we have an excuse to arrest the mongrel." Said Glen hopefully, his morale rising.

"That grasping at straws boss." Commented Mike, "He could be out of the country by now."

"We will have his picture plastered throughout the country and in Brazil at our Embassy in Brasilia and our consulate in Rio de Janeiro, have all our people on the lookout for him. If he still here we will get him, Mike."

Over the next few weeks, they followed up every report that came in but to no avail.

Either Fernandes had gone to ground or had left the country. It was two days later that Glen received a report from the Australian consulate in Rio de Janeiro. That their man had been sighted in a leading restaurant by one of the senior government staff.

"That's it, boss," said Mike, "He has escaped."

"This isn't over by a long shot, mate. You can take my word on it. I'll be waiting, he doesn't know we have a photograph identifying him. If he ever comes back, he's mine - so help me god." Swore Glen venomously, as an image of his wife and daughter lying in their coffins flashed into his mind. Strengthening his determination to catch the last man responsible for their death.

The End

Bibliography

General References

Style manual Sixth edition,
Macquarie dictionary, Roget's Thesaurus.

Author biography

The author was born in Western Australia. Left there in his twenties and travelled throughout Australia and New Zealand. Thirty years ago he moved into a small rural village to raise his family in NSW. He has worked in various jobs from oil rigs, security guard, shed hand, wool presser, courier driver, sales rep to sales manager. In his fifties completed his Higher School Certificate, then went on to complete a Bachelor of Arts in photography. He also finished several college courses in children writing and mystery and crime writing.

Printed in the United States
By Bookmasters